Magick & Magnolias

By

D1710548

Ellen Dugan

Magick & Magnolias
Copyright @ Ellen Dugan 2018
Cover art designed by Kyle Hallemeier
Cover image Fotolia/Adobe Stock: millaf
Legacy Of Magick logo designed by Kyle Hallemeier
Editing and Formatting by Libris in CAPS

This is a work of fiction. Names, characters, businesses, organizations, places, events and incidents either are the product of the author's imagination or are used fictitiously. Any resemblance to actual persons, living or dead, events, or locales is entirely coincidental.

No part of this book may be reproduced, or stored in a retrieval system, or transmitted in any other form or by any means electronic, mechanical, photocopying, recording or otherwise without the express written permission of the publisher.

Published by Ellen Dugan

ACKNOWLEDGMENTS

As always, thanks to my family, friends, beta readers, and editors. To Crystal who was a voice of calm reason when I started to slam my head against the writing desk. To M and P who let me bounce crazy ideas off of them, and don't seem to mind. Finally, to Katie, Meme, and Necole for the information and insight into modern-day witchy Southern women.

Other titles by Ellen Dugan

THE LEGACY OF MAGICK SERIES

Legacy Of Magick, Book 1

Secret Of the Rose, Book 2

Message Of the Crow, Book 3

Beneath An Ivy Moon, Book 4

Under The Holly Moon, Book 5

The Hidden Legacy, Book 6

Spells Of The Heart, Book 7

Sugarplums, Spells & Silver Bells, Book 8

Magick & Magnolias, Book 9

Mistletoe & Ivy, Book 10 (Coming 2019)

THE GYPSY CHRONICLES

Gypsy At Heart, Book 1

Gypsy Spirit, Book 2

Gypsy Soul, Book 3 (Coming 2019)

DAUGHTERS OF MIDNIGHT SERIES

Midnight Gardens, Book 1

Midnight Masquerade, Book 2

Midnight Prophecy, Book 3

Like the magnolia tree,
She bends with the wind,
Trials and tribulation may weather her,
Yet, after the storm her beauty blooms...

-Nancy B. Brewer

CHAPTER ONE

"Mama, are we there yet?"

I'd lost count of the number of times I'd heard that question over the past two days. Gripping the steering wheel tighter, I resisted the urge to scream. "No, sugar pie, we're not. But we're close."

"We are?" My daughter, Willow, bounced in her booster seat, and I flashed my eyes to the review mirror in time to see her kick her snow boot-clad feet in the air.

With relief, I checked the GPS. "We should be arriving in less than a half hour." A massive double bridge came into view, and I counted five lanes heading west and five heading in the opposite direction. "See that bridge?" I desperately pointed out. "Once we cross that we'll be almost at our new house."

"Will I get to use my snow boots?" It was her second favorite question.

"I'm sure you will." I smiled when I said it, but internally I was thankful our trip up north had *not*

1

included me driving through a snow storm—for the very first time.

"Can I see the pictures of our house, again?"

"Sure," I patted around, found my cell and handed her my phone without taking my eyes off the road. With terrifying skill she opened the photo app and began to scroll through. "Do you see the pictures of the cottage?" I eased into the far right lane of the bridge. Everyone was driving so fast, it was more than a little intimidating.

"Uh-huh I see it," she said. "I get my own room."

"Yes you do."

"Will my toys be there?"

"Yes. Remember that cousin Thomas called yesterday, to tell us that all our boxes had been delivered?"

"What if my dolls are lonely?" Willow asked.

"You can reassure them soon enough."

I thought to the pictures Thomas Drake had sent me. The stone cottage on his estate—*his estate*—I thought, was charming. The fully furnished rental property was small, but we didn't need much. The two bedrooms with one and a half baths would be plenty for Willow and me. I hoped the fireplace in the living room worked. I was looking forward to building a cozy fire and sitting in front of it.

"How come you don't have any pictures of Thomas?" Willow wanted to know, as she went through the photos.

I thought back to the elegant older man who'd swooped into our lives a few months before and saved the day. "Because he didn't send me any." It was the most honest thing I could think to say.

"Mama, I like our cousin. He's nice." Willow sang as she entertained herself looking at the pictures of the cottage on my phone.

He certainly was, I thought to myself. Thomas Drake was also powerful, and if every story that my mother had ever told me was true, the man had descended from some pretty powerful modern-day magicians as well.

Since I'd been young, my mother, Patricia, had told me that she was the secret love child of a Witch and a Magician. Her birth mother, Irene Bishop, had hidden her away with the only couple she could trust—her best friends—Vance and Taylor Sutton. The story went that Irene had given up her baby girl to keep her safe from an evil man who threatened her very existence.

At first, I'd been spellbound by it all. What little girl doesn't want to believe in faery tales? But after I'd grown up I'd begun to doubt my mother's claim, figuring she was simply making up stories about her biological family for attention, or so she could brag to her friends about being a hereditary Witch.

Then out of the blue, her biological family had contacted me. When I'd met my mama's family—her cousin, I wasn't sure what to make of Thomas Drake. Somehow, I had felt a connection to him from the first moment we met: A soul-deep, quiet, yet powerful recognition.

The older man had carried himself with a sort of dignity, or polite arrogance I supposed. Honestly, his wardrobe, fancy car and bank account hadn't impressed me much. But copies of my mother's birth certificate and her adoption papers certainly had. In the short week he'd spent in town, he had humbled me with his quiet generosity, compassion, and sincere desire to help.

"You are family," he'd said, and proceeded to steamroll his way through every obstacle that I had faced.

When all was said and done, he'd terrified my ex who had caused Willow and me nothing but pain, found me an excellent realtor, and had hired the best damn attorney money could buy. Now my child was safe. My mother's house was sold, and her medical bills were paid off from the sale. I was free to get the hell out of Louisiana, far away from nasty gossip and bad memories. I was finally able to start my life over in Missouri.

It was risky. Probably the craziest thing I'd ever done...but desperate times called for desperate measures.

Truth be told, I could work almost anywhere. As an event coordinator, or bridal consultant, I had that luxury. I had built a solid professional reputation for myself. I'd even landed some bigger events in Shreveport. I was confident that I could do the same up north. All I had to do was prove myself with my new cousin's wedding that I'd been hired to coordinate.

It was probably a sympathy job, I knew. *They'd asked me to take the job out of kindness, but I wouldn't let them down.* I squared my shoulders. *They were about to learn that Magnolia Irene Parrish was a consummate professional. I could wrangle* any *bride and deal with* any *wedding crisis.* My stomach gave a nasty pitch, and even as I told myself not to worry...I did anyway.

I'd get a second job in an office if need be. Hell, I'd work as a waitress until I established myself as an event coordinator in William's Ford. But I'd pay my own way. I didn't want to be beholden to my new-found family, and lord almighty, but Willow and I had fallen hip deep into family. From both my maternal grandmother—the Bishop's, and grandfather—the Drake's side of the tree.

After Thomas had left, I'd started emailing back and forth with the family bride, my third cousin, Autumn Bishop. We'd kept in touch over the past few months, and I was curious to meet her in person. After all, it was she who had started everything by finding an old strongbox that contained family papers, including my mother's birth certificate, her adoption papers and photos.

While my mother Patricia had known her biological mother, Irene Bishop, throughout her life, it turned out that the rest of the Bishop family had been *shocked* to learn of my mother's existence.

Autumn seemed nice enough, and she had assured me that my grandmother's people were excited to meet me...and there was a mess of them.

First, there were the Drakes, my maternal grandfather's biological family. They had the means to pay for us to move cross-country and had accomplished it in the blink of an eye. All that had been left for me to do was pack a few travel bags, gas up the car, and head north.

Now our journey was almost at an end. I took the first exit after crossing the bridge and in a few minutes found myself driving through the river town of William's Ford, Missouri.

Picturesque was the word that came first to mind, and thankfully the streets were dry and clear. I passed a smattering of restaurants, banks and stores. I spied two national chain pharmacies, a massive grocery store, and the University campus on my left.

The winter-bare trees had a dusting of snow on their dark branches, and there were a few inches also blanketing the grass. While Willow cheered over the snow, I admired the fancy decorative street lights along the roads. I cruised along with the local traffic, following the directions of the GPS. I rolled my shoulders against the tension gathered there and drove into a gorgeous neighborhood filled with large Victorian-era homes.

The brick sidewalks were also clear, and I slowed down, enjoying the view of the pretty homes and the large trees. I tried to imagine what it would all look like in the spring. I spotted the Drake mansion, stopped my car in the middle of the street, and sat there like a rube. "Lord have mercy!"

The house truly was a mansion. Three stories of gray stone, the huge house sprawled out impressively. The grounds of the estate were large, ensuring that no neighbors were particularly close—save one. A tad off to one side, surrounded by trees, nestled a charming cottage built from brick and trimmed out with the same stone as the mansion.

"Look Willow, here's the cottage." I carefully eased into the driveway while my girl cheered. I took a deep breath, blew it out slowly and told myself to stay calm.

My cell began to ring, and Willow answered it. "Hello?"

"Willow, give me the phone." I held out my hand.

"Hi Cousin Thomas!" Willow said. "We just got here. You have snow!"

How had he known we'd arrived? I wondered, then gave up waiting for her to give me my phone. I turned off the car and climbed out. The cold was a shocking slap to the senses. *This Southern girl needed to thicken up her blood,* I thought. Reaching quickly for my new winter coat, I shrugged it on and zipped it up. Willow was already unbuckling herself from the car seat as I walked around to the passenger side of the car.

"Did you hang up?" I asked as she tossed my phone aside and bounced out of the back seat.

"Cousin Thomas says he's coming over to help us settle in." Her breath made white clouds against the January air. "Mama, it's cold!"

"Yes, darlin' it is." I immediately tried to zip her coat. "Willow, stand still." I finally got the zipper pulled up, and as soon as I let go she took off for the nearest snow-covered surface.

Willow entertained herself by jumping in a pile of snow, as I retrieved my phone and purse. I grabbed Willow's backpack and shut the door, heading to the trunk for our luggage.

"Hello," a male voice said. "You must be Magnolia and Willow."

I saw a gorgeous, dark-haired man, who I estimated to be in his early thirties. He walked through the snow wearing a smart navy overcoat, dark jeans and boots.

"Hi!" Willow ran past him. "Look, I made footprints!"

"I'm your cousin, Julian." He smiled. "Thomas is my father."

"Hello, Julian." I nodded, recalling that Thomas had given me a rundown on the current Drake family. "It's a pleasure to meet you."

He walked over and extended a hand. "It's lovely to finally meet you, Magnolia."

"Oh, honey please, call me Maggie." I automatically shook his hand. "Only my mama called me Magnolia." I smiled politely, met his eyes, and felt a jolt go all the way to my toes. My cousin's eyes were a startling combination of blue and brown. One eye had a ring of brown against the electric blue, and the other iris was brown with patches of that same bright blue color.

"Is something wrong?" he asked.

"Your eyes," I said, tugging him a bit closer. "Sectoral heterochromia." *I'd seen eyes like his before.*

"Hi cousin Thomas!" Willow launched herself at the older man, who'd suddenly arrived. To my surprise, he scooped her up despite his elegant clothes and settled her—snowy boots and all—on his hip.

"Hello Princess," Thomas said, smiling fondly at her. "How was your trip?"

"We drove forever!" Willow declared.

I finally remembered to release Julian's hand. "Well, I guess I've got the answer to the question that's puzzled me for the past four years." I unlocked the trunk and raised it.

Julian cocked his head. "Oh, what question is that?"

"I'd always wondered where my daughter's unusual eye coloring came from." I gestured to where Thomas stood with Willow. "Now I have my answer."

Thomas walked closer, and Julian glanced over at Willow. He narrowed his eyes for a moment, and slowly, he began to smile.

Willow's right eye was blue, and her left was almost equally divided between both brown and sky-blue colors.

"Her eyes are like mine." Julian sounded awed.

"It's a Drake family trait," Thomas said to me.

"Phillip—your grandfather, had the same mixture of eye colors."

"Funny old world, isn't it?" I put my hands on my hips as I looked from Julian to my daughter. For some reason, all the nerves that had been dancing in my belly smoothed out.

Julian laughed and tugged a suitcase from the trunk. "Welcome home, cousin."

***

Thomas led the way down the front walk with Willow's hand in his. He stopped long enough on the tiny front porch to open the door. Willow rushed inside with an excited shout, and I followed behind them hauling my suitcase and purse. Julian was right behind me and was carting in the rest.

The cottage was charming as advertised and smelled sweet of lavender. It was, as I'd been told, furnished in comfortable and child-friendly furniture. The kitchen was U shaped, on the small side, but gorgeous with cabinets in a soft blue-green with crystal knobs. The countertops were white flecked with gray, and the white subway tile backsplash gave it all a crisp, clean look.

There was just room enough for a drop leaf table, and my eyes widened at seeing the obviously new appliances. Someone had placed a small vase of daisies on the counter and it made me smile.

A loud knock sounded on the cottage door and

before I finished turning around, a pretty brunette in a bright royal blue coat let herself right in. "You're here!" she cried and moved directly to me with her arms out.

"Er...hello." I managed, then found myself in a surprising but welcoming embrace. I recognized her from her social media page. Autumn Bishop—my cousin on my grandmother's side and my first bridal client in William's Ford.

"Finally!" She pulled back and held me at arm's length. Her green eyes shone behind trendy glasses. "Good god, you're totally gorgeous, aren't you?" she said. "You've got the same dark hair as Julian." Before I could respond, she was turning and speaking to a blonde man who'd come in with her. "Duncan, come meet your cousin."

"Hello, Magnolia," Duncan said, and held out a hand.

"Please, call me Maggie," I said, and when Autumn released me, I stuck my hand out.

"Maggie." Duncan smiled and took my hand, and I found myself being measured by my new cousin. His blue eyes were intense but smiling. His casual work clothes and old bomber jacket, in comparison to the rest of the Drake family's elegant apparel, had me relaxing slightly.

"I'll take your suitcases to the bedrooms for you," Julian announced, and carried them to the back.

"Oh, thank you," I managed.

Willow discovered that all her toys and dolls were

unpacked and promptly hauled Thomas off to go see them. Before I realized what had happened, Autumn had cheerfully herded me to the kitchen and put on the water for some tea. She filled up the cottage with energy and enthusiasm.

"This isn't necessary," I tried to tell her, but found that my words fell on deaf ears.

"I made sure they stocked the pantry and fridge for you," she said, and proceeded to show me the staples in the cabinets.

"Thank you," I said, peering in the refrigerator, and seeing eggs, juice, milk, butter and fresh fruit. "That was very considerate."

Autumn turned and bumped into me. "Oops, sorry. Have a seat, sit down and relax."

"Well, I—" My voice trailed off as she steered me to the table and pulled out a chair. Amused, I sat.

Only after she'd poured me a mug of tea, and had plied Willow with cookies and juice, did she decide we were all right to be left on our own. "Now, if you need anything, you have my cell phone number, right?"

"I do." I nodded.

"I'll let the two of you settle in, and we'll see you both at dinner tonight."

"If you want to walk over," Julian said, "follow the path from the back porch and through the gardens. We had it cleared."

"Thank you," I said.

"Be at home," Thomas said with a small smile.

Autumn shooed the men out of the cottage and with a cheerful wave to Willow, she shut the door behind them all.

The silence in the cottage was profound.

Willow looked up from her snack at the kitchen table. "She sure talks fast, doesn't she Mama?"

I bit back a laugh. "Yes, darlin' she does."

"I like her," Willow said around a mouthful of oatmeal raisin cookie.

"So do I," I admitted, and with a sigh, went to my bedroom and began to unpack.

It hadn't taken long to put our things away. Thanks to the Drake's thoughtfulness, the majority of our belongings were already hanging in closets or folded in drawers. I discovered a bowl of dried lavender potpourri in the bedroom. *That explained the fragrance,* I thought. While I rearranged a few of my clothes to suit my own preferences, Willow ran around the little cottage exclaiming over everything she found.

When it was time for dinner, I changed into dress slacks, low-heeled boots, and a new chunky knit sweater. I touched up my makeup, deepening the taupe shadow so my eyes appeared to be a darker shade of blue. After running a brush through my long dark curls, I spritzed on some perfume and called it good. Willow insisted on wearing her snow boots with her blue dress, and she was so excited that I had trouble getting her to stand still long enough for me to braid her brown hair down her back.

Eventually, I had the two of us bundled up, and we were able to leave the cottage. As directed, I followed the path that went from the back door and across the lawn. Solar lights ensured that the path was well lit, and I found myself holding my breath at the beauty of walking through the snowy gardens. We came to a tall brick wall which had been softened by ivy, and as we walked through the archway, I took in the pretty courtyard and the back door of the mansion.

"What will it all look like in the spring?" I wondered, studying the garden. The minute I took my eyes off her, Willow stomped into a deep pile of snow.

"It's like where Elsa lives..." Willow breathed.

I grinned down at my daughter. Through her eyes, it did resemble a snowy faery land. Holding hands, I helped her out of the snow pile, and we made our way to the family entrance of the Drake mansion. The quick walk had been good for the both of us, and though the air was cold, it was bracing and helped to clear my head.

I needed to make a good impression on both Autumn and Duncan. I fully expected that the topic of dinner conversation would be on their upcoming wedding, and my part as the wedding coordinator. Which is why I had a small notebook and pen in my bag.

I knocked on the back door, that was painted an eye-popping shade of teal, and was surprised when Julian opened the door himself.

"Welcome," he said, holding the door open.

"Hi Julian!" Willow said loudly.

"Wipe your boots," I warned her, but it was pointless. My daughter stomped her feet once on the mat, and was hurrying straight across the parquet floors, leaving a trail of melting snow.

"I'm sorry about that," I began and tried not to be intimidated by the sheer size and scale of the house. I twisted the antique ring I wore on my right hand. The ring had been a gift and was set in silver with pave diamonds arranged in a small crescent around a central blue sapphire. Fiddling with the ring was a nervous gesture that I'd never managed to break. Even as I made myself stop fidgeting, I remembered that sapphires were good for calming the mind and clearing away negative thoughts. *Work your mo-jo, please.* I thought to the ring.

"Don't worry about the snow. It's fine," Julian assured me. He took our coats and ushered us to a dining room. I took my daughter's hand, hoping to avert any disasters. As we walked into the dining room I had only seconds to gather impressions of the opulent space. Warm taupe walls with bright white trim and crown moldings, and a huge whitewashed fireplace where a blaze crackled. A tasteful crystal chandelier was centered above a massive dining room table that could seat at least twelve.

"Thank you, Nina," Thomas was saying to a striking young woman with midnight hair as she placed a tray of roast beef, carrots and potatoes on the dining room table.

"Hi!" Willow said loudly. "We're here for supper!"

Thomas, Duncan, Autumn, and the woman all turned our way expectantly.

I clutched Willow's hand. *Breathe, Maggie,* I flashed a smile and reminded myself that I'd coordinated four-course dinners for some very posh and upper-crust weddings in my day. I wasn't intimidated by a display of wealth.

"Breathe," Julian whispered, and his fingers grazed my back in a supportive touch.

I shot a glance at him. I'd been intuitive all my life, and I put it to practical use when working with brides. It often kept me a few steps ahead of potential disasters at weddings. But while I was quiet about it, I'd rarely met anyone else who had the same kind of natural ability. Yet his comment, so similar to my own thoughts, made me wonder. Perhaps—not unlike the eye color—the intuition might be another family trait. I quickly set that all aside, as Thomas was there smiling and welcoming us to the table.

The woman was introduced to us as Nina Vasquez, and I was informed she'd recently taken over the house manager position for the Drake's.

"We're lucky to have Nina," Julian said. "She studied at le Cordon Bleu Academy."

Nina beamed at the praise. "Enjoy your dinner." She nodded to us all and left the room.

The food was gorgeous, but thankfully it was served

family style. As we passed around that pretty roast beef and vegetables, Thomas sat at the head of the table with Willow on his left. I sat beside Willow with Julian on my left, while Duncan and Autumn were across from me.

Willow was sitting on top of a few plump pillows, chattering away to both Autumn and Thomas, and having the time of her life.

Duncan smiled at me from across the table. "Did you get settled in?" he asked.

"We did," I said, cutting up Willow's roast beef for her.

Willow swung her feet. "Can I have a roll, Mama?"

Before I could speak, Autumn passed a buttered roll across the table, sliding it on Willow's plate. "There you go, short-stuff."

"Short-stuff?" Willow laughed.

Autumn winked, then shifted her attention to me. "I can't begin to tell you how happy I am that you're here to help with the wedding, Maggie. There are far too many details...and I'm in way over my head."

I met Autumn's eyes and sent her the same smile I'd given dozens of other nervous brides. "Don't you worry now. That's what I'm here for. To take care of all those details."

Duncan slipped his arm around his fiancée's shoulders. "Autumn's been trying to do everything for the handfasting herself."

"If only I could find the right kind of cords for the

ceremony…I suppose I could make some myself."
Autumn frowned. "But should I use ribbon or satin
cords? Multi colored or all white?"

I nodded, reminding myself that the bride and groom
were having a handfasting ritual on their wedding day.
During which their hands would be bound together with
a ceremonial cord. The old tradition was where the term
'tied the knot' came from. "I can help you with that," I
said. "I have a few ideas."

"Good." Autumn nodded. "It's one less thing for me
to worry about."

"Well, you can stop worrying, because I'm on top of
this," I said soothingly. "We should all have a sit-down.
Say...day after tomorrow?"

Thomas sipped at his wine. "There's no rush,
Maggie, we want you to take all the time you need to
feel at home."

"I want to hit the ground running," I said. "As a
matter of fact, I have meetings scheduled with the
baker, and your florist tomorrow afternoon—right after
we go and visit Willow's pre-school."

"I get a new school," Willow said.

"Which pre-school?" Thomas asked.

"The one that you recommended," I answered him.
"The pre-school on the University campus."

"My nephew, Morgan, goes there," Autumn said.
"He's younger than Willow, but he loves it."

"Your nephew, he's going to be the ring bearer,
correct?" I remembered.

Duncan grinned. "He is. The kid's a pistol."

"You have two flower girls as well," I said to the couple. "Sophia and Chloe. The girls are nine and seven years old."

"Wow. You remembered their names and ages." Autumn smiled.

"I'm all about the details," I said. "Nothing slips past me, I promise you."

"I can't wait for you to meet the bridesmaids." Autumn grinned. "We have several."

"So you have a final number." I nodded and reached down for my bag that I'd left beside my chair. Quickly I pulled a notebook and pen out. I unsnapped the monogrammed cover and began to take notes.

"There will be five," Autumn said. "My cousins Ivy and Holly, sister-in-law Lexie, and my friends Candice Jacobs and Violet O'Connell."

I added the names dutifully. "Speaking of which," I said, "when are you going shopping for the bridesmaid dresses? That should have been done a month ago, Autumn."

"Well..." Autumn shifted her utensils. "I had a challenge getting everyone together, so I thought maybe we could order the dresses online."

"Absolutely not," I said. "I have the notes about the style and colors you were wanting to go with for your enchanted garden theme." I had previously underlined the words 'rainbow' and 'different pastel colors' in my notebook. I nodded to the bride. "I'll confirm the appointment for your bridal party in the morning and get everyone together by the end of the week."

Autumn tilted her head. "You can get an appointment for us that fast?"

I closed the notebook with a quiet snap. "I already made the appointment a few weeks ago."

Her jaw dropped. "But how will we get everyone together?"

"You leave that to me. I know a thing or two about wrangling bridesmaids." I smiled at the couple. "Once we have the dresses nailed down, Duncan, we're going to want to take the groomsmen to get all the men measured, so the tuxes, vests and ties can be ordered."

"I'm suddenly afraid," Duncan said, staring at me.

"I'm not." Autumn gave Duncan a little elbow nudge. "I told you, I did my homework. Our cousin Maggie has a solid reputation as an event planner." She toasted me with her wine glass. "One of the weddings you coordinated last year was even featured in a national bridal magazine."

I was close to blushing, and I covered it by tucking away the notebook.

"It was clever to feature that write-up on your website," Thomas said. "Smart business sense."

Now it was my turn to blink in surprise. "I didn't realize that y'all had been aware of that." The knot I'd had in my belly for weeks started to loosen. *I'd gotten the job on my own merit after all, it seemed. Not because of any pity or familial sympathy...*

"I also contacted a couple of the brides you worked with last year through social media," Autumn said. "They couldn't stop raving about you."

I lifted my water glass, took a sip and made sure my expression was neutral. "Thank you, that's certainly nice to hear."

"Mama works with brides," Willow said. "Sometimes I get to help."

"How do you help, short-stuff?" Autumn wanted to know.

"I pass out the programs, or make sure the flower girls don't run off. They can be slippery," Willow said earnestly.

Duncan's lips twitched. "Sounds like a serious job."

I almost choked on my water. The last thing I needed was for my new family to think I had my four-year-old working because I couldn't handle an event...I cleared my throat. "Willow attended our friend's wedding last fall. While I worked, she kept the flower girls entertained."

"Mama says sometimes you gotta wrangle those bridesmaids." Willows statement had the adults chuckling.

Oh my god. I was mortified, but smiled easily.

I felt the lightest of touches on my arm. "Relax, Maggie." Julian's voice was the barest whisper of sound as everyone talked around us. "They aren't judging you."

I nodded in silent acknowledgement of his words.

I watched as Willow picked up her roll and took a huge, enthusiastic bite. "Be careful honey," I warned her. I'd barely finished my words when she dropped it. The bread bounced off her plate and disappeared under the table.

Willow lifted very large eyes to Thomas. "I'm sorry," she said contritely.

"Butter fingers." Thomas smiled at the girl.

Willow nodded solemnly. "It was slippery." She started to lick the melted butter off her fingers, when she figured it out. "Butter fingers!" She let loose a belly laugh and everyone began to chuckle in response.

"Now that's a sound I've missed," Thomas said with a nod to Willow. "It's good to hear a child's laughter in this house again." He lifted his wine glass. "To family," he said.

I tapped my glass to Julian's and then over to Thomas. "To family," I said.

***

After dinner, Willow and I walked back to the cottage. The cold was bracing but pleasant. I stopped on the back porch to unlock the door, and Willow suddenly bent down.

"Mama, look what I found!"

I pushed the door open. "What'd you find, honey?"

Willow held up a tattered, dirty and broken fashion doll to show me.

"Baby, put that down. It's dirty." I said, automatically.

She ignored me and was now holding the doll at eye level and studying it.

"Willow." I said her name again.

My daughter didn't answer. She stood, frozen in place staring vacantly at the doll.

"Willow!" I said, sharply.

She started, blinked and tipped her face up to mine. "Yes, Mama?"

I took the old doll away from her. "Give me that," I said, holding it by the fingertips. I ushered her inside and dropped the old doll in the kitchen trashcan, immediately. While Willow tugged her mittens off and unzipped her coat, I washed my hands in the sink.

"You threw it away?" she asked sadly.

"Yes honey, it was all broken and dirty," I said.

"But it was for me!" she said crossly.

"Baby, no it wasn't." I dried my hands. "It was an old doll someone left behind."

I bundled Willow off to bed, and once she was down for the night I took advantage of the logs that had been laid in the fireplace. I lit them and sat on the couch watching the flames for a while, thinking over my first day in William's Ford.

Autumn and Duncan appeared to be happily in love, and the Drakes had been nothing but welcoming and generous to Willow and me. It gave me hope that my daughter and I could make good lives for ourselves here. Free from the shadows of the past.

A prickling at the base of my neck had me glancing warily over my shoulder. I'd heard nothing, yet I got up and went to double check the locks on the back and front doors. I felt exposed almost. Pulling the shade down over the kitchen window, I wondered what had made me feel so tense, and my gaze landed on the metal kitchen can.

"You're being paranoid, Maggie," I muttered to myself. But I crept cautiously to the garbage can, slowly peering over the edge anyway.

The face of the doll was battered in and the dark hair was tied in intricate knots. Old strips of fabric were tied around it in a sort of crude dress. I couldn't say why that old doll had my feathers ruffled. Yet it did. All I knew was that I wanted that thing out of my house, or better yet, destroyed.

Going with my gut, I snatched a paper towel, used it to fish the doll out of the garbage, and marched directly to the fireplace. The fire wasn't very big, but I tugged the pretty glass doors open and tossed the doll in the flames.

The flames grew large and engulfed it immediately. Before my eyes, the ratty fashion doll began to burn impossibly fast. With a loud pop that sent sparks shooting out onto the brick hearth, the doll started to melt. The plastic made the oddest sound when it burned —a sort of high-pitched squealing noise.

The smell from the burning plastic was vile, and I

looked around hoping for something to toss on the fire to cover the stench. My eyes landed on a basket of lavender potpourri resting on the end table.

"Lavender is excellent for cleansings," I said, thoughtfully. Even though I'd cut myself off from magick many years ago...old habits still died hard. Picking up the basket, I chucked the fragrant contents onto the fire.

To reinforce the action, I added a spontaneous protection charm. "Lavender burn and take away; any evil sent to us this day."

The lavender did the trick and the foul odor from the plastic was suddenly gone. The potpourri's smoke rolled up the chimney, the flames went down to a low simmer, and the tension left my shoulders as suddenly as it had arrived. I was probably overreacting, but I didn't want to take any chances. No one in William's Ford knew about my past.

I'd been very careful. I'd made sure that nobody had any reason to dig into Magnolia Sutton's troubled teenage years. All anyone saw of me these days was Maggie Parrish, mother, professional event coordinator, and mundane.

I intended to keep it that way.

Satisfied that I'd taken care of it, I shut the doors on the fireplace and headed to bed.

CHAPTER TWO

The visit to the preschool did more to soothe *my* nerves than Willow's. She dragged her feet going into the building and spoke quietly to her teacher. She took in everything with wide eyes and had very little to say —which was a sign of nerves for my girl.

As we drove across town for the meetings with both the baker and the florist for Autumn and Duncan's wedding, I tried to broach the subject of her new preschool. "Your teacher, Miss Tamira seemed very nice."

Willow shrugged.

"What did you think of your cubby being all decorated and ready for you?"

Willow heaved a mighty sigh, closed her eyes, and leaned her head against the back seat. But still, she remained silent.

"If you aren't feeling well darlin' I can take you home instead of going to see the baker." I waited a beat, before adding smoothly. "She makes cookies, cupcakes, and cakepops, I hear."

Willow's head snapped up. "What's a cakepop?" she asked suspiciously.

I hid a smile. "Let's go find out."

I managed a parking spot a few doors down from the bakery—which was conveniently next to the florist. I'd previously exchanged emails with both the florist and the baker, and I'd checked out their websites online...however nothing beat seeing how they ran their businesses first hand.

I went around to let Willow out of the car, and hand-in-hand we walked into *Charming Cakepops.* The bakery's display window featured a Valentine's Day motif—lots of pink and red cupcakes, a sprinkling of artisan chocolates, many cakepops, and heart shaped cookies.

In the display, the cookies appeared to spill out of an old vintage, glass cookie jar that was lying on its side, and everything else was artfully arranged on tiered trays. It took seconds to sum it all up, but the display had my mouth watering, *and* looking forward to seeing the inside of the bakery.

I pushed open the wooden door that was painted candy pink and an old bell sounded.

"Be right out!" a woman's voice called from somewhere in the back.

Willow went straight for the display cases holding the treats and tugged me along with her. While she perused the baked goods, I took the opportunity to check out the set up. Old hardwood floors gleamed in the winter light. Beautiful white shelving covered the entire wall behind the cases and was trimmed out with fancy gingerbread woodwork. The background of the shelves was painted the palest of pink, and lighting brightened each shelf. Gleaming white pendant lights illuminated the cases and the confections displayed inside.

I studied the large chandelier that hung in the center of the room. The light fixture was painted in an eye-popping shade of hot pink. *The décor was clever,* I thought.

It was vintage meets new, with rustic wood, glossy white shelving and cases, gleaming glass, and the barest hint of dusty rose on the walls. A half dozen metal café tables and padded ice cream chairs allowed for seating. At the moment, a pair of college students was sitting together at a table, each with a cupcake and a coffee. A self-serve coffee and tea center was arranged along the far wall, and a sign above it proclaimed: *Cake Fixes Everything*.

No doubt about it, the bakery had style and atmosphere...but best of all, it smelled incredible inside the shop. I was never going to walk out of there empty-handed.

"Hi. Can I help you?" came a cheerful voice.

I discovered a petite woman standing behind the front counter. A tumble of platinum blonde curls were pinned to the crown of her head. It added a few inches of height to her, but at a guess she couldn't have been taller than five foot two.

"I'm Maggie Parrish," I said. "I have an eleven o'clock meeting with Candice Jacobs to discuss the Bishop - Quinn wedding."

"I'm Candice." Dark brown eyes danced as she came out from around the counter. She was wearing a white chef's coat with pink trim, but also jeans and neon green tennis shoes.

"Hello," I said, and smiled at her outfit. When she reached for my hand and shook it, my shoulders dropped. I immediately felt at home. There was something...well...charming about Candice.

"It's nice to meet you in person, Maggie." Candice turned her attention to my daughter. "And you're Willow. I'm glad your mom could bring you along."

"Thank you for understanding," I said. "Willow starts preschool tomorrow, and—"

"You've only just moved here." Candice tipped her head. "Your accent is awesome. Where are you from?"

"Louisiana," I said.

"Autumn mentioned you were from out of town but I didn't realize you were from out of state."

I dropped a hand to my daughter's shoulder. "Willow, say hello to Ms. Jacobs."

"Hi." Willow reached back for my hand and gripped it tightly.

Candice motioned us to a table and went to go gather her notes for the wedding. I helped Willow unzip her coat and she climbed onto the ice cream chair and swung her feet. "It smells yummy in here, Mama."

"This won't take long," I promised Willow. "When we're finished we can go get lunch."

"Can I have a cheese burger?" Willow wanted to know.

Before I could answer her, Candice came back out carrying a tray. As she walked closer I saw that the tray held a notebook, three short bottles of water, and a small plate of cakepops. Quickly, she set the tray down, passed out the water, and put the cakepops in the center of the table.

"Ooooh," Willow breathed as she studied the sparkly cakepops in pink and white. "Mama, look!"

"Do we have any food allergies?" Candice asked me.

"No." I shook my head.

"Good." Efficiently, Candice placed tiny white paper doilies in front of Willow and then me.

"I didn't expect you to bring out samples," I started to say.

"Think of these as less of a sample, and more of a 'Welcome to William's Ford' offering." Candice placed one white and one pink cakepop in front of both Willow and me. "What do you think of our town, Maggie?" she asked.

"It's lovely," I said.

"You moved into the brick cottage on the Drake's property, right?"

"Yes, they're a family connection."

"I see." Candice's expression was carefully neutral as she took her seat.

My stomach dropped. I didn't know why it had become suddenly awkward, yet I felt the best course of action was to change the subject. Deliberately, I picked up the white cakepop. "How did you decorate these so perfectly?" I asked, admiring the swirls of glittery pink. "They're almost too pretty to eat."

"That one is red velvet dipped in white chocolate," Candice explained, and reached across the table to open Willow's bottle of water for her. "The pink has white cake on the inside."

Willow took a bite of the pink cakepop, and she started to smile. "Mama, these are yummy!"

I tried the red velvet expecting a nice treat, but the flavors that melted in my mouth had me sighing and leaning back in my chair. "Oh, my." I took another bite. "Candice, you are an artist."

Candice smiled and took a sip of her water. "I'm glad you like them. Autumn and Duncan have chosen those two cake flavors for their wedding." She flipped open a notebook and rotated it to face me. "While the color of the candy coating will be different, here is a photo of the tiered setup they've chosen for the reception."

We spent a pleasant half hour going over the details of the wedding dessert. The delivery time, set up, and so forth. Now that I'd sampled the cakepops for myself, I could see why Autumn had been keen to have them at her wedding reception. Beyond the taste, which was extraordinary, the rainbow of different pastel colors would be gorgeous in the tiered display.

I confirmed Candice's Saturday appointment with the bridal party for bridesmaid dress shopping, and she promised me she'd be there 'with bells on'. Before we left, she boxed up a half dozen more cakepops for Willow.

I pulled my wallet out of my bag. But she waved me off.

"It's on the house." She winked at Willow.

Since Willow was in such a good mood from the two cakepops she'd eaten, we went directly next door to the O'Connell florist shop before getting lunch.

The florist was a wonderland of spring in the middle of winter. Lush green plants, orchids, blooming house plants, and a glass-fronted cooler full of flowers greeted us, as did a large gray cat that hopped out of the front window and marched right up to Willow.

"*Meow*," the cat cried. It sounded exactly like he'd said *hello*. Without further ado, he plopped himself down on Willow's snow boots.

Willow giggled. "Mama, the cat said hello."

I couldn't help but laugh too. "Hey there, kitty-cat."

"That's Tank." Came a woman's voice. "He's friendly."

The blonde woman stood behind a sturdy workstation. She had long, straight hair pulled back in a ponytail, and I saw as she walked forward that the bottom half of her hair was dyed purple.

Purple hair, I thought. *Land sakes.*

"You must be Maggie and Willow," she said, holding out a hand. "I'm Violet O'Connell. Welcome to William's Ford."

"Pleasure to meet you in person, Violet." I tucked the box of cakepops under my arm and shook her hand.

"I love your accent," Violet said. "Where are you from?"

"Louisiana."

Another woman came out from the back. She was middle aged, blonde and looked enough like Violet that I guessed they were mother and daughter. She introduced herself to me as Cora O'Connell. "What brought you to Missouri?" Cora asked, shaking my hand.

"Besides coordinating the wedding," Violet added, making me smile.

"I have cousins in William's Ford," I said.

"Anyone we know?" Cora asked.

"Jeez, Mom." Violet rolled her eyes. "Let the woman take her coat off and sit down, before you begin the inquisition."

Violet led the way, and before I knew it I found myself seated in a chair at a wooden consultation table, while Willow dragged a ribbon across the store for Tank to chase. Cora took over answering phones and running the shop while Violet and I had our meeting. I'd honestly expected to have a more formal sit-down type of meeting with the baker and the florist, but clearly, that wasn't how they did things here in William's Ford.

I had to admit, it was an unusual set-up. Both the baker and the florist were bridesmaids in the wedding they were vending for. But after fifteen minutes with Violet O'Connell, I could see that the woman was a consummate professional, *and* she was well organized. After subtly checking out the arrangements in the cooler and viewing the photos of the other weddings she had done, I felt relieved that my bride and groom had chosen both their baker and florist well.

Violet confirmed her bridesmaid dress appointment for Saturday, but before we left, she threw me a curve ball.

"So, Maggie." Violet folded her hands in her lap. "Have you ever organized a child's birthday party? A really extravagant one?"

"Yes." I nodded. "And I've done event planning for a few over-the-top sweet sixteen parties, and also a debutant ball."

Violet leaned forward. "There's a special little girl in my life and she's about to turn six. She lost her mother a few years ago, and I recently found out from her father that she's never had a real birthday party."

I opened my notebook and got out my pen. "The date?" I asked briskly.

"Well that's the thing," Violet said. "It's on Sunday, and with Valentine's Day so close the flower shop is crazy busy. I don't have the time to do this properly.

Not in the way she deserves."

I jotted the date down. "Do you have a theme in mind?"

"Sugarplum Fairy," Violet said. "It's a long story, but that's how we met. Her father and I took her to see *The Nutcracker* ballet over the holidays, and Charlie's become obsessed."

"The birthday girl is named Charlie," I said as I began to take notes.

"Charlotte, actually. I call her Charlie," Violet explained.

"How many guests?" I asked, as I wrote down: *ballet, pastel colors, sparkle, snowflakes.*

"Eight—maybe ten children."

"Budget?" I asked.

"I know it's last minute," Violet said. "How much would you charge to take care of *everything*? We're talking cake, decorations, games, goodie bags..."

I sat back and considered. "It would be a nice touch if the children could make something at the party, too," I said. "A simple craft that goes with your theme. Something they could take home."

"That's perfect!" Violet began to smile. I know I'm asking for a lot in a short amount of time, but what do you think you would charge?"

I swiftly considered the costs and more importantly the benefits...*This could get my name out there as an event coordinator, quickly. One gorgeous, fancy little girl's birthday party and I'd have parents standing in line wanting a party for their own princess.*

Even as my heart pounded in excitement, I calmly named a fee, double what I would normally charge. My intuition said she'd go for it, but I held my breath wondering how she would react to the price.

Violet O'Connell never even blinked. "You're hired," she said.

Willow giggled as Tank grabbed the ribbon away from her and romped across the sales floor. "I like your cat, Violet!" Willow said, coming to stand by me.

Tank suddenly jumped to the top of the table. With a sort of feline mutter, he walked over to head-butt Violet.

"Yes, Tank. I agree," Violet said to the cat.

"Sorry," I said. "What do you agree with?"

Violet's blue eyes shifted from the cat's to mine. "We would like to invite Willow to the birthday party as well."

Surely she didn't mean we—as in herself and the cat? "We would?" I asked, out loud.

"Sure." Violet ran her hand over the cat's head. "It would be a great way for Willow to meet some of the other kids in town."

Willow's eyes lit up. "I wanna go to the Sugarplum Fairy party!"

"That's very kind of you," I said, ready to politely decline, and Tank reached over and gently patted at the top of Willow's head. The cat shifted his gaze to me as if to say, *What's your problem, honey?*

I studied my daughter who now stood between Violet and I. Willow was currently making kissy noises to the huge cat and he was leaning against her and purring like a freight train. I wondered if the cat was Violet's familiar...but after watching them interact, I had my answer.

I hid my discomfort behind a professional smile. *Just because a woman had a psychic bond with an animal didn't mean she was slinging hexes and curses,* I reminded myself. *First off, the plants in the shop would never have been able to withstand the negativity. The fact that everything around us was lush, vibrant and healthy, reinforced that* if *Violet and her familiar were working magick, it was the positive and life affirming variety.*

"Please, Mama. Can I go?" Willow interrupted my reverie.

There was no way to decline without sounding ungracious. So, I gave in. "Yes you may." *I'd be at the party anyway,* I thought. *Where I could keep a watchful eye on things, and no one would even know.*

"Hooray!" Willow did a little dance.

Tank walked across the table and nudged my hand, wanting to be petted.

"Thank you, Mr. Tank," I said rubbing his gray ears.

"Meow," Tank cried.

I couldn't help but chuckle. "Thank you for the invitation as well, Violet," I said, meeting her eyes. "This will be lovely opportunity for Willow to make some friends."

***

Willow and I stopped at her favorite fast-food place, and once again I was asked where I was from. I tried to take it in stride, but I was sorely tempted to reply with something sassy as opposed to a polite response, but I held my tongue.

After Willow ate, we moved to the indoor play area. I sat on a bench where I could keep an eye on her and brainstormed. I took notes as fast as I could while Willow ran around and climbed all over everything.

I already knew the name of the local party rental vendor, as Duncan and Autumn were renting tents for their reception from them. One quick phone call confirmed I could indeed order helium balloons in whatever color I would need.

As to a location for the Sugarplum Fairy birthday party, I immediately thought of *Charming Cakepops.* I checked to see that Willow was still happily playing, and then on a hunch, I contacted Candice to inquire about renting out the space for a few hours on Sunday.

My instincts were right on target. Candice was delighted to reserve the bakery, as she and Violet were friends. Candice assured me there would be no problem at all with providing the cupcakes and cakepops needed for the Sugarplum Fairy party. I promised to call her the next day to discuss the details of the desserts and ended our call. I tucked my notebook away and rounded up my daughter for the trip home.

By the time we returned to our cottage, Willow was happy to cuddle on the sofa and watch an animated movie. I sat at the drop-leaf table in the kitchen and got to work on my laptop. In a few hours I had a list of vendors and craft stores to visit, and had ordered ballet-themed party plates and wintery types of decorations. I ended up paying extra to have everything overnighted from my favorite online wholesaler, but it would be well worth it.

With hands trembling from nerves, I shut down the laptop. I sincerely hoped that, in my efforts to dazzle the residents of William's Ford with my event coordinator skills, I hadn't over-extended myself. I had five days to pull off a child's elegant birthday party, and in four days, I had the bridesmaids dress selection to oversee.

I blew out a long breath. When my stomach growled, I checked the clock on the kitchen stove and saw it was 5:00. I frowned, wondering what I could put together for dinner with the supplies I had on hand. My plans to go grocery shopping had been demolished by the impromptu birthday party planning.

A knock on the front door had me rising. I opened it and discovered my cousin Julian standing on the front porch, wearing a fancy winter jacket and dress slacks and holding a large pizza box.

"I had a feeling you might need a hand with supper

tonight," he said. "Do you like pizza?"

My smile was automatic. "Cousin, you and I are going to be very good friends." I stood back so he could enter, and Willow saw him and let out a cheer.

He carried the box to the kitchen. "I know where everything is," he said. Julian shrugged out of his jacket and proceeded to get out plates and glasses. "Sit down and tell me about your first day."

It was a pleasant surprise to spend a little alone time with Julian. For such a sophisticated man, he was easy company—and Willow seemed to adore him from the moment they'd met. Truth be told, Willow was a damn-fine judge of character, and her comfort with Julian told me quite a bit. After dinner, Willow climbed right in his lap and told him about the cakepops, meeting Tank the cat, and the birthday party.

Before I knew it, Julian had volunteered to keep an eye on Willow when I ran the bridesmaid's dress appointment on Saturday. While he and Willow ate a few cakepops, Julian assured me he had plenty of practice babysitting, as he sometimes watched his god-daughter, Isabel.

I surveyed the elegantly attired man in front of me and had a hard time imagining Julian Drake as a babysitter. "You have a goddaughter?"

"Isabel Julianna. She's nine-months-old and gorgeous." He grinned. "Her parents and I are friends. As a matter of fact, you met her mother last night, Nina Vasquez."

"Oh." I recalled the pretty woman who'd cooked such an amazing meal. "That's right."

Julian nodded. "Nina took over managing the house and the staff, when Mrs. Johnson retired last month."

"Dinner was absolutely wonderful," I said.

"Wait until you taste her lamb chops," Julian said. "Nina's a fantastic cook, we're lucky to have her and her family with us. She's exactly what we needed to get the house running smoothly again."

"Oh?" *With us?* I wondered at that, but before I could even open my mouth to ask, Julian continued.

"There's a housekeeper's suite on the first floor of the mansion. Mrs. Johnson never lived there, so Duncan updated the rooms for the Vasquez family."

"That sounds lovely," I said. "Autumn mentioned that Duncan restored and remodeled houses."

Julian stood and began cleaning up from the pizza. Willow raced to help, asking questions about baby Isabel. I sat back and discovered that it was a refreshing change to see a male rolling up his sleeves and happily clearing away a meal—even if it was a pizza.

I'd never had so much cheerful help from good-natured people in my life. I supposed I was going to have to get used to it. It wasn't until after Julian had left for the evening that I realized he'd shown up right as I'd been thinking about supper. *Almost as if he'd had a sixth sense about it.*

I wondered again if he, like me, was intuitive. Despite my mother's old story, so far I'd seen nothing that led me to believe the Drakes were involved in any sort of sorcery. The Drakes appeared to be upstanding members of their community and damn fine people.

They were simply helping out a relative, because they could afford to be generous.

***

Saturday morning dawned bright, sunny and cold. I'd never experienced single digit temperatures, and it was an awful shock. My quick trip to warm up the car had resulted in me dashing back inside the cottage to add another layer of clothing. Julian arrived on time to pick up Willow, and they trooped off to the main house together. As I drove shivering across town to the bridal salon, I figured I had just enough time to grab a coffee before the bridal appointment.

Julian had recommended the *Black Cat Coffee House*, and since it was only four doors down from the salon, I parked my car and hustled out of the cold as quickly as I could.

The coffee shop was a delight. I smiled over the feline theme framed artwork and enjoyed the pretty brick walls and gleaming hardwood floors. I paid for my cappuccino and was moving down the row to the pick-up area when I heard my name being called.

Duncan Quinn sat at a table with another man. Duncan appeared comfortable slouching in his chair, wearing boots, jeans, fleece-lined bomber jacket and a blue scarf. While his companion sat perfectly straight in his chair, almost as if he were either nervous, or very uncomfortable in his surroundings.

His companion was trim, I noted. The man's winter coat was a dark gray wool peacoat. I could see the edge of a plaid shirt, and he too wore jeans. He had an intriguing face, and shaggy dark brown hair that brushed the tops of his shoulders. In contrast to the mop of hair, the man sported a close, well-trimmed mustache and beard.

"Hello, Duncan," I said, walking over to their table.

"Maggie," Duncan said, gesturing to his companion. "I'd like you to meet my friend. Wyatt Hastings, this is Magnolia Parrish."

"Hello, Magnolia." The man nodded his head in greeting, but didn't offer his hand.

I was startled at the striking contrast between his light blue eyes and his dark lashes and brows. Recovering my composure, I gave him a nod in return. "Please, Mr. Hastings. Call me Maggie."

"Maggie," he said, studying my face. "Magnolia, suits you better."

"I prefer to be called Maggie."

"Maggie is our wedding coordinator," Duncan told his friend.

"Yes indeed." I smiled. "And I recognize your name, Mr. Hastings." At my words his shoulders stiffened, but I continued on smoothly. "You're one of the groomsmen."

He gripped his coffee cup tighter. "Yes, I am."

I turned as the barista called my name. "Excuse me, gentlemen." I walked over to the counter and picked up my drink.

As I walked back to their table, Duncan pushed out a chair for me. After checking my watch, I saw I had five minutes to spare, so I sat next to Duncan and tucked my monogrammed tote bag on my lap.

"Your accent," Wyatt said. "It's beautiful. Where are you from, originally?"

The man wasn't flirting, but the way he watched me made me think he was taking a sort of inventory. I considered him as I took a sip of my coffee. "I'm from Louisiana."

"What part?" He leaned a bit closer. "Your accent doesn't sound at all like the ones from New Orleans."

"The northwestern corner of Louisiana," I explained. "A small town close to Shreveport." I left it at that. I had good reasons for not wanting folks to know exactly where I'd grown up.

Wyatt nodded, took out his cell phone and apparently began to tap in notes to himself.

"What on earth are you doing?" It concerned me, but I forced myself to act casual.

"Better watch out, Maggie." Duncan gave me an elbow nudge. "Wyatt's a writer."

"And nothing and no one is safe." Wyatt's lips turned up, as he agreed with his friend.

Duncan chuckled. "You never know...you could find

yourself or that Southern drawl in his next book."

I frowned as the man continued to enter notes on his cell phone with blinding speed. "Y'all act like I'm from Mars or something. Louisiana's hardly exotic."

"It's different and fabulous," Wyatt muttered as he typed.

Oh, I realized. *The man was simply a sucker for an accent.* I sipped my cappuccino and told myself to act casual. "Don't get out much, do you Mr. Hastings?"

"I make myself get out of the house once a week," he said soberly, and set his phone aside on the tabletop. "Besides, sitting here and having a coffee is a good way to get ideas for new characters, or...to figure out ways to kill people."

I choked on my drink. The man had been completely serious. "What sort of books, *do* you write, Mr. Hastings?"

"Mysteries," he said.

"Murder mysteries. Really *gruesome* ones," Duncan added, with relish.

I raised my eyebrows at the writer. "Well, isn't that nice?"

Wyatt began to chuckle. "I'm almost disappointed. You didn't call me, 'sugar'."

My lips twitched, but I refused to smile. Wyatt Hastings was certainly an odd duck. "Well, if y'all will excuse me." I stood. "I have several bridesmaids to wrangle."

"Good luck with that," Duncan said cheerfully.

I nodded to Mr. Hastings. "It was certainly interesting meeting you." I waited a beat until those pale blue eyes met mine. "Sugar."

The smile Wyatt Hastings flashed my way almost made up for him taking notes on me and my accent. I allowed myself a slight smile, slung the tote bag over my shoulder and headed for the bridal shop.

***

I had several different styles of the chiffon gowns Autumn had indicated she preferred hanging up by the fitting rooms. Going from my notes, I made sure to have the correct sizes pulled, as well as a petite size for Candice, *before* the bridal appointment. As I hung the last dress, the bridal store manager introduced herself and we exchanged a few pleasantries. Which of course began with: I love your accent. This was naturally followed by: What brings you to Missouri?

"Where are you living now that you're our newest resident?" the manager asked.

I gave her a polite smile. "I'm renting a cottage here in town."

"Oh? There are some charming properties in the historic district. Did you nab one of those?"

"Yes, I'm staying in the cottage on the Drake property."

The woman flinched. She tried to cover up her reaction, but I'd already seen it. "Do you know that family well, dear?" Her voice sounded strained.

I frowned. "The Drakes are a family connection," was the most information I was willing to share.

"I didn't know you were related to the Drakes." She cleared her throat and flashed a nervous smile. "Excuse me while I go get the spring color swatches for the bride to choose from."

I watched as the manager went behind the front counter. She said something to her co-worker and the co-worker stopped what she was doing. The pair of them stared blatantly at me from across the floor.

Must be a small town gossipy thing, I decided, as the women began to whisper. Although it made me uncomfortable, I shrugged their odd reaction off. Glancing at my watch, and seeing that I had a moment, I double-checked my appearance in the mirror before everyone arrived.

The sleek ponytail I wore was a calculated move— one must never outshine the bride. It was a hard cold fact that brides were often uncomfortable with a coordinator who was prettier than they were.

My whole life people had cast judgments on me because of my appearance. They'd figured I was either a prize to be won, someone's trophy wife, or that I was looking for a man. When I disabused them of that notion, then I was accused of being aloof, cold, or a bitch.

When it came to the bridal industry my best bet was to simply tone my looks down with a careful choice of apparel and subtle cosmetics. My black slacks were a basic element in my consultant's wardrobe. Typically I wore heels, but in concession to the winter weather, I'd switched out the pumps for a pair of black suede, low-heeled boots. The crisp white blouse served me well in Louisiana, but with the colder temperatures up north I'd added a mock navy turtleneck underneath and looped a camel plaid infinity scarf around my neck.

With a final adjustment of the scarf, I reminded myself to remain calm. I was about to meet more of my grandmother's people, and I wanted to be prepared, polite, and in control of the situation when I did.

I had exchanged emails with all of the bridesmaids but had only met Candice and Violet face-to-face this week. There were still three more to meet—relatives all. Lexie Bishop: Autumn's sister in law, and Holly and Ivy Bishop, Autumn's twin cousins.

"Hi, Maggie!" Violet arrived first, announcing that she'd ducked out of the flower shop and had walked the few blocks to the bridal salon. "Are you ready for the craziness that's about to go down?" she asked, unbuttoning her heavy coat.

"I can more than handle ten children for a birthday party." I held my hands out for her deep amethyst wool coat. "Everything will be beautiful tomorrow. Don't you worry."

"No, not the party," Violet chuckled. "I *meant* the bridesmaids."

I passed Violet's coat onto a staff member of the

salon. "They won't break me," I said.

I heard the ruckus outside before the door to the salon swung open. Autumn was surrounded by four women, all who were chatting at the same time with a great deal of enthusiasm.

"Hello." I gave them all a professional smile.

"Hello cousin Maggie!" A dramatic-looking brunette with dark-rimmed eyes marched straight to me and enfolded me in a big hug. She added a squeeze before pulling back to hold me at arm's length. Eyes the same shade of green as Autumn's grinned up at me. "I'm Ivy," she said. "It's great to finally meet you."

"Hello." I smiled politely at the gothic looking young woman. "Let me take your coat."

"Don't you worry about that." She quickly peeled out of her black coat, tossed it to a sales associate, and grabbed my arm. "Come with me, there's more family for you to meet."

All my plans for a quiet smooth entrance and seating of the bridal party went straight out the window. Ivy steered me over to a woman with dark blonde hair and serious blue eyes, and introduced her to me as Lexie. Before I knew it, I was coming face to face with the third of my cousins, Holly.

"Hello," she said, shaking my hand. "Welcome to the family."

"Thank you," I said, as the volume of happy voices rose around us. Holly, I discovered, looked nothing like her twin sister. She was a bit taller and in direct opposition to her sister's sleek, dark bob and green eyes, Holly's eyes were aqua-blue. Her hair was a wild tumble of ginger curls that hung halfway down her back. "Let me take your coat."

"Thanks." Holly relinquished her teal coat, and I, in turn, passed it on to the store manager.

"Miss Parrish, I thought you said you were related to the Drakes," the manager said, softly.

I didn't respond to her comment and gave her a stern look instead.

"I'm sorry. Maybe I'm confused." She flashed a nervous smile. "Didn't I just hear the Bishop girl welcome you to the family?"

The woman was nosier than I was comfortable with, and it was time to put my foot down. "I fail to see what business it is of yours."

Her eyes grew round. "Are you somehow related to *both* the Bishops and the Drakes?"

"And if I am?"

"Oh my goodness." She backed away from me and hustled to the far side of the room.

Old busy-body, I thought and deliberately ignored her. "Ladies," I said to the bridal party, "if I could have y'all take a seat."

Lexie—the matron of honor, nudged everyone to the seating area. I managed to keep Autumn in the center while Holly and Ivy sat to her left. Lexie sat on the bride's right, Candice squeezed in and Violet sat on the arm of the sofa. They all turned to me expectantly.

I took immediate advantage of the temporary silence. "Now that I have your attention, we'll get started."

CHAPTER THREE

I needed a cigarette. Probably a stiff drink, or maybe both.

The bridesmaid dress fitting had been a success, but the strangest thing had happened. It was toward the end of the appointment, when Ivy and Holly had been standing in front of the three-way mirror. Ivy had been trying on the one-shouldered variation of the chiffon bridesmaid's dress, and her sister had on a softer, more romantic version that featured fluttery short sleeves.

I had suggested adding an embellished sash to the dresses to doll them up a bit. And as I tried to hand the sash over to Holly, it had instead, somehow, flown out of my hand and straight into Ivy's.

I didn't recoil from the girls, but it was a near thing. I stood completely still as my mind raced to make sense of what it had seen. Telekinesis was rare. Typically only the most powerful of practitioners could control it. However, that sash certainly hadn't slipped...

Before I could comment, Lexie walked up behind

Ivy and had lightly cuffed her on the back of the head. "Knock it off, Ivy," she'd said.

Ivy's response was an unrepentant grin, and everyone had started to snicker...except for me.

"These beaded sashes are very pretty," Holly said, gently taking a second embellished sash from my hand and tying it at her own waist. "Good thinking, Maggie."

It had to have been an odd reflection of the three-way mirror, I decided. The only way I'd ever seen the gift used was to intimidate and control... Surely the young woman wouldn't waste that sort of ability on a light-hearted prank. Would she?

I swallowed my unease and acted as if I'd seen nothing, and instead focused on the task at hand.

When all was said and done, Lexie, the matron of honor, had picked out a knee-length chiffon dress that featured a scoop neck, tank straps and a pleated bodice. Holly had selected the V-neck dress with soft fluttery cap sleeves. Candice had preferred a Y-neckline with a gently gathered skirt. Ivy had gone for the more dramatic, goddess-style, one-shoulder dress with a cascading side gather. Violet had favored a strapless version of the chiffon dress with a sweetheart neckline and ruching detail that cascaded down the front, adding a little dimension.

After much debate, Autumn had settled on the individual colors for her bridesmaids as well. Lexie had a pale lemon yellow, and Ivy a mint green. Holly was wearing sky blue, Violet would have the lilac—a wise choice considering her hair color—and finally, Candice would be in soft pink. The embellished sashes were unanimously approved, and the bridal salon gave us a discount since we were buying five of them. It was agreed that shoes would be nude and flats as the wedding ceremony and reception would be on the grass in a garden.

The dresses and sashes were ordered and had been guaranteed to be delivered to the shop by early April. Which was cutting it closer to the May wedding than I would have cared for, but I made sure that everyone had ordered their sizes correctly, so there shouldn't be any problems.

As Holly paid for her gown, the cash register crashed. To my surprise, Holly backed up several paces and told the sales associate to try again. The computer blinked back to life, the sale went through, and the store manager apologized for the technical hiccup.

"Of course, Lexie didn't whap you upside the head for that..." Ivy said to her sister.

"Perhaps that's because this was involuntary, while you were showing off," Holly said with an arch look at her twin.

I was standing right behind the sisters during this exchange, waiting to buy the fabric swatches that matched the bridesmaid's gowns. My stomach tightened at their words. "Is everything alright?" I asked them.

Ivy smiled. "Absolutely."

Her smile read false to me, and the coffee I'd had earlier wasn't sitting well on my stomach. Perhaps I was under more stress with meeting all of them than I had realized. At any rate, I kept a smile on my face and shuffled the lot of them out the door.

***

I went to pick up Willow and headed to the kitchen door of the Drake mansion as instructed. I found her in the family kitchen with Julian, Nina Vasquez, her husband Diego and their daughter Isabel.

The nine-month-old sat in a high chair squealing happily and banging a plastic spoon on the tray, while Willow was helping Nina bake cookies. My original plan to go directly back to the cottage was sidetracked. Willow was blissfully happy working elbow-to elbow with Nina.

"Would you like a cup of tea?" Nina asked me as I shrugged out of my coat.

"God, yes," I hung my coat over the back of a kitchen chair. Julian introduced me to Diego and Isabel, and I sat beside the baby.

"Better make that chamomile," Julian said to Nina.

"Problems with the bridesmaids?" Nina asked as she pulled down a big tin of tea and rummaged through.

"Nothing more than the usual." I said and smiled at the baby. "Hello, pretty girl."

Isabel stopped her happy squeals and gazed at me

solemnly.

"Isabel has a bit of a temper," Diego warned me. "She doesn't like strangers."

"Is that right?" I smiled at her father. While the man was covered in tattoos and looked rough around the edges, his voice was quiet and calm.

"She gets that from her father," Nina said tartly, placing a mug in front of me.

"I can make the tea myself," I said, starting to rise. "Nina, you don't have to wait on me."

"I'm not." Nina poured hot water from a bright red kettle. "I simply don't like people poking around in my kitchen."

"She has a system." Diego smiled, and he went from tough and intimidating to bad-boy handsome in the blink of an eye. "Don't mess with her spice rack—it will get ugly."

Nina fired something off at her husband. It sounded Spanish but wasn't...*Maybe Portuguese*, I guessed. While I couldn't interpret her, the tone was crystal clear. Diego only laughed in response. I opened my tea bag, dunked it in the hot water, and told myself to relax.

Nina went back to helping Willow put the cookie dough on baking sheets, and Isabel decided at that moment to throw her spoon to the floor, arch her back in a tantrum, and let out an impressive howl.

Automatically I leaned over, unbuckled the high chair strap, and picked up the baby. "What's the problem, sugar pie?"

Isabel stiffened her whole body and I ignored it. Holding Isabel under her arms, I stood her on my lap so we were eye to eye. Her face wrinkled up.

"You gonna have yourself a little hissy fit?" I asked her.

The baby seemed to reconsider and studied me carefully with dark brown eyes.

"No. I didn't think so," I said. Turning Isabel around so she faced outwards, I tucked her on my lap.

Isabel began to happily bang her hands on the table, and I eased my mug further away.

Diego stared. "How did you manage that?"

"I'm a mother," I said, dropping a kiss on the top of the baby's dark hair. "I know a thing or two about strong-willed babies."

"She doesn't like most people she meets," Diego said.

"Especially my father," Julian agreed. "They glare at each other most days."

Willow climbed down off the step-stool she'd been standing on at the counter and walked over to the table. She bent over and got up in the baby's face. "Hi, Isabel!" she said too loudly.

Isabel responded with a bounce and a happy squeal as she reached for Willow.

"She likes my mama, and she likes me," Willow pointed out, taking the baby's hand.

"Thank you for helping keep Willow entertained today," I said to Nina. "If I can ever return the favor, please let me know."

"Yes!" Willow bounced up and down. "I wanna watch Isabel!"

"Deal," Nina said, slipping a batch of cookies from the oven. "I miss date nights."

"Are you trying to take over my babysitting job?" Julian asked Willow.

"Oh, sorry. Don't you have another job?" Willow asked him seriously.

In answer, Julian threw back his head and laughed.

By the time we arrived back at the cottage, it was suppertime. I started some water for elbow noodles for the mac and cheese Willow loved and slid a ham steak into the oven. After the meal I supervised Willow in the tub, and once I put Willow to bed I double-checked and organized all of the decorations, games and goodie bags for the Sugarplum Fairy party.

Satisfied everything was set, I made a quick run through the cottage, straightening as I went. I walked across the living room and whacked my shin on the coffee table. "Ouch!" I grabbed at my leg and saw that I'd hit the table because it had been moved. It now sat more central on the area rug as opposed to closer to the sofa. "How in the world did it end up in the middle of the room?" I asked myself.

As a matter of fact, the pillows on the sofa had been rearranged, and all the wholesaler catalogues I'd left neatly stacked on the end table appeared to have been gone through. I stopped myself from automatically straightening them and cast my gaze cautiously around the cottage. Which is how I noticed that the framed personal photos I'd added to the mantle had been shifted slightly.

The framed photo of myself, and a three-year-old Willow, was no longer central on the mantle. It wasn't moved by much, but it made my stomach drop in anxiety. *Willow could have messed with the pillows...but she couldn't reach the mantle.* "Or maybe you're being paranoid," I muttered.

The urge to scan the cottage for unwanted or intrusive energy was damn near overwhelming. Biting my lip, I waited until the urge passed. I hadn't practiced magick in almost fifteen years. I hadn't relied on dark magick during my divorce, nor had I used it when I'd been fighting off a custody battle. In my experience, almost all spell-craft was a dangerous crutch, and I'd been standing on my own for a long time now.

I certainly wasn't going to take up with the dark arts again because I was fatigued from relocating half way across the country and stressed out from the bridal appointment.

You did a banishing spell the other night over that ugly doll... my inner voice pointed out.

"That was different," I muttered. I rolled my eyes for arguing with myself, shut off the lights, and headed to bed. Tomorrow was a big day, and I needed to be at my best.

***

It had taken me two hours. Probably less if I hadn't had Willow with me, but I had transformed the seating section of *Charming Cakepops* into a young girl's fantasy. Crepe paper streamers swooped festively around the space. I'd set up an eight-foot table and covered it with pale aqua cloth and layers of iridescent tulle. Pastel pink feather boas served as a table runner and white sparkling snowflakes—old Christmas ornaments from Violet O'Connell—had been worked into the arrangement.

Candice had created a two-tiered display of her cakepops in lavender and pale pink with crystal like sugar sparkles. Next to that, a platter held cupcakes all decorated in pink and pale lavender, each with a tiny ballerina dancing on the top.

To add to the fantasy effect, a dozen pink, lavender and aqua helium balloons wrapped in tulle floated around that dessert table at various heights. They swayed back and forth, their ribbon streamers weighted to the floor with a Mylar base.

I'd commandeered three of the café tables for the guests and covered them with more layers of tulle. One table had a Nutcracker for a centerpiece, another had a pair of satin toe shoes, and the third held a trio of tiny white bottlebrush trees. I'd cut another pink feather boa into thirds and had looped the feathers around each of the centerpieces.

Willow walked around the guest tables placing smaller snowflake ornaments in the feathers at the tables...and I snuck around behind Willow readjusting the snowflakes for maximum impact. When that was finished, I sprinkled confetti on the tabletops. Once I had the main components on the tables arranged to my liking, I positioned the paper plates, paper cups, coordinating napkins, and finally the glittery place cards.

I allowed Willow to 'help' by setting out the goodie bags on another table and she amused herself with that, and by running back and forth to see what Candice was doing in her bakery kitchen.

I was standing in my stockinged feet on a café chair, tying a final cascade of snowflakes from the hot pink chandelier, when I heard a tap on the bakery door. I saw Violet outside the door holding baskets full of flowers. I hustled to the door, flipped the lock, and let her inside.

She passed me a basket. "I wanted to get these here before Matthew brings Charlie."

I couldn't help but sniff at the basket of pink roses, baby's breath, white daisies, and purple carnations. "These are adorable," I said, and took the second bouquet from her.

"I came early," she said. "In case you needed my help but..." her voice trailed off.

I glanced over to regard Violet standing frozen, with very wide eyes.

"Is something wrong?" I asked.

"Oh my goddess, Maggie." Violet breathed. "It's *beautiful*! Like a faery tale. I never expected anything like this!"

I smiled. "I believe you requested an elegant fantasy of a birthday party for Charlie, did you not?"

Walking directly to the main table, I shuffled a few things around to make the flowers work. I peeked up at Violet. She was still looking around at everything with a mile-wide grin.

"Charlie is going to lose her mind," Violet predicted.

"I'm very glad that you're pleased with it," I said.

I slipped my shoes back on, took my phone out of my pocket, and snapped several pictures of the dessert tables and the entire party set-up. It *had* turned out well, and I intended to add the photos to my website.

***

The birthday party was a smashing success. I watched as the parents dropped off their children for the party, and their reactions to the décor and accessories was very satisfying. Charlie and her friends all had a grand time. Willow fit right in with the older children and enjoyed herself. I had the chance to meet Matthew Bell, Violet's partner—and Charlie's father. He thanked me for making his daughter a birthday party she'd never forget.

As the guests departed I stood by the door, passing out goodie bags. They were filled with cookies wrapped in a sparkly iridescent bag, the craft the children had made, and personalized aqua and pink chocolate candies that matched the party décor. Several mothers had asked for my business card, and I slipped them discreetly out of my jacket pocket and into their hands.

By the time the clean up was finished, Willow was snoozing in a café chair, and I gently bundled her back into her coat. To my dismay it had begun to snow during the party, and I'd had to cart the left-over decorations and tulle through what—to my eyes— seemed like a significant snowfall. Fortunately I was parked directly in front of the bakery, but I still was sliding around in my heels. I started the car to let it warm up, hurried back inside to say goodbye and thank you to Candice, and carried my sleepy daughter out.

I was reaching for the car door when someone walked right into us.

It was a fairly solid hit, my shoulder went back and I almost lost my balance. "Well, excuse you!" I said, shocked. The other person—a woman—tossed a glare over her shoulder and kept on walking.

"How rude," I muttered, and loaded Willow in my car. I buckled her into the booster seat and shut the passenger door.

The snow was really coming down, I realized. Frowning up at the sky, I swallowed a sick sense of anxiety at driving in the stuff and picked my way around the car and eased behind the wheel.

"Stay calm," I told myself, and switched on the

wipers. There was only an inch or two on the ground, but it *was* sticking to the streets, and I'd never actually driven in snow before. I was more nervous than I cared to admit, and my fingers itched to draw a protective pentagram over the steering wheel. *Stop that*! Silently, I scolded myself. *You're a professional, 'normal' woman, remember? Mundanes don't resort to the dark arts to drive in a snow storm!*

Blowing out a long breath, I cautiously backed out of the parking space. "It's a five minute drive to the cottage," I said, for the comfort of hearing a voice. "Girl, you've got this."

I eased the car down the street and was horrified that everyone else was blazing right along without a care in the world. The driver behind me honked impatiently at my slow speed, and I gulped and stepped on the gas a tad harder. The windshield began to fog up and I turned the airflow on the defroster to high. But somehow, it only made it worse.

I wiped the interior of windshield clear with my gloved hand, and suddenly there was a black dog standing right in the middle of the snowy street. "Shit!" I stomped on the brakes, and my car slid out from under me. I gasped, hanging on to the steering wheel for dear life, and my car swung sharply sideways, crashing into another oncoming car.

The impact was all on the driver's side. I felt the force of the other car's front bumper push my door inward and smack against my left arm. My head bounced off the driver's side window, and the noise was incredibly loud. Willow's startled cry at the sound made it worse.

Then it was suddenly over. "Are you alright, baby?" I asked, turning to reach for her. I couldn't go very far. I tried to undo my seatbelt, but found myself trapped. "Are you okay?" I ran my hand over her leg. "Baby can you move your hands and arms?"

There was a ruckus outside the car. "Mama what happened?" Willow craned her neck to see what was happening, and it relieved my fear. If she was moving freely, she was probably fine.

"The car slipped in the snow," I said. "We hit another car."

"We did?" Willow tried to look.

There was a man standing outside my car door calling for me to open it. The windows were so fogged up that I couldn't see him. I lifted my left arm to try, and immediately regretted it. Pain radiated up my arm and had me wheezing. I clenched my teeth against a litany of cuss words my daughter shouldn't hear.

"Mama?" Willow's voice trembled.

I tried to open the door with my other arm but it was stuck. "I can't open the door!" I explained.

"I called 911!" His voice carried clearly. "Are either of you hurt?"

"My daughter seems to be fine," I said.

"Can you unlock the passenger door?" He wanted to know. "Put the car in park, turn it off, see if the locks pop open."

I did still have my foot stomped down on the brakes. I quickly shifted the car into park, switched off the engine and the locks popped.

The passenger door was pulled open. "Magnolia?"

I blinked at the handsome, bearded man as he leaned down to look in the car. He seemed familiar. "Yes?" My voice sounded strange to my own ears.

"It's Wyatt Hastings. Do you remember me?"

"Hastings?"

"Duncan's friend," he said.

"Oh, the odd man who writes the gruesome mysteries." I tried to focus on him and shook my head to clear it. I grabbed my temple with my good hand and moaned. "Son of a bitch."

"Hey." He leaned further into the car.

"Did I hit your car?" I asked.

"No, not my car," Wyatt said. "I heard the collision from inside my house and came out to see if everyone was okay."

"Is the other driver alright?" I wanted to know, and trailed off as something trickled into my eyes.

"He's fine." Wyatt climbed across the passenger seat. "Magnolia, you're *not* okay. Your head is bleeding."

Automatically, I wiped at my forehead. It was sticky, and when I looked down at my fingers they were bloody. "Next time I'll draw the damned pentagram..." I muttered.

"What did you say?" Mr. Hasting asked.

I caught myself and tried to focus. "Is the other driver okay..." I frowned at him as Willow started to cry. "I asked that already, didn't I?"

"Magnolia." His voice was firm. "Look at me. Do you hurt anywhere else?"

"My arm," I said as spots appeared before my eyes. "Please, Mr. Hastings, check on my daughter," I told him, and then everything went dark.

When I opened my eyes again, I found a paramedic in my face. "There you are." His voice was cheerful. I was still in the front seat of my car but now my driver's door was open. Snow continued to fall.

"Where's my daughter?" I asked, lurching forward, and the pain that blasted through my arm had me cringing. "Shit!" My stomach roiled at the pain.

"She's fine. Officer Bishop is keeping her company while we check you out." He eased me back.

My stomach lurched. "I beg your pardon," I managed to say. "But I think I'm going to throw up."

At least I didn't vomit on the nice EMT. Afterwards they had to stabilize my neck of course, and my shoulder. While they secured me on a backboard, I heard Willow crying, and it broke my heart. Once I was on the gurney, Lexie Bishop appeared at my side.

I blinked at her uniform. "You're a police officer?"

"I am." Lexie nodded. "It's going to be okay, Maggie. I've got your girl. She's safe and warm."

"Don't let her see me, Lexie," I said. "It'll scare her

too much."

"I won't," Lexie said, giving my fingers a brisk pat. "She's in the back seat of the squad car, wrapped in a blanket, and talking to my partner. We'll be following you to the emergency room. Maggie, is there anyone you'd like me to call?"

"Thomas," I said, as they put me in the ambulance. "Call Thomas Drake."

***

I was headed off to X-ray when the entire Drake family descended on the emergency room. Thomas stopped them long enough to speak to me.

"Hey," I said, still strapped to the backboard. "Sorry about the fuss, y'all."

To my surprise Thomas was a tad pale, but he smiled and brushed the hair back from my face. "We'll be right here waiting for you."

"Please, would you stay with Willow?" I asked him.

"I will. Don't you worry," Thomas said soothingly. He gave a nod to the technician and EMTs and they rolled me off.

A short time later, I was returned to the treatment room, sans backboard, and discovered there was a crowd waiting for me: Thomas, Julian, Autumn, Duncan, and Wyatt Hastings. Thomas told me that Willow was sitting in a treatment room across the hall with Lexie Bishop, that the doctors had checked her out, and she was just fine.

I frowned at Wyatt. "Why is Mr. Hastings here?"

"The accident happened in front of Wyatt's house," Thomas explained. "He wanted to make sure that you and Willow were alright."

"Don't you remember talking to me after the accident?" Wyatt asked with a hint of a smile. "You were a kind of out of it."

I frowned, wondering what I'd said. "You're the one who told me to open the door."

"That's right." He nodded.

"You climbed over the car seat to check on me," I suddenly remembered.

The doctor walked in and nodded respectfully to Thomas. As a matter of fact, the whole staff was moving double-time. I'd never been treated so well at an emergency room in my life. I wondered what was going on.

I'd been very lucky, the ER doctor said with a calm smile. I only had a mild concussion from hitting my head on the window. "A stitch or two will take care of the cut, and the shoulder dislocation isn't severe. Once we put her left shoulder back in place, she'll only need to wear a sling for a few weeks."

"Back in place?" I asked nervously.

"I don't want her to be in too much pain." Thomas frowned.

"You leave that to us," the doctor said, and proceeded to usher everyone out of the room.

"I'm staying," Thomas announced, and sat in the chair beside the bed.

"You don't have to," I began.

"Yes, I do." He folded his arms across his chest and made himself comfortable.

Once they'd dealt with my shoulder, taken care of the cut at my hairline, and *after* they'd cleaned up the blood, only then would I let Willow come and see me.

She was fine, and was holding a small teddy bear. She walked back into the room with Lexie. "Hi Mama!"

"Hi baby." I smiled and held out my right hand to her.

But she didn't run to me. Instead she stayed where she was. "Lexie said you hurt your shoulder and I shouldn't jump on the bed."

"That's probably true." I sighed. "Thank you, Lexie, for staying with her all this time."

"You're family." Lexie smiled easily. "It was the least I could do."

"A nurse gave me a bear!" Willow held it up.

"I hope you said, thank you," I began as Julian, Duncan and Autumn came back in.

"Mama, did you know that Lexie says, I have two *more* cousins?" Willow smiled shyly up at her.

"You sure do. We're everywhere," Lexie said, placing a hand on Willow's shoulder. Although she had smiled warmly at Willow, the look she sent to Thomas Drake afterward seemed significant to me.

Maybe it was because she was standing there in her

police uniform, I thought. *Or maybe it was from the pain medicine they'd whacked me up with before they'd put my shoulder back in place.* I squelched down a giggle, and realized I was feeling more than a little strange.

"Morgan, he's a boy, and three years old," Willow was saying. "The baby is a girl and her name is...Be—Lynn?"

"Belinda," Lexie corrected.

"Belinda is six months old," Willow announced importantly. "Lexie showed me pictures on her phone."

"I'm happy to see that you're doing okay," Lexie nudged Willow toward Julian and Willow happily took his hand. "You'll need to see about getting some snow tires for that car."

"Oh no!" I started to sit up. "My car! How bad is it? Is the other driver hurt?"

Thomas eased me back. "The other driver is fine. His truck only had minor damage on the front bumper."

"My car?" I asked.

"We'll get it repaired," Thomas said, "don't worry."

"I'm going to head out," Lexie said, stepping back. "Maggie, I'll come and check on you in a couple of days."

"Oh, that's very kind of you," I began.

Lexie winked at Willow. "Take care of your mom."

"I will," Willow said solemnly.

Lexie flashed a smile. "Be safe, everyone." And she left.

I was discharged shorty after. By the time the paperwork was done, Autumn and Duncan had gone home. Willow and I were driven back to the Drake estate in Julian's Range Rover. It hadn't been easy climbing up into it, but the SUV handled the slippery roads beautifully. Willow exclaimed over the snow—which was still falling—and I wondered how in the world I was going to manage a four-year-old when I was down to one arm.

"Maggie," Thomas said, laying his hand on my good arm.

I startled. "I'm sorry. What?"

"I was saying I think you should stay in the mansion with us for the next few weeks. At least until your shoulder heals."

I leaned my head back against the car seat. "That's probably a good idea—at least for the next few days" I said.

"Excellent." Thomas nodded.

"We'll have to stop at the cottage and get our things."

Thomas smiled. "That's already been taken care of."

***

When we arrived back at the mansion, Nina was waiting for us. Thomas helped me up the stairs and I discovered that Nina had sent one of the staff to go and fetch our things, while another had prepared two guest rooms. They featured an attached Jack and Jill-style bathroom, so Willow and I could share and be next to each other.

To my surprise it was Nina who had shooed the men out of the way. She might have been young, but Nina Vasquez brooked no-nonsense as she helped me change into a nightshirt. We managed to work around the sling, and it was odd having a woman who was eight years my junior cluck over me like a mother hen, but Nina was kind and efficient and it kept me from feeling too embarrassed.

No sooner had I been tucked into bed did Julian poke his head in the room. "How's the patient?" he asked, bringing in an ice pack.

I took it gladly and placed it on my shoulder. "A little sore," I said over Willow who was running around the large room whooping it up. She was wired after everything that had happened: The party, the accident, the police, and the ER. "Willow," I said. "That's enough."

"I'm like a plane!" Willow ran past Julian with her arms out making airplane noises.

Nina laughed. "You're like a girl who needs to go to bed, *amada*."

"I don't wanna!" Willow laughed and 'flew' into the adjoining room.

"This should be fun." I groused, set the icepack aside, and pushed the covers back with my good arm.

"Whoa, wait," Julian said. "What do you think you

are doing?"

"I'm going to need to get her to bed," I explained.

"No you're not." Thomas walked in and my jaw dropped. "You were told by the doctors to take it easy."

I begrudgingly pulled the blankets back up while he gave me a lecture about keeping ice on my injury. Thomas reminded me what the doctor had said at the ER about the importance of the ice. I opened my mouth to argue, but he put the ice back in place himself. When I started to ask about repairs to my car, Thomas waved my questions away.

"We'll speak of it the morning." He walked over to the door. "Get some rest."

Willow zoomed past Julian and Nina again, and Julian started to laugh.

"When she gets like this," I warned them, "it takes a while to wind her down."

"I've got this," Nina said. "It will be good practice for me when Isabel is older." She rubbed her hands together and marched after Willow. A moment later I heard Willow begin to laugh and then the water in the bathroom turned on.

"Can I get you anything, Maggie?" Julian asked.

"No." I yawned.

"If you need anything, or some help, let us know." Julian walked over and demonstrated how to use the household phone on the nightstand. "My room is right down the hall. Either Dad or I will come in and check on you later."

"Thanks, Julian," I said when he clicked on the lamp on the nightstand. He walked across the room, shut off the overhead light, pulled the door almost closed behind him, and left.

Well, I thought, *I guessed they'd shown me.*

Apparently I was resting whether I liked it or not. I shifted, trying to get more comfortable, and clenched my teeth when I moved the wrong way.

"Can I have a bubble bath, Nina?" Willow's voice drifted clearly to me.

"Not tonight," Nina said.

"Can I braid your hair?" Willow asked next.

"Perhaps tomorrow," she answered. "Get in the tub."

"I could take a shower," Willow said. "I'm tall enough."

"Well you could, but tonight it's a bath and then bed."

I knew what was coming before Willow spoke. "Mama reads me a book before bed."

My girl was a champion wheedler, no doubt about it. The whole thing struck me as hilarious, and I figured the drugs were still in my system. Before I knew it I fell asleep, still propped up on the pillows.

CHAPTER FOUR

I woke up early the next morning. Cautiously, I got out of bed and shuffled my way to the bathroom. My eyes glanced toward the window and I was amazed. The snow had accumulated to several inches overnight. I'd never seen that much snow in my life. I paused at the window, marveling at the quiet. No one was out or moving in all of that. Willow was going to go crazy when she saw it.

I walked to the adjoining room and saw that Willow was sleeping peacefully. Carefully, I closed her door and headed for the bathroom, took care of business, and when I got a look at myself in the mirror...I was appalled.

Magnolia Irene Parrish, the professional event coordinator, the calm and cool bridal consultant looked like she'd been ridden hard and put away wet. I had a lovely bruise along my left temple. A neat bandage covered up the stitch I'd gotten, but my long, dark hair was a wreck and there was still some blood in it. I leaned against the bathroom counter with my good arm, wondered how to wash my hands—one-handed—and swore.

"That's no way for a Southern belle to talk." Julian's voice from the other side of the door had me jumping.

"Are you decent?" he asked.

"Yes."

The door swung open. "What are you doing in here?"

"Take a wild guess," I said, trying not to act like I was uncomfortable standing in front of him in my nightshirt. Julian was standing there in only a pair of sweatpants and no shirt. The man—my cousin—was seriously gorgeous, and embarrassed, I yanked my eyes away from his bare chest.

He crossed his arms. "I knocked on your door, when you didn't answer I wanted to see if you were alright. You shouldn't be out of bed."

"I'm not an invalid," I complained as he led me gently back across the room.

"No, you're just stiff and sore." He pulled the covers back and I slowly sat on the bed.

"I need to wash my hair," I said, and felt ridiculous.

"I can help you with that," he said, casually.

"Oh? How's that?" I asked suspiciously, as he helped me get situated.

Julian snorted with laughter. It was such a silly sound, that it made me smile, despite everything. "Magnolia," he said between laughs, "I wasn't inferring anything improper. Actually, I'm seeing someone and she—"

"Oh!" I blushed. "I didn't mean to imply—"

"—has very long hair." Julian finished with a grin. "I thought we could probably use the kitchen sink to deal with washing your hair more comfortably."

"Will Nina let us in her kitchen?" I managed to smile.

"For this, I'm sure she will," Julian said. "Why don't you try and relax, and I'll bring you a fresh ice pack for your shoulder."

"Okay," I said, and tried not to sound ungrateful. "Thank you, Julian."

He nodded. "That's what family is for."

I leaned back and listened as he padded down the hall.

A few minutes later and he was back wearing workout clothes and running shoes. Julian carried a mug of tea in one hand and a freezer bag full of ice cubes in the other. He paused long enough to grab the remote from across the room and brought them both over. "Here you go. Might as well watch some television while you're laid up." He set the mug down within reach and pulled a bottle of ibuprofen out of his pocket.

"This is very kind of you—" I began.

"Willow woke me up earlier," he announced, securing the ice bag in place.

"What?" I sat straight up.

Julian eased me back. "It's fine. She found my room, and told me she wanted me to go build snowmen with her. I think she was sleepwalking."

"She does that sometimes. I was so out of it last night I forgot to warn y'all. I'm sorry."

"No worries." He shrugged. "I steered her back to her own bed and she fell right back to sleep." He chatted for a few more moments, made a comment about hitting the treadmill, and left.

I took the pills after Julian left and I marveled at the generous hospitality they'd all shown me. I'd never had siblings, and my own mother wasn't exactly very...mothering. Growing up I'd yearned for a normal family, people who were there for each other no matter what.

I wondered if this was how it felt.

***

For the first week after the accident I was absolutely miserable, even with my arm in the special sling/brace the doctor had given me. Not that it was so painful, just that I was sore, down to one arm, trying to run my own business *and* caring for a four-year-old. Thank heavens I had help. I don't know how we'd have managed without it.

While my car was being repaired, I'd gone ahead and purchased snow tires. Thomas had made noises about replacing the car for me, but I turned down his offer. The car might be old, but it was mine.

Willow thrived under the extra attention of Thomas, Julian, and Nina Vasquez. Julian had indeed taken her outside the day of the big snowfall, taught her how to make snowmen, and Willow was thrilled. Thomas took several pictures of them in the snow for me with his cell phone, and I was stunned to discover that he'd had a few printed and had added the photos to a collection of framed family pictures in the library.

Lexie was true to her word and dropped by to check on me a few days later. She also brought her daughter, Belinda, along with her. The baby was all wrapped up in a pink snowsuit and had the same dark blonde hair and blue eyes as her mother. Belinda drooled and grinned as we sat and chatted about the upcoming bridal shower and the wedding. I thanked Lexie again for her help the night of the accident, and after a brief visit, she and Belinda left.

Wyatt Hastings came to visit me a week after the accident. I'd been sitting in the family's gorgeous library in a big comfy chair working on my laptop one-handed. I was enjoying the fire while Thomas pretended not to hover.

To my surprise, Wyatt gifted me with three of his mystery novels. Saying he thought I might enjoy having something to read while I recovered. While I was touched at the gesture, I was also apprehensive. I hesitated, and he asked what was wrong.

"I recall Duncan saying your stories were

gruesome...and I don't like gory books," I said, as he held them out.

"I think you'll like these," he said. "They're from a new series of mine, and are more in the style of a cozy mystery."

"Oh, really? I enjoy cozy mysteries." I said, happily accepting the paperbacks. When I took the books from him, I saw burn scars on the back of one of his hands. Red, and thick, they disappeared under the cuff of his long sleeve shirt. They were severe, and I instantly felt sympathy for him.

He saw that I'd noticed, and I watched his shoulders stiffen, as if he expected me to ask about them, or worse, recoil at the sight. I did neither. Instead I smiled. "If I have nightmares from your novels," I said, "I'm going to be very cross with you."

"Fair enough." When he smiled, his ice blue eyes crinkled at the corners.

I glanced over the cover art on the books and got a jolt of recognition when I saw the author's name was listed as *Ford Williams*. "You use a pseudonym?" I asked.

Thomas dropped a hand on Wyatt's shoulder. "He does. It's a play on words—"

"For the town of William's Ford," I finished. "Of course."

"It's also a way to maintain some privacy," Wyatt said.

"My old boss loved reading your books," I said.

"Annie always swore they took her mind off the crazy brides, and the scarier the story the better. She's a big fan."

"That's good to hear." Wyatt nodded. "I'm honored that she enjoys them."

"Thank you, Mr. Hastings." I tucked the paperbacks beside me.

"Call me Wyatt," he said, making himself at home in the opposite chair. "After all, I sort of rescued you. We should be on a first name basis, don't you think?"

I nodded. "Thank you, Wyatt. I look forward to reading them."

We chatted for a few more minutes and Wyatt left, saying he was on a deadline and needed to get back to work. Thomas walked him out, and I waited until Thomas came back to ask about Wyatt and how he'd gotten the scars.

"It's a sad story," Thomas said. With a quiet sigh, he sat in the chair Wyatt had vacated. "When Wyatt was ten-years-old, there was a fire at his family's home."

"Oh no," I said.

"The fire trapped Wyatt and his brother on one side of the house," Thomas explained. "The boys had tried to get to their parents but couldn't. Even though he was injured, Wyatt still managed to help his younger brother, Xander, climb out the second-floor window. They jumped down and dropped to the ground."

"What happened to his parents?" I asked.

Thomas shifted in the chair beside me. "They both

died in the fire. Smoke inhalation."

"Oh, that's so sad." My heart ached for those two young boys.

"Wyatt was in the hospital for weeks recovering from the burns, and other injuries. After he was well enough to be released, he and Xander lived with their grandparents until they went off to college."

"So now Wyatt is a writer." I nodded. "I recognized his pen name, but would never have put it all together unless he'd given me his books."

"Our Wyatt likes a quiet life and he's very protective of his privacy."

"The first time I met him, he made a joke about getting out of the house once a week, whether he needs to or not."

Thomas chuckled. "That's actually true. He stays at home writing for the most part. He doesn't tour, and rarely does publicity events for his novels."

I tucked a pillow under my injured arm for more support. "How did he and Duncan become friends?"

"He'd hired Duncan to remodel a few rooms and build him a writer's studio, about five years ago. Wyatt and his brother had inherited the house from their grandparents and it needed some modern updates. It's a lovely, old Greek Revival Italianate built in 1857. It's only a few blocks from here."

"What does his brother do for a living?"

"You've already met him." Thomas smiled.

"I have?" I smiled. "When?"

"He was one of the EMTs who tended to you after your car accident."

***

Time flew by, my sling came off and suddenly it was March. My first taste of a mid-western winter was quite the eye opener. I was shocked to see that winter showed no signs of abating, and Thomas explained that they often had more snow in Missouri in the month of March than in January.

We'd been staying in the mansion for over three weeks, and during that time I'd grown closer to Thomas and Julian. I also felt fortunate to have started a real friendship with Nina.

Once the orthopedic doctor gave me the all-clear, I was more than ready to return to the cottage, drive again, and get back to a regular routine. I worried it would hurt Thomas' feelings when I moved out—even if it was only across the lawn. But I needed to be on my own.

I had a big wedding to coordinate in less than sixty days, and I'd also managed to pick up a few new events as well. The Sugarplum Fairy birthday party I'd done for Charlie Bell had worked wonders in getting my name out there. I managed to meet with a few interested clients—even while still in my sling—to go over proposals for parties, and a small wedding in September.

The first official day back in the cottage had been easier than I'd thought. After I'd taken Willow to preschool myself, I returned to find some of the staff from the main house had brought all our things back for us. Kindly, one of the cleaning ladies stayed for an hour and even helped me unpack and settle in.

After she left, I puttered around the cottage and felt content to be at home. The little house felt warm and welcoming again. I took my time and got re-dressed to meet a client at the *Black Cat Coffee House*. After that, I had an afternoon appointment at the bridal salon to oversee Autumn's wedding gown fitting.

The roads were clear as I drove through town, and now that I was able to drive, I needed to take Julian up on his offer of teaching me how to maneuver in the snow. I could privately admit to being a bit paranoid about the winter weather these days. I'd had weather alerts set up to send me push notifications on my cell phone. I didn't ever want to be caught unaware or unprepared for snow again.

I walked into the coffee shop carrying my monogrammed tote bag and headed for the counter. It was lovely to be welcomed by name, and it made me feel like a local. I picked up my coffee and selected my favorite table in the back. From there, I could watch all the comings and goings on Main Street, and still keep an eye out for my bride and groom. I popped open my laptop and got to work answering emails from potential clients and my vendors. Business was picking up. If things kept moving as they were I might need to look into renting office space.

When the chair pulled out across from me I lifted my eyes and was surprised to see Wyatt Hastings, as opposed to my September bride and groom.

"Magnolia," he said, sitting in the chair across from me.

I hit *send* on the email I'd finished, and smiled. "Hello, Wyatt."

"Working today?" he asked.

I closed down the email screen. "Yes, I'm scheduled to meet a new couple for their September wedding."

"Oh." He started to rise. "Do you need me to leave?"

"No." I waved him back in his seat. "They're not due for another ten minutes." I slid the laptop aside. "Besides, I wanted to say thank you for the novels you brought to me."

He met my eyes. "They weren't too creepy for you?"

*He'd be horrified if he ever knew what I actually did find 'creepy'...*I thought. *Nothing like growing up seeing your mother perform black magick rituals to skew your outlook on horror.* I yanked my thoughts to the here and now. "No, the books weren't too scary for me," I said, smoothly. "I enjoyed them."

The small smile he flashed changed his whole face. "I'm glad, and you're welcome."

I glanced deliberately around the coffee shop. "See any likely victims—I mean, 'fictional character inspiration' in today's patrons?"

Wyatt chuckled and rubbed a hand thoughtfully over his beard. "You never know..." he said dramatically.

I grinned, enjoying his sense of humor.

"There's something about you," he said, almost as if he was speaking to himself.

"It's the accent." I rolled my eyes. "I get asked on a daily basis *where I'm from.* Y'all act like I'm from Mars instead of the South. Maybe you should write a story about a Southern woman, driven mad by folks asking her about her accent."

"Maybe..." He seemed to think it over. "But if I did, I'd have to make her a gorgeous brunette with dark blue eyes."

I couldn't help but react to his words. My shoulders stiffened. *Just once,* I thought. *It'd be mighty nice to be appreciated by a man for something other than my looks.*

"I've offended you." Wyatt tipped his head to one side, considering me. "You're uncomfortable with compliments?"

"Not uncomfortable, merely disappointed that men aren't able to see past *this.*" I pointed to my face.

"I see more than your face, Magnolia. I see a loving mother, and a clever, capable business woman." He sipped at his coffee. "Even down to one arm you were back to work within a week. You're determined and a hard worker, I'll give you that."

My stomach actually fluttered over the compliment, and I smiled at him. "Thank you," I said, and meant it.

"You're welcome." Wyatt nodded, his expression remaining sober. "Now, would it piss you off if I said you have a beautiful smile?"

I tossed my hair over one shoulder. "Are you flirting with me, Wyatt?"

"If I were?"

I sat back in my chair. "You know, I used to think you were shy and quiet. Now I'm not so sure."

"I am *not* shy." Wyatt frowned over my description.

"No." I narrowed my eyes as I considered him. "You are direct though, in a very odd sort of way."

"I prefer to think of myself as thoughtful, or studious." He sounded completely serious.

"I'm sure you would, sugar." I added the last bit in the hopes that he'd smile again. He didn't disappoint me. "You have a very nice smile." I told him. "You should use it more often."

"Are you flirting with *me*, Magnolia?"

"Honey, I'm a Southern woman. If I flirt with you...believe me, you won't have to wonder. You'll know."

His brows disappeared beneath his shaggy hair. "I'll consider myself warned."

I was saved from making a clever come back by the arrival of the September bride and groom. When the couple hailed me, Wyatt stood.

"I'll let you get to your clients. Goodbye, Magnolia." He gave me a polite nod and left without another word. Compared to the happy chatter of the bride, Wyatt literally slipped into the background.

I blinked, and he was quietly easing his way out the door.

***

The fitting for Autumn's bridal gown went smoothly. There were only minor adjustments to be made and afterward I found myself face-to-face with Autumn's great Aunt—and mine—Faye Bishop.

I couldn't say why, but I had the strangest feeling of disapproval from the older woman. She lounged in the chair at the bridal salon like a queen, and the associates at the salon apparently thought the same, as they scurried to do her bidding.

When Autumn asked me what I thought of the gown, I'd told her honestly that I thought her choice was perfect for a garden wedding. The white floor-length gown featured an illusion neckline with a sleeveless lace bodice topped by an A-line chiffon skirt. She'd opted out of a veil and explained that Violet was working up fresh flowers for her hair.

I noted the hair accessory and, while the bride changed back into street clothes, made my best effort to be polite to my grandmother's sister. "Autumn tells me you're wearing a soft gray suit dress and matching hat to the wedding."

"I am." Her silver eyes narrowed on me. "I'm walking the bride down the aisle as well." Her tone of voice sounded like a challenge.

"Yes ma'am, I have that in my notes." I smiled. "How lovely for you both."

"You have my sister's eyes." Faye frowned.

I closed my notebook and took my time slipping it back in my bag. "I wouldn't know, I never met Irene Bishop."

"Truth be told, you look more like your grandfather, Phillip." Faye sniffed in derision. "Clearly, you're more Drake than Bishop."

"Hmm," was the most polite response I could offer. The woman's attitude put my back up, but I was determined *not* to let her know.

"I suppose we have to invite you and your child to the bridal shower," Faye continued with a scowl. "Autumn would want that."

"But you don't," I said, twisting my ring as I watched her.

"No," she said bluntly, "I don't." Her eyes narrowed on my hands.

"Where did you get that ring?" Faye demanded. "How long have you had it?"

I automatically dropped my gaze to the antique sapphire ring on my right hand. "It was a gift from my Grandma Taylor when I graduated from high school."

Faye rose to her feet and snatched my hand. She lifted it to eye level and studied the ring. After a moment she lifted her eyes to mine. "That ring originally belonged to my sister, Irene."

Her words jolted me clear to my toes. "Are you sure?"

"Yes. I'm absolutely positive." Her voice was serious and low. "See the crescent around the sapphire?" She let go and pointed to the design of the ring. "The crescent moon is our family's magickal crest."

"I had no idea," I said.

"That ring is a Bishop family heirloom," she said. "It belongs with the Bishop family."

"Well it's been in *my* family for over fifty years," I argued. "Taylor and Vance Sutton were the only grandparents I ever knew. If you think I'm going to hand over a gift from my Grandma Taylor you are vastly mistaken."

"I can prove it." Faye held up her left hand. "My father had matching rings made for both my sister and I."

On her pinky finger was the twin of the ring I'd worn for over ten years.

"I suppose Irene must have given the ring to my Grandma Taylor." Even as the words left my mouth I knew that was the case.

Faye stared at me hard for a good thirty seconds. Her eyes were darting back and forth almost as if she were reading a book. "Taylor knew what she was doing giving the ring to you instead of your mother...That would have been disastrous." Her voice was flat, almost trance-like.

My mouth went dry as Faye continued to speak.

"Taylor had always worn the ring, but on your graduation day she insisted that it was important for you to have it...she took it from her own finger and put it on yours." Faye blinked and came back to herself. "And you haven't taken it off since the day she gave it to you."

The woman was dead on, but I went for a casual air as if she hadn't plucked the memories straight out of my mind. "That would be correct." I brushed my hair back and tried to act nonchalant like nothing weird was happening.

Faye scowled and took a seat again. "Well at least you didn't steal it."

Insulted, I drew myself up straight. "Why, Faye...aren't you precious?" I said, my smile just this side of polite.

Faye opened her mouth to snap, but the bride came bouncing out of the fitting room. "Ta-da!" Autumn sang. "All done!"

I felt a tightening in my stomach—a warning—and immediately shifted my attention to Autumn. Good thing too, as she promptly tripped on the carpet. "Careful, darlin'!" I grabbed her arm in the nick of time.

With my help she managed not to face-plant, but instead dropped the shoebox she was carrying. "Aw, jeez," she said. "Ask me again why I'm wearing flats with my wedding gown."

I smiled and bent down to pick up the shoes myself. "I think that's very sensible, considering you'll be in the grass." I tucked the shoes back inside and closed the lid. They were a pretty choice. The satin flats had pointed toes and were a soft sky blue.

Autumn accepted the shoebox. "The shoes take care of the 'something blue' part of the day, anyway."

I smiled at her. It was impossible not to like my cousin. *Of course, we were more like third cousins...but still...*

"Hey, Aunt Faye," Autumn said, interrupting my thoughts.

The old woman stood. "Yes dear?"

"Did you talk to Maggie about bringing Willow to the bridal shower?" Autumn linked her arm with the older woman's.

"She sure did," I said with forced cheer. "Willow and I are both looking forward to it."

"As are we," Faye said smoothly.

When pigs fly, I thought to myself.

"Great!" Autumn was all enthusiasm. "We'll see both you and Willow on Saturday."

***

The day of the bridal shower had temperatures that rose to above freezing. The sun was shining, the snow was finally starting to melt, and forty degrees felt like heaven. I truly did not want to attend, especially after

Faye's rude behavior and accusations, but I had better manners than that.

We arrived at the Bishop's precisely ten minutes early, and I was glad that I had, as parking was at a premium. The driveway was occupied, and the entire street was filled with cars. I drove down the block and ended up parking several houses down.

Silently, I psyched myself up and exited the car. I waited before opening Willow's door while a woman walked her Rottweiler past. The dog was large and although he was leashed, I moved well back, instinctively not trusting the animal.

The brunette smirked rudely as she passed, and the dog didn't spare me a glance. I watched and waited as they walked farther down the street. For some reason, I was hesitant to open Willow's door. I wanted to make sure they were gone.

"Mama?" Willow called.

I breathed a sigh of relief when the woman and her dog were no longer in sight. I silently scolded myself over my reaction and helped Willow climb out of the car. *I was plainly more wound up than I'd realized.*

"You ready, honey?" I asked Willow, with a bright smile.

"Yes!" Willow said with a big smile.

"Well, let's go." Taking Willow's hand in mine, I tucked the gift under my good arm and started down the sidewalk, keeping an eye out for ice or slush. Together we walked past Autumn's craftsman style bungalow, and then farther along the street until we came to the entrance of the Bishop's manor home.

"That's a pretty house, Mama," Willow said.

I tipped my head back and took in the fancy gingerbread trim and the round tower with its dramatically pointed roof. "Yes, it is."

"I like Cousin Thomas' house better." Willow said loyally.

The comment made me laugh, and with a smile on my face, Willow and I marched up the front steps and knocked on the door.

The shower was an eye-opener. There were twenty guests, not counting the wedding party, and several children. Lexie was keeping everyone in order, and Ivy was everywhere at once, passing out sparkling cider to the children or champagne punch to the adults.

Holly took our coats and our gift was added to the pile. I chose a seat close to the fireplace and toward the back of the family room. Willow and I had no sooner taken our seats when I finally met the flower girls, Sophia and Chloe, and their mother, Shannon Proctor-Jacobs.

I'd spoken to Shannon on the phone a few times over the past few months, and we'd exchanged emails about the girls' dresses for the wedding, but it was good to put a face to the voice. Shannon sat next to me, and the girls—who were spunky but well behaved—sat on the floor by their mother's feet.

Violet arrived with her mother Cora, and they'd

brought Charlie along. Charlie took one look at Willow and the girls and made a beeline for them. She began chattering away with Willow, Sophia and Chloe Jacobs. Before I knew it, Holly had perched on the arm of the couch next to me, and I discovered that I was actually enjoying myself.

"I saw the photos on your website of the party you put together for Charlie," Shannon was saying.

"Willow, behave yourself," I said, as she and the other girls had gone from talking to bouncing up and down on the area rug.

"It was fabulous." Shannon said enthusiastically.

I smiled in response. "Thank you."

"Anyway, I was wondering, have you ever done a gender reveal party?"

I studied the blonde. Her loose sweater had quite camouflaged her baby bump. "Of course." I smiled. "When are you scheduled to have your ultrasound?" I asked.

"In three weeks."

I reached for the planner/ notebook I always kept in my purse. Shannon pointed out the date of her appointment. It was on the second Thursday in April, and as we discussed it I agreed that the Saturday after would be ideal. "Did you want the party to be elaborate or simple?" I asked.

Shannon laughed. "Somewhere in between."

"Dinner or *hors d'oeuvres*?"

"I was thinking of appetizers and some really

extravagant sweets—all in pink and blue," Shannon said.

I nodded. "Why don't we have a sit-down next week. I will put some ideas together for you, and then you and your husband can choose what you like. How's that sound?" I scribbled the date on the back of one of my business cards.

"That'd be great." Shannon smiled. "This baby was a big surprise and it's definitely going to be the last one for us. So we decided to do something different and do a gender reveal."

I slipped her my card, and I added her contact information in my phone. Lexie announced that there were refreshments in the kitchen, and I mentally sighed when Willow, Charlie, Sophia and Chloe all went stampeding for the food.

On the surface, the bridal shower seemed perfectly normal...until you tuned in and caught the conversations that were flowing as the guests helped themselves to the buffet.

"...and I told Kyle," this was from Shannon. "I'd prefer to rely on the good old-fashioned ultrasound for the gender results, as opposed to him scrying."

"What'd he have to say about that?" Lexie wanted to know.

Shannon cocked a brow. "That I was practically insulting his family's heritage and he was shocked at my lack of faith in his clairvoyant abilities."

"As if," Lexie snorted with laughter. "The Proctors

have nearly as many Seers in their line as the Jacobs do."

Faye Bishop selected carrot sticks from the vegetable crudité. "Well," she said to another woman, "the handfasting ceremony won't fall on Beltane proper, but at least we have the energies of the sabbat and the waxing moon in play..."

I managed to not bobble my plate. All around me folks were casually talking about magick, and that was something I'd done my best to cut myself off from a long, long time ago. *Hell's bells!* I thought as a bead of sweat rolled down my back. I looked at the shower guests with new eyes, suddenly noticing lots of magickal jewelry.

While the women continued to discuss the astrological aspects of the wedding date, I selected a small sandwich with great care, reminding myself to keep my facial expressions neutral. I tried to be casual as I checked my surroundings and suddenly saw a few witchy decorations in the home too.

Almost every woman at the shower was a practitioner. *God almighty,* I thought. *I'd avoided situations like this for years. But now, I was in fact, surrounded by Witches.* The realization made my self-imposed exile from magick even harder. I blew out a careful breath, shuffled forward in the food line, and tried to act like a completely clueless mundane.

Cora O'Connell stepped behind me, helping herself to a small sandwich. "Violet," she said to her daughter, "you're going to have to have a talk with next weekend's bride. I'm washing my hands of her. I swear to goddess if she calls the shop and changes her mind on the centerpieces *one more time,* I'm going to cast for an ice storm to hit on her wedding day."

Violet rolled her eyes. "I'd prefer you cast for snow instead of ice, Mom."

Cora frowned. "Why's that?"

Violet picked up a carrot stick and bit in. "Cause we'll be the ones stuck delivering flowers in bad weather, and snow is much easier to deal with than ice."

"Good point." Cora laughed. "Maybe I'll have Marie sweeten the Bridezilla up with some Hoodoo."

A stunning woman with micro braids joined the buffet line. "Somebody call my name?" The woman was tall, curvy and covered with tattoos. A myriad of different tattoos ran down her arms and over the back of both her hands. What skin wasn't adorned was a beautiful shade of *café au lait.*

"Mom's threatening to jinx next weekend's bride," Violet explained. "This one is being a real Bridezilla."

"Maybe you should ask the expert on how best to handle that." Marie tossed me a wink. "What do you say, Maggie?"

I cleared my throat. *Play it cool, Maggie, I warned myself.* "It's been my experience that Bridezillas are usually insecure and frightened. They often require extra hand-holding. In these situations there's always a deeper issue that's the true problem," I said, nodding to

Cora and Violet. "The centerpieces have simply become a safe target for her to focus her anxiety on."

"There, you see?" Marie smiled across the table. "The event coordinator has spoken."

I moved forward in the line, picked up a cup of sparkling cider and returned to my spot on the sofa. My shoulders felt tight even as I sat and made small talk with Shannon about her daughter's flower girl dresses. The conversations around me were of the wedding, of course, but also about the metaphysical: astrology, crystals, herbs, and I almost choked when I heard Ivy casually talking about spell casting in front of the children.

The last thing I needed was for Willow to overhear any of that. "Excuse me," I said to Ivy, but she didn't seem to notice.

From where she sat beside me on the couch, Holly nudged her sister with her foot "Ivy," she said.

"What?" Ivy glanced at her twin first, and then to me.

"Y'all need to be careful what you're saying in front of the little ones," I said to the dramatic looking brunette.

"Seriously?" Ivy raised one darkened eyebrow.

"Your topic of conversation is making Maggie uncomfortable," Holly said.

Ivy blinked in surprise. "You're not a practitioner?" she asked me.

Not anymore. "No," I said, out loud.

"Really?" Ivy tipped her head to one side, studying me. "Sorry if I offended you."

I nodded, and the conversations resumed around us. I took a sip of the cider and made an effort to unclench.

Holly's hand lighted on my arm. "Are you alright?" she asked me quietly.

As I focused on Holly, I saw for the first time a scar that ran through her left eyebrow. It held my attention for a moment, until I noticed that her eye color had shifted to an uncanny shade of aqua-blue. Brighter than they'd been even a few moments ago. I swallowed nervously. "Yes, I'm fine," I said, even though it was a lie.

Holly gave my shoulder the gentlest of squeezes. "No one here expects you to be anything other than what you are, Maggie. It might help to remember that."

Before I could reply, I caught Faye Bishop staring at me. The woman had her brows raised and was wearing a slight sneer. Without a word it let me know she found me beneath her. Determined to not let her know how uncomfortable I was, I smiled at the old woman, and deliberately re-started the conversation with Shannon about the gender reveal party that she wanted.

Eventually the food was consumed and it was time for the bride to open her bridal shower gifts. I was relieved when everyone stopped chatting and focused instead on the presents. As matron of honor Lexie sat beside the bride, dutifully recording each gift and the giver.

Only after the gifts had been opened and the cake sliced and passed around was it polite for Willow and I to leave. Willow had a great time sitting with the other girls. Even though they were older, each of them had been very kind to her. Which made it hard to get Willow to want to go.

As smoothly as possible we took our leave, and I didn't fully exhale again until I was out of the house and back in my car.

CHAPTER FIVE

It wasn't until later that evening that I managed to snag a moment to let myself relax. I'd been wound up since the bridal shower, and I'd even snapped at Willow a few times over supper. But now it was finally quiet, and the cottage was still and silent.

Willow was sound asleep, and shortly before midnight I stepped out on the tiny back porch of the cottage, took a seat at the wrought iron café table and chairs, and allowed myself a single cigarette. Even though I smoked rarely these days, I still saved a few for emergency situations.

While the waxing moon cast pretty shadows over the grass and a few patches of the snow left in the yard, I let my mind go back over the afternoon. On the plus side, I'd secured another event—the Jacobs' baby gender reveal party. On the negative side however, the Bishop half of my family tree were all obviously practitioners.

I shook my head over the snippets of conversations

I'd picked up on at the bridal shower. All that talk of magick was an uncomfortable blast from my past, reminding me too much of when my mother would invite her so-called magickal study group over to the house. Of course, my mother's excursions into spell casting had typically been met with disasters. As in anything that could have gone wrong...typically did.

I remembered all too clearly being a smug girl of sixteen and trying out spells for myself, confident that I could do better than my mother...and they'd all worked, while my mother's magick had flopped. When she caught me casting a healing spell on our old cat she'd been furious—not because I'd been working magick—but because it was white magick, positive magick. The healing spell I'd done had worked, while her own spells never did.

That old scruffy tomcat had managed another six months living out his last days in comfort, and my mother had been infuriated.

Then came her group of wanna-be-witchy-friends, and they'd all decided that whatever white magick I'd been working had somehow sabotaged my mother's darker spellwork. After their interrogation and accusations, I'd left magick alone. Turning my back on anything to do with *their* version of magick, I abandoned my practice. I'd gone cold turkey on witchcraft and had stayed away from any spell-casting from that point on.

Stubbing the cigarette out, I picked it up and carried

it to the bottom of my garden, to drop it in the outdoor garbage can. Making me wish I could dispose of those unhappy memories much in the same way.

I'm not sure whether it was movement or a sound that had me looking up quickly. The back of my neck prickled, and all I knew for sure was that I was no longer alone in the yard behind the cottage. I froze in place, holding my breath.

The area of the property that adjoined my garden and the rest of the Drake property boasted many trees and shrubs. It was fairly secluded and dark, even with the low-watt landscape lighting that illuminated the winding path from the cottage to the mansion. As I stood there trying to figure out what was out there, the lights suddenly blinked out.

For a wild few seconds I was truly afraid, and silently began berating myself for walking around alone in the yard, late at night. My eyes finally adjusted to the deeper darkness as a person walked into my view. I was vastly relieved to recognize Julian. I started to call out to him, but stopped.

He wasn't alone.

My cousin Julian was walking through the trees with someone—a woman. Gradually the couple came nearer, and it took me a moment before I realized that she was covered in a dark blue hooded cloak.

The long cape made her practically blend into the darkness. I blinked a couple of times in surprise. Having removed myself from the Craft and contact with other Witches, I hadn't seen anyone wear a cloak in years—unless it was for a Halloween costume. As I watched, the couple sank to a concrete bench in the secluded side gardens of the manor.

Stuck, I stayed where I was. Nervous that any movement I made would reveal my presence. I was slightly embarrassed to have accidentally stumbled upon a private moment, but yet I was curious. Especially since Julian had told me he was involved with someone, but he'd never mentioned who. Their kiss became more heated, and the woman's hood fell back revealing long ginger curls.

It was Holly Bishop.

My jaw dropped. I'd estimated Holly to be twenty-two, so she had to be at least eight years younger than he was. From the way they held each other, it was clear they were lovers.

Holly tossed a leg over Julian's lap, straddling him on the bench. "Here. Now," she said.

I heard the low murmur of Julian's reply. When they shifted to deal with their clothes, I scrambled back as noiselessly as possible.

And, I'm out! I thought, moving across the yard and farther away from them.

Obviously they believed that they were alone, because the sounds they soon began to make left no doubt as to what they were doing. Smothering a nervous laugh, I tiptoed back to my porch and eased the door open, making sure to shut it behind me gently.

It must be some sort of insane desperation that had Julian and Holly making love outside on a bench in the gardens while the snow melted around them. While part of me tried to imagine how one would ever get comfortable having sex on a bench...another part of me wondered what it would be like to want someone so badly, that you simply couldn't wait to have them. With a sigh, I locked up and headed for bed.

That night I dreamt of the garden, but instead of being surrounded by snow there was soft green grass and pink tulips everywhere. I heard a low voice call my name and I turned with a smile on my face, fully expecting to see the love of my life...but instead all I saw was shadows.

***

Spring had finally arrived in William's Ford. The temperatures grew steadily warmer and before I knew it, daffodils were breaking the ground. I found the first clutch blooming by our back porch and smiled over them.

The gray buds on the magnolia trees in front of the cottage started to swell, and it would only be a matter of time before they started to bloom. Thomas had told me the tree was the saucer magnolia variety, and I looked forward to its pink flowers.

On the first warm evening, I invited Nina Vasquez and Isabel over to the cottage, and while the baby sat on the blanket in the new grass, Willow settled beside her making Isabel laugh at her toys.

I handed Nina a glass of white wine and we sat at the café table and chairs on the back porch, appreciating the pretty evening.

"How was the bridal shower?" Nina asked. "Did you enjoy spending time with the other side of your family?"

I shot a look toward Willow and lowered my voice. "It was an *interesting* afternoon."

"How so?"

"My grandmother's people sure are different." I took a sip of my wine and thought it over. "As a matter of fact, lots of folks 'round town act a tad, *eccentric*."

Nina snorted out a laugh. "You've been living in William's Ford for a over three months, and you're only now figuring that out?"

"Exactly!" I gestured with my wine glass. "Everyone talks about spells and charms right out in the open. It's shocking. They're not even trying to be discreet."

"I'm surprised to hear you say that, considering your lineage."

"What? Why?"

Nina set her glass on the table. "Because of the Drakes and the Bishops...and their history."

"Oh, that." I shrugged, hoping it came across as carefree. "I seem to recall my mama talking about an old feud. Very Hatfield and McCoy type of thing."

"Maggie." Nina rested her hand on top of mine.

"You do understand what the Drakes are, don't you?"

I glanced up in her face. "You said *what* not *who*."

"I did." Nina held my gaze.

"I'm afraid I'm not following you, Nina."

Nina gave me a withering look. "You're far too smart to play dumb, Maggie. I'm talking about magick —and you know it."

I scoffed. "Come on Nina. The Drakes are successful, intelligent people. I haven't seen *any* sign of them being into the occult. Believe me, I'd know."

"You might be surprised." Nina sat back in her chair. "My grandparents immigrated to the Unites States from Brazil, and my *avó*—my grandmother—she told me that her grandmother was a *Curandeira*."

"What's a..." I tried to sound it out. "Coo-run-deria?"

"*Curanderia,* is Portuguese for healer," Nina said matter-of-factly, sampling the wine.

"Like an herbalist or wise woman type of thing?"

Nina toasted me with her glass of wine. "Exactly. One who heals with spells and charms. Like your mother's family does on *both* sides."

"Bullshit! My mother certainly never healed anyone. That would take—"

Nina's laughter had me stopping mid sentence. She set the wine down and proceeded to laugh until she cried.

"It's not funny. Why on earth are you laughing?" I asked while the children stared at Nina.

"I've never heard someone say 'bullshit' with a Southern accent before. It's hysterical!" She wiped her eyes.

"I'm not the only one with an accent, sugar." I pointed out.

That only made Nina laugh harder.

"What's so funny?" Willow wanted to know.

"Grown-up stuff, *amada*," Nina replied.

"What's *amada* mean?" Willow wanted to know.

"Sweetheart," Nina answered.

"Oh. Okay." Willow left to go race across the yard.

"Are you telling me that you don't believe in magick?" Nina asked, once Willow was gone.

I made sure that when I spoke, my voice would be calm. "Oh, I believe. I've seen enough of *magick* to last me a lifetime."

"How do you mean?" Nina asked.

"My mother. She was into the occult." I struggled to maintain my composure. "She liked to think she had power, but she had no real talent for spells—which was probably a blessing. And please, don't get me started on how the other children in town treat me. I was always 'Crazy Patty's kid'."

"I'm sorry," Nina said, contritely. "What about your father?"

"He left my mother when I was a toddler. Mama always said it was because he was narrow-minded and refused to accept her spirituality." I blew out a breath. "More likely he couldn't handle the stench of the nag-champa incense. Not to mention my mother trooping off every weekend to go to some Pagan festival or coven meeting."

"So she was a free-spirit?" Nina asked.

"That's a generous assessment." I took a sip of wine before continuing. "She'd been horribly spoiled by her adoptive parents. Mama came from money, was beautiful, and indulged for most of her life. People always gave into her. She manipulated everyone around her—like a true narcissist."

"That's horrible." Nina shook her head sadly.

"When I grew older, she started to become jealous. Envious of my looks, and of the attention it caused from boys and men."

"Good god," Nina swore.

"The thing is, she was convinced she had these potent magickal powers, but fortunately she didn't." I took a careful breath. "I grew up learning magick, but it was the kind that my mother believed in—and it was mostly self-aggrandizing, dark and chaotic."

"Not all practitioners are like that," Nina said.

"The folks my mama associated with were cut from the same cloth. So convinced of their own importance. They were always fixin' to get even with someone, or hexin' a different coven or group because of some spat. That's the sort of magick I was taught. Manipulative and cruel."

"Were you able to have any sort of regular life?" Nina asked. "What about your friends?"

"I didn't have any real friends. I didn't dare have the kids from school over to the house, and my high school years were hell. But I studied, and received a partial scholarship. It was a chance to get out and I went after it hard. When I went away to college, I finally found some freedom." I took another sip of wine for fortification. "That's how I met Willow's father. He was so blessedly *normal*. And I thought he loved me."

"You were young," Nina said.

"Please," I rolled my eyes. "I was practically the same age you are now."

"Did your mother approve of him?"

"God, I never introduced her to him, it was too embarrassing. We ran off to Las Vegas and got married right after graduation from LSU. Stupidest thing I *ever* did."

"What was he like?"

"When I met Beau Parrish, he was a handsome college football star, with dreams of playing in the pros. He never made it though, and it turned him bitter. He'd traded on his celebrity status after college for a year or so...Alumni or football fans were always happy to give him a pseudo job. But when the pros didn't pan out, he started drinking, and pretty soon there wasn't any money coming in. I was pregnant with Willow, with a ton of student debt, and determined to somehow give my child a better life than I'd had. A good life. A *normal* life, with a happy, pretty home, school friends, and playdates...so I applied for a job as an assistant to a big event coordinator in Shreveport."

"Obviously that worked out well for you," Nina said.

"I paid my dues and learned the ropes from Annie Cormier. She's a hell of a woman. Tough as nails." I smiled, remembering. "Pregnant or not, I've never worked as hard in my life as I did for her. I had a knack for weddings, and a way with even the most difficult of brides. She noticed and took me under her wing. A year after Willow was born, she even helped me hire a divorce lawyer and held my hand during the divorce proceedings."

"What about your own mother?" Nina asked. "Where was she?"

"Who knows?' I shrugged. "I hadn't seen or heard from her in years. Once the divorce was final, I continued to work my way up from assistant to event coordinator in my own right. About seven months ago, I got a call from a lawyer, informing me that my mother had passed away. I hadn't even known she was ill."

"What did you do?" Nina wanted to know.

"I went back home and discovered that all my mother had left was an old life insurance policy, a trashed home, a mountain of unpaid bills, and the house her adoptive parents had given her—which had somehow been left to me."

"What a mess," Nina said.

"The insurance policy barely covered the funeral costs, and a few weeks later when Beau found out I'd inherited the house, he decided to sue me for custody of

Willow—unless I handed over half of what the house was worth. He started some ugly gossip about my mother's friends, and life style. After her death it all got brought up again. Beau began insinuating that I was the same. Before I knew it, I started losing clients."

Nina hissed out a breath. "Bastard."

"That he is," I agreed. "It didn't matter that there wasn't any money in her accounts. Beau figured he'd finally landed on a way to get even with me for divorcing him. The last thing he'd ever expected was that the woman he'd thought of as a trophy wife was smarter than he'd realized. Anyway, while I scrambled to do damage control and keep the creditors at bay, the probate lawyer discovered that my mother had given most of her money away to some shyster who claimed to be a 'natural healer.' Seems she'd blown whatever money she did have on sage sticks, chakra alignments and more bogus spells."

Nina reached out for my hand. "I'm so sorry, Maggie."

"And then Thomas contacted me." I blew out a long breath. "He'd hired an investigator to find his Uncle Phillip's descendants—my mother and me. I honestly couldn't believe it...not at first. All those wild stories Mama had told me, were based on *real* people."

"No one could blame you for being suspicious, not after everything you'd gone through."

"That I was, but I was also desperate at the time for any sort of help, and the next thing I knew Thomas showed up at my apartment. He was so kind, and in a matter of days, he managed to work miracles."

"Julian told me that Mr. Drake hired you a lawyer and a realtor."

"He sure as hell did." I took another sip of wine. "That new realtor managed to sell my mother's house within a week. And I *still* don't know what Thomas did or said to make Beau back off, but he absolutely terrified him, and the custody suit was dropped."

Nina got up and went to go pick up a fussy Isabel. "No wonder you decided to make a fresh start for yourself."

I couldn't believe I'd told her all of that. Mortified, I tried to apologize. "I beg your pardon, Nina," I said, twisting the sapphire ring. "I shouldn't have dumped everything on you."

Nina simply sat again and reached over to give my hand a squeeze. "Don't be silly, Maggie. What are friends for?"

"I can't imagine what you must think of me. I'm truly sorry."

"I think you are a strong woman who made her own way. And considering everything you've told me, that's truly remarkable."

We sat in companionable silence for a few moments while Willow raced around the yard counting daffodils. I desperately tried to come up with a different topic of conversation, and asked Nina how she had met Diego.

Nina explained they had met at the restaurant she

was working at to pay her way through culinary school. Diego had taken a second job at night, as a dishwasher trying to make extra money to pay for his mechanic classes. I giggled as Nina recounted that they had hated each other at first. He'd thought she was a pampered princess, and she though he was a smart-mouthed jerk with too many tattoos and a superiority complex.

"So how'd y'all end up together?" I couldn't resist asking.

Nina bounced Isabel on her knee. "One night when I was closing up the restaurant I was mugged—at gunpoint."

"That sounds terrifying."

"It was," Nina admitted, "but then Diego came from out of nowhere and saved me. He wrestled the gun away from the mugger and proceeded to beat the hell out of him for threatening me."

"Wow," I said as Nina smiled over the memory.

"After he dealt with that, we called the police and Diego stayed with me the entire time. He took me out for a coffee afterward. We ended up talking until dawn. That was when I realized although he looked like a thug, he was in fact, a gentleman."

"His mama raised him right, clearly."

"No actually, he'd been in the foster care system his entire childhood. He even did a stint in rehab, but he's worked hard to improve himself, and has taken the opportunities he's been given to build a better life."

I was impressed. "That takes a lot of courage."

"That's how he and Julian met," Nina said.

"I'm sorry." I shook my head, not following her. "*How* did they meet?"

"In rehab. That's how they became friends."

Rehab? I did a double take. "I had no idea."

"It was Julian who pulled some strings and arranged for Diego to get a scholarship to the auto-mechanics school," Nina said.

"He did?"

"Julian has walked his own dark path, but he came out of his experience a better man." Nina smiled. "I'm so happy that now he has someone who loves him, and accepts him for who he is. Julian deserves some happiness in his life."

My mind was reeling at the revelations, but I zeroed in on the last bit. "Speaking of that..." I checked to make sure Willow was still out of earshot. "I got an eyeful of Julian and his lady friend the other night in the gardens."

Nina lifted her eyebrows. "Oh?"

"It was an accident, I assure you," I rushed to explain. "I'm not into voyeurism."

"Oh shit," Nina chuckled a bit.

"I have to say, I was surprised...she's a might younger than he is."

Nina sent me a bland stare. "You don't approve?"

"It's not for me to approve or disapprove," I said. "They seem to be crazy about each other."

Nina said nothing, she simply sat and studied me

carefully.

"Why do I have the feeling that their relationship is a secret?" I asked.

Nina shifted the baby on her lap. "Because it is."

"Why on earth would it be?"

"You should probably ask Julian about that. *Discreetly.*" Nina suggested.

"I see." I nodded. "And I will. Be discreet, that is. Nina, I've seen too little kindness or generosity in my own life to betray Julian and Thomas. They've both been wonderful to me."

Isabel started to fuss, and Nina stood. "I better take her back to the house."

"Oh, alright." I stood too.

"Thanks for the wine, and the company," Nina said.

I nodded. "You're welcome." I had to stop myself from wringing my hands. I hoped I hadn't offended her.

Willow came running over. "You're leaving?"

Nina bent down and gave Willow a one-armed hug. "This baby girl needs a bath and bed," she explained.

"'Night, Isabel!" Willow patted the baby's chubby thigh.

"Next time you'll have to come over to our apartments," Nina said. "We have a miniature patio of our own. I want to show you the herb garden that Autumn is designing for me."

Relieved, I smiled. "I'd enjoy that."

"See you later." Nina waved and headed down the path.

Willow came and stood beside me. Together we watched as Nina and the baby traveled down the winding footpath towards the mansion.

"*I* don't need a bath," Willow said, before I could suggest it.

I smiled down at her. "Yes, darlin' you do."

"Nuh-uh," Willow argued.

With a laugh, I gathered up the wine bottle and glasses and herded my reluctant daughter inside the house.

***

The magnolia trees in the front of the cottage didn't disappoint, and when they bloomed, the exterior of our cottage was more romantic than ever before.

I met Duncan, Thomas, all the groomsmen, and the ring bearer for their tuxedo fittings and was satisfied that everything was well in hand. Duncan had been nervous, and while I found it endearing, Julian, Wyatt, his brother, Xander and Duncan's friend Marshall had managed to keep him grounded and on task during the appointment. The suits and vests for their wedding were going to be a soft silvery-gray. The men would wear white shirts, and the ties would all be a warm ivory. For fun, I'd purchased different colored socks for the groomsmen to match the bridesmaid they were partnered with. That touch had made Duncan roar with laughter.

Morgan, Autumn's nephew and the ring bearer, had chattered up a blue streak the entire time. He seemed very interested in Thomas, and while everyone else was relaxed and happy, I had picked up on some tension between Thomas and Bran, Autumn's brother. They were perfectly civil to each other, but yet I felt it none-the-less.

A few days later I was working at the kitchen table, enjoying the peace and quiet as Willow was at pre-school. I'd just finished unpacking the decorating supplies for the Jacobs' gender reveal party, when Autumn dropped by with a gift.

"For you," she said, holding out a book.

"Oh." I had no choice other than to accept the book she cheerfully shoved into my arms. "Thank you." I stepped back and allowed her to enter the cottage.

"Your grandmother has been hounding me for weeks to give that to you," she said, and shrugged her jacket off.

"My grandmother?" I asked, flipping through the pages. It was an old vintage cookbook and a tad worn. I shrugged and shut the door behind her.

"Yeah, Irene wants you to have it," Autumn said, walking over to the couch. She caught the toe of her shoe on the rug and tripped.

"Careful!" I called out.

"I swear," Autumn grumbled as she caught herself. "If I didn't trip on something at least once a day, I'd wonder what was wrong..." She heaved a mighty sigh and sat on the couch. "Anyway, what was I saying? Oh, yeah, Irene. She wants you to have the book now."

I frowned over her use of present tense as opposed to past. "Don't you mean she *wanted* me to have it?"

Autumn met my eyes. "No," she said calmly and clearly. "She *wants* you to have it. Irene reminded me herself this morning."

I bobbled the old cookbook, but managed to set it on the coffee table as I took a seat beside her. "Autumn, my grandmother has been dead for thirty years."

Behind her trendy glasses, those green eyes considered me. "Maggie, your grandmother has been haunting the house I own for decades. When I bought the property last year and moved in, Irene came out to play. She's a *very* active spirit."

"Well, isn't that nice..." the comeback was automatic. I realized it probably sounded condescending...but in all honesty, I didn't know how else to respond.

"You don't know." Autumn shifted on the couch to look at me fully in the face. She gently laid one of her hands on mine. "Maggie, I'm a psychic sensitive. I can see and hear spirits on this plane."

I studied the pretty brunette that sat cheerfully on my sofa. *Bless her heart,* I thought. *The porch light's on but no one's home.*

"What's that about a porch light?" Autumn asked.

I flinched.

Autumn grinned. "Didn't anyone ever tell you to be

careful with your thoughts around a psychic, Maggie?"

"I..." I stopped and considered her. "Are you telepathic?"

"Not normally, no. I'm more of a Seer." Autumn shrugged. "However, I sometimes *can* pick up on people if their thoughts are directed at me, and if I'm touching them."

Even as my mind raced with questions, the urge to yank away from her was damn near overwhelming. I forced myself to sit still and brazen it out. "So you're a real psychic?"

"Among other things." Autumn wiggled her eyebrows. "I had a vision of you and Willow long before we ever found that lock box with all the information in it about your mother."

"You did?"

"Um, hmm." Autumn flipped her hair over one shoulder. "I saw a child, a girl running down the sidewalk in front of the cottage. The magnolias were in bloom...Her hair was in two long pigtails, and she wore a blue dress and white shoes. You were standing on the porch waiting for her and you called her, 'Sugar pie'."

My heart slammed against my ribs. "How long ago was this?"

"Last fall," Autumn said. "Ask Thomas about it, if you don't believe me."

"I believe you." I blew out a long shaky breath. "When Willow left for school this morning she had on a blue dress, and I'd put her hair in two pigtails...she was wearing her white dressy shoes as well. We'd argued about her wearing them to school, but I'd given in."

"Really?" Autumn smiled, and swiped a mark in the air as if keeping tally on a scoreboard. "Score another one for the Seer."

Here was a chance to learn more about my own intuition. From an actual psychic, I thought. "So..." I said slowly as my curiosity got the better of me. "What other things can you do?"

"I can show you." Autumn gave my hand a gentle squeeze. "But you'll have to let me in," she said.

"Let you in?"

"Yeah, open up," Autumn said. "Let me see."

I suddenly understood. "You want me to drop my energetic shields, don't you?"

"Exactly," she said. "It's a hell of a lot easier to scry if you let me in voluntarily."

I never in my life thought anything I learned from my mother would actually prove useful, but...*what the hell*, I decided. "You'll have to give me a moment. It's been a long time since I tried anything metaphysical."

"That's okay," Autumn said. "Take your time."

"I can't believe I'm doing this," I grumbled and shifted to face her.

There we sat, cross-legged on the sofa and facing each other. When Autumn silently held her hands out to mine I took a deep breath, reached for her hands, shut my eyes...

And I dropped my shields.

It was like being on a carousel, but one that went impossibly fast. There was a blur of color, sound, and movement all melding into each other. Images from my past flashed in front of my eyes. I bore down, gripping onto Autumn's hands like a lifeline, and then something surprising happened. I started to see pictures. No. Not pictures...it was more like seeing a movie play out...they were memories, I realized. Yet they weren't my own.

They were Autumn's.

She knelt in the grass planting flowers with a man with brown hair and green eyes. He said something silly to her, and I heard her laugh as she called him, "Dad"...She was driving an old pick-up truck cross country from New Hampshire to go to grad school in William's Ford. She pulled up to the manor, and parked her truck at the curb for the first time...She collided with Duncan and they tumbled to the ground, landing in each other's arms. They were both wearing athletic wear and hers was an eye popping clash of colors...Ivy and Autumn sat face-to-face, in a similar pose as we were now. They were in a park under an old tree. A pink light illuminated the pair of them and I felt, as much as saw, a shield of energy around Autumn. It cracked, shattered and fell to the ground.

Autumn holding her cell phone while she argued with her mother...the call ended. I felt tears in my own eyes as I understood that she'd been disowned for embracing her magickal heritage.

Autumn placing a long stem rose on top of a casket...next, a neon green ball of fire curved down from the sky, and lighting struck the roof of the Drake mansion. The explosion was deafening, and Autumn was huddling with Julian and Faye on the wet, brick pavers of the courtyard...A large group of people gathered in a circle in the same courtyard, and crows watched them all from the limbs of a massive old tree...

The pictures in my mind snapped forward again. *I saw Autumn cuddled on a couch, but this time she lay in the arms of a gorgeous man. "Rene," I hear her say his name as he pulled her protectively close and simply held her.*

The bungalow she lived in now, as it was when she bought it. Another fast shuffling of images as it went through a rehab process and Holly bringing Duncan to the bungalow. He was shoved through the door, bumped into Autumn and they landed in each others arms, yet again...Autumn and Duncan kissing in the kitchen... Duncan pulling a lockbox out of it's hidey hole, and the two of them sitting at the kitchen table going over the contents...

I came back to my body with a thump. It wasn't pleasant. My stomach lurched as the room took a lazy turn, and then stopped. Belatedly, I remembered to let go of Autumn's hands.

"Well, god damn, cousin Maggie." Autumn didn't sound upset...more like satisfied. "Here I thought I was going to be the one doing the reading and yet, you managed to scan me at the same time."

"I'm sorry," I managed. "I knew I had some intuition, but I didn't know I could do that!"

"Don't apologize." Autumn waved it away. "I wondered what talents I'd find if you let your shields down."

"That was intense," I said, and leaned back against the cushions.

"So you *do* have some psychic ability, and a real working knowledge of magick, despite everything. I won't ask why you don't practice." Autumn patted my leg. "I saw how it was for you growing up. That'd be enough to make anyone shy away from the Craft."

CHAPTER SIX

My shoulders dropped. I was so relieved that I didn't have to explain it to her, that it bordered on ridiculous. "Exactly."

"So you're a Witch after all," Autumn said.

"Not really."

Autumn shook her head. "You're a reluctant Witch. How interesting."

I jerked a shoulder at her assessment. "I don't think of myself as a Witch. Not anymore."

"You did when you were a teenager," Autumn raised her brows. "Honey, I *saw* you. That cat you did the healing spell on. His name was Binx."

Tears sprang to my eyes as I remembered my old cat. "Yes." I nodded. "That was his name. Like the cat Binx, from *Hocus Pocus*. Not a very original name for a black cat, but I loved him."

Autumn tapped a finger to her lips. "No wonder Irene's ghost has been so demanding." Autumn reached out for the book she'd brought. "This cookbook, it belonged to your grandmother. But it's much more than a cookbook, Maggie." Autumn open the book and spun it to face me. "You see all the notes in the margins?"

"Yes."

"This cookbook is filled with spells and charms—"

"You're saying that's a grimoire?"

"That's right." Autumn smiled. "But I'm warning you now...The annotated recipes? Don't play around with them." Autumn set the book on the table in front of us and scooted forward. Motioning me to join her.

I swung my legs around and leaned forward to look at the cookbook. "What do you mean?"

Autumn flipped a few more pages searching for something. "You see this one?" She pointed at a recipe called *Lies Be Gone Lemon Bars*. "When I made this recipe, I was unaware that it was a culinary spell. I took a pan of this dessert to work, for a pot-luck. Everyone who ate a lemon bar told me the truth, or they blurted out whatever was on their mind. Things they normally would never say out loud...and let's just say that I learned *way* more than I ever wanted to know."

I felt my eyes go wide. "So you're saying that you accidentally spelled your co-workers?"

"Yeah." Autumn grimaced. "It wasn't one of my finest moments."

"My mother would have considered that a success," I said. "Then again, for Mama it had been all about power: As in power over another."

"Which is probably why her spells were so

disastrous," Autumn pointed out.

I blinked. "I never thought of it that way."

"If I've learned anything since I moved to William's Ford, it's that magick is all about what's in the heart of the practitioner. Their intentions, personality, and who they truly are...inside. That force shapes and colors their magick."

I nodded. "I never thought about it that way. But that makes a certain sort of sense."

Autumn flipped a few more pages. "See this recipe?"

I read the title of the cake recipe that she pointed to. It was called *Chocolate Sin*. I glanced over the notes written on the side and flinched. "This was my grandmother's work? Lord have mercy! That's a deity invocation wrapped up in a sex spell if I ever saw one!"

Autumn's shoulders dropped. "You literally saved me about an hour of explanations."

"You honestly didn't work that, did you?"

"Yeah," Autumn said, with a grimace. "In my defense, I didn't know that this was a spell book. I thought I'd simply found an old family cookbook. It was a major rookie-Witch mistake. After I served the cake for dessert, things got a little wild."

I was torn between shock and laughter. "Dare I ask who you served the cake to?"

Autumn smiled. "To Duncan. Last summer."

I pressed my fingers to my lips to keep from snorting with laughter.

"We were exes and trying to be friends at the time."

Autumn rolled her eyes. "Boy, did it take a lot of willpower to keep things from getting too crazy that night."

"So if I'm following you correctly, my grandmother Irene dabbled in the darker aspects of the Craft?" I shook my head. "Could that be where my mama got her predilection for manipulative magick?"

"No. I doubt it," Autumn said. "Listen, when I first moved into the bungalow, I heard a lot of nasty rumors about Irene Bishop and the sort of magick her clients paid for."

"Oh Lord." I grimaced. "You mean she was like a Witch for hire?"

"Not exactly." Autumn flipped her hair over one shoulder. "After a while I learned there were two sides to the story. Irene Bishop was many things, and while I don't approve of taking money for spell craft, she *wasn't* dark. She worked some amazing magick for her clients."

"Such as?"

"Successful spells for women who desperately wanted children, and more than a few healing spells. Irene was clever, ambitious, and generous to her friends. And let's not forget that your grandmother was willing to sacrifice a great deal to keep her only child safe. She's a hell of a woman."

"Was," I corrected automatically.

Autumn grinned. "I'll have to have you over to the bungalow. You can meet your grandmother and see for yourself."

"I have only a smidgen of feminine intuition. I'm no psychic, not like you are."

Autumn gripped my hand. "Magnolia Irene Parrish, you are *much* more than you realize."

The pages on the cookbook began to rifle...on their own. With a gasp, I jerked farther away from the coffee table.

"Oh." Autumn smiled at me innocently. "I probably should have warned you about that. Don't be scared. The cookbook has a mind of its own."

The pages stopped, and I cautiously peered down to see what recipe they landed on. "*Avalon Apple Pie*," I read out loud. "A recipe guaranteed to invoke the magickal wisdom of your ancestors..."

"That's a new one," Autumn chuckled. "I suppose Irene wants you to go ahead and embrace your heritage. Reluctant Witch or not."

"No thank you, Irene," I said out loud—in case she was listening somehow.

As the pages began to turn again I probably should have been frightened, but at the moment I was too amazed to do anything other than sit and stare. Finally they came to rest, and together, Autumn and I leaned forward to see where the pages had landed this time.

"*Make New Friends Manicotti,*" we read out loud.

She nudged me with her elbow. "She's subtle, our Irene." Autumn rolled her eyes.

I couldn't help it, I began to laugh.

After Autumn left, I spent some time studying the cookbook. Eventually, I put the cookbook away in a kitchen cabinet, high enough where Willow wouldn't reach it. The first night I had it in the cottage, my eyes kept traveling to the cabinet, half expecting it to come bursting out and land on the table. If I hadn't seen for myself what the book could do, I would never have believed it.

The recent visits with Nina and Autumn had brought up many memories for me of my teenage years. Back when I'd been attempting to take the magick I'd learned and apply it in a more affirmative way. What I wouldn't have given to have known about these other Witches...good Witches.

Despite the rudeness of their Aunt Faye, The Bishops appeared to be a normal, well-adjusted family. Clearly my cousins practiced a very different sort of magick than my own mother had. The fact that they lived regular and happy lives, despite being Witches, was somehow reassuring to me.

The next morning I sat on the front steps of the porch after I'd dropped Willow off at preschool and watched as the first of the pink petals from the magnolia began to fall. The old trees were sliding past their peak of blooming, and I was determined to enjoy them for as long as I could.

I tipped my face up to the morning sun and on impulse went and plucked a seed pod from the nearest magnolia tree. I tucked it in a niche in the stones surrounding the front door for good fortune. It was more a folklore thing than witchcraft...it couldn't hurt, and I could certainly use the luck.

I'd ended up relocating to a town surrounded by modern practitioners of the Craft. While I'd yet to see any signs that the Drakes were practitioners as well, I was going to have to pull my head out of the sand and start paying closer attention. There was an energy here in William's Ford. Perhaps it was ley lines, or maybe it was something else. But my instincts told me I needed to keep watch. I did feel safe in the cottage, and deep in my heart I knew that coming here had been the best move for both me and for Willow.

As if to confirm my thoughts, several magnolia petals dropped from the tree and landed gently in my lap.

***

Shannon dropped by later in the week with a sealed envelope containing her ultrasound gender results. After she left, I sat on the couch holding the envelope, and decided to see if my intuition worked for more than knowing when a bride was about to have a meltdown, or a situation was about to pop up at a wedding reception.

I held the envelope in my hands and closed my eyes. I calmed my breathing, and focused. *Boy* popped into my mind suddenly. I took a deep breath, opened my eyes, and read the results. With a chuckle, I got up and added the appropriate color confetti to the uninflated gender reveal balloon.

On Saturday afternoon Willow stayed with Nina and Diego, and I swung by *Charming Cakepops* for the pink and blue cakepops and cupcakes. Today I was dressed business casual with my dark blazer, slacks, and an amethyst tone blouse. I'd added my Grandma Taylor's pearls at the last second. I'd debated on wearing them, but my intuition insisted that it would be a good move today.

Even though it felt odd to have my intuition push me into a specific fashion choice, I went ahead anyway. Besides the ring, they were all I had of the woman. After she'd passed away two years ago, her pearls had been sent to me instead of her adopted daughter—my mother.

With the desserts safely stowed in my car, I drove to the party rental center to pick up the white, pastel blue and pink balloon arch, and to have the oversized gender reveal balloon filled with helium.

Getting all the balloons in my car was tricky, but I managed it. I arrived at the Jacobs house at two o'clock to set up their decorations, the balloon arch, and the dessert table. Moments before their guests were scheduled to arrive, I brought in the gender reveal balloon. I managed several photos of the party décor, intending to add the pretty photos of the party set up to my website later in the evening.

When Shannon asked me to stay for the reveal I was surprised, but touched. I felt a real need to hurry home, but I brushed it off. There were plenty of familiar faces here today. I was surprised to learn that Lexie and Shannon were first cousins. I'd already known that Candice was Kyle's sister, and I was introduced to their father, Oliver, who I was informed made the best doughnuts in the county.

Autumn and Duncan were also in attendance, as were Holly and Ivy Bishop. I offered to make a video recording on my phone for Shannon, and I made sure to get the set-up in the background of the video. While the family and friends all gathered around for the big reveal, I chatted casually with Lexie's husband, Bran, as he held their infant daughter Belinda.

Bran was acting as a groomsman in the upcoming wedding, and his son Morgan—the ring bearer—was there at the party too. The little boy had the same red hair as his father and a mischievous light in his eye. If it wasn't for Lexie and her no-nonsense attitude, I'd have been worried that the ring bearer-to-be would be a real handful.

When the time for the big reveal had arrived, Shannon and Kyle stood together holding hat pins in one hand, and the ribbons on the oversized black balloon in place with the other. Their girls Sophia and Chloe stood next to them and with the countdown of *three, two, one*! The Jacobs popped the big balloon and a shower of blue confetti burst out and all over the four of them. The party guests' reaction was priceless. Obviously, everyone was pretty excited that there would be a boy after two girls.

I texted the thirty second video to Shannon and Kyle's phones, passed the ultrasound photos and results off to Lexie to give to the parents, and made a discreet exit.

I made the quick trip back to the cottage, parked the car and headed over to the kitchen of the main house to pick up Willow and Isabel. I'd promised to swap babysitting favors today, and Willow and I would be babysitting Miss Isabel this evening so her parents could enjoy a long-overdue date night.

I pushed down my impatience to leave and ended up lingering at the main house while Nina showed me her new herb garden that Autumn had designed. There were dozens of young plants already in place. I imagined it would be stunning by the end of summer.

An hour later, Willow and I had finally waved off Isabel's parents, and I was pushing the baby in her stroller back through the property and to the cottage. Willow insisted on hauling the diaper bag. She slung it cross-body the way I had my purse, and I struggled not to smile at her seriousness. It took twice as long getting to the cottage as it should have, and eventually I took the bag from her and let Willow "help" push the stroller. Together, we eased it up the back porch steps, and I pulled the house keys from my purse to unlock the door.

The door didn't seem to want to open. Annoyed, I gave the handle a good shake. The key turned in the lock and finally we were able to get in. "Here we go." I scooped up the baby, set her on my hip, and pushed the back door open.

I felt it the moment my foot hit the threshold. *Something was wrong.* Instinctively, I froze in my tracks, pulled the baby closer, and blocked Willow from entering the cottage.

"Mama?" Willow said.

"Just a minute, honey." I held up a hand, urging her to wait on the back porch as I stood in the doorway surveying the kitchen and living room.

The kitchen had been trashed. The refrigerator door stood wide open. Both chairs were knocked over and all the staples in the canisters had been dumped on the floor. I could see, as I looked across to the living room, that the cushions had been flung about as well.

Not sure if I'd walked in on the middle of a burglary, I eased back out the door and shut it quietly. "Willow." I herded her back and off the porch. "Can you reach the phone in the outside pocket of my purse?"

"Yes, Ma'am." Willows voice was uncertain. "What's wrong Mama?" She pulled it free.

"Baby, call Julian for me." I said it softly, hitching Isabel higher on my hip. "Do you remember how?"

"I know how." Willow pushed the home button, catching her tongue between her teeth. "Call Julian," she said into my phone and it automatically began to dial.

I scooped up Willow with my other arm, kicked my heels into the grass, and hauled both the girls away from the cottage as fast as I could. "Hang on, honey," I told Willow, as she tightened her arms around my neck.

"Mama! Are we playing a game?" Willow wanted to know. She began to laugh into the phone. "Hi Julian!"

"Julian," I pitched my voice so he would hear me. "Y'all need to come to the cottage right now. It's been broken into."

I heard his startled reply but kept moving.

Julian met us at the halfway point between the cottage and the mansion, and he wasn't alone. Wyatt Hastings was with him. "Magnolia!" Julian called to me and both men were running full out.

If I wouldn't have been out of breath from jogging while carrying two children, I would have reassured them that we were alright. As it was, I was struggling to catch my breath and hold onto a giggling four-year-old and a squirming, unhappy Isabel.

We met at the stone bench. The same one where I'd seen Julian and Holly...I snapped my mind away from that, focusing on the here and now. "We're okay," I panted, as Willow had almost cut off my air.

Julian scooped Willow up in one arm and Wyatt reached out to steady me. "Did you walk in on a burglary?"

"I don't know." I huffed.

"Wyatt," Julian said, passing Willow over to him.

"Take the girls back to the main house and call the police."

"What are you gonna do?" I demanded.

"I'm going to go see if the intruder is still there."

Before I could argue, Julian was off like a shot and moving towards the cottage.

"Is he crazy?" I asked Wyatt. "What if someone is still in the cottage? What if they have a gun?"

Wyatt smiled. "Julian can more than take care of himself."

"With *what*? That great wardrobe isn't going to protect him."

Wyatt held out an arm for me and began to usher us toward the main house. "Trust me. He's got an ace up his sleeve a criminal would never see coming."

"What do you mean?" I cut myself off, it was pointless arguing. I hustled back to the main house and called the police.

***

The police arrived and took over the cottage. I'd half expected Lexie to show up, but she wasn't one of the responding officers. When they asked me to come back and let them know if anything was missing, I left Willow and Isabel with Thomas, who insisted he was more than up to the task of watching the girls, and walked to the cottage with Wyatt and Julian as my escorts.

Once they let me inside the cottage and I could look around, I was stunned to see that the bedrooms had also been trashed. The good news was I hadn't left any cash in the cottage and nothing had been stolen. They'd ignored the television and my laptop.

The bad news was that all of the dresser drawers had been dumped, and the contents rifled through. The kitchen had taken the worst of it. Flour and sugar had been thrown around, ketchup and mustard was dripping from the walls, and a jar of pickles had been smashed on the floor.

My jewelry box had been dumped, but as far as I could tell nothing had been taken. The costume jewelry was piled in a tangled mess, but still there. The only real items I had of value were my sapphire ring, and Grandma Taylor's pearls...It hit me hard suddenly that it was a damn good thing I'd followed my intuition and worn the necklace after all, otherwise they'd have probably been stolen.

The front door had been the point of entry. When Julian asked if I'd set the alarm code, I told him no. I'd never even used it since we'd moved in. When I admitted that, it made me feel pretty foolish. If I would've set the stinking alarm, none of this would have probably happened.

The police asked if I had any enemies, and other than my ex—I couldn't think of a single person petty enough to have done something like this, so I told them no. The police called it malicious mischief, took photos and filed their reports, and Julian told me Thomas would file an insurance claim, so all that was left to do was clean up, and try and put everything back to how it was.

I put the bedrooms back to rights, and Wyatt and Julian tackled the kitchen. Once that was done, I wanted to go back and check on the kids. Julian re-showed me how to engage the security system, and the three of us went back to the main house.

I was shocked to discover Thomas and Willow sitting on a big overstuffed sofa, watching *Frozen* with surround sound. Isabel was snoozing peacefully, propped up in Thomas's lap while he sat beside Willow with his feet up on one end of the in-home-theater-style furniture.

I did a double take as Willow shared her popcorn with Thomas. Julian and Wyatt had stepped in the room behind me, and I shot a glance at the two men, watching them grin in reaction to what Thomas was watching.

I smothered a chuckle. "Hey y'all." I walked into the room.

"Oh." Thomas checked over his shoulder, giving us a casual wave. "You're back."

Willow bounced on the fancy leather. "We're having a movie night, Mama!"

"I see." I walked around the big sectional sofa. "How's Isabel? Any troubles?"

"None at all," Thomas said casually.

"*Frozen*?" Julian asked his father. "Dad, you're watching *Frozen*?"

"I've never seen it before," Thomas said straight faced. "It's a wonderful movie. I especially like how Elsa must learn to embrace her magickal powers...and no longer be frightened of them."

He seemed to be looking right at me when he said that, but I shrugged it off.

"Sit with me, Mama," Willow said. "You can have some of my popcorn."

"How did everything go?" Thomas asked.

I sat on the big couch next to Willow, taking a handful of her popcorn. "Nothing that a little elbow grease couldn't cure." I said, purposefully keeping my answer vague in front of my daughter.

Julian stood behind me and rested his hand on my shoulder. "Maybe you two should stay here tonight."

I reached back for his hand. "That's probably a good idea."

Wyatt plopped down in a chair to my left. "I love this movie."

I snorted out a laugh. "You like Disney movies?"

Wyatt smiled as Willow started to sing along with the rock trolls. "Sure, what's not to like?"

***

The following morning, Thomas announced he was taking Willow out to breakfast, and she was thrilled. I took the opportunity he'd given me to do a thorough cleaning of the cottage. He'd generously offered to send some of the staff over to help, but I wanted to do it myself.

It had dawned on me in the middle of the night that I had completely forgotten about Irene's cookbook, and I was relieved the next morning to see that it was still in the cabinet above the refrigerator, exactly where I'd left it. I wiped down the kitchen cabinets, the inside of the refrigerator, re-mopped the kitchen floor, and scrubbed the devil out of every inch of the cottage. It made me feel slightly more in control. I was dumping the mop water down the kitchen sink when a knock sounded on the cottage door.

I opened it to find Wyatt holding a couple bags of groceries. The spring breeze had his brown hair blowing in his eyes. He was wearing a pair of jeans and a long sleeved, button down pale green shirt. The color made his eyes pop, and I immediately regretted my current choice of outfit.

"Good morning." He smiled.

"Wyatt." I smiled and tried not to be embarrassed that I was wearing a ratty old t-shirt, cut off shorts, and had my hair clipped in a messy twist on top of my head. I also tragically didn't have a stitch of makeup on. My Grandma Taylor would be rolling in her grave. *Southern ladies should always be prepared to receive a visitor.* "Sorry," I said pointing at my hair, "I've been cleaning, and wasn't expecting anyone."

"You look stunning just as you are." He sounded sincere, and held out the bags. "I brought some things to replace what was ruined last night."

"Oh." I took the bags. "Thank you, that was very nice. Would you like to come in?" I stepped back and allowed him to enter.

He walked in and I took the groceries to the kitchen.

"It looks great in here," Wyatt said as he followed me back.

"Thanks." I set everything on the counter. "I've been scrubbing for an hour."

To my surprise he nudged me aside, opened up the bags, and started to tuck things in the fridge himself. "I got you a carton of milk, more eggs, some ketchup and mustard." He smiled over at me. "Basically, I replaced all your condiments." He pulled out a jar of mayo and another jar of sweet pickles and put those in the fridge.

I reached in the other grocery bag, saw bags of flour and sugar. "Thank you." I was touched at the thoughtfulness of his gesture. He'd noticed all the food that had been smashed or thrown around the kitchen and had replaced every single item.

He shut the refrigerator door and smiled at me. Good manners had me automatically ask him if he'd like to have a seat, but instead of going to the living room as I'd expected, he sat in one of the kitchen chairs.

Not sure what else to do, I went ahead and refilled the canisters, while Wyatt asked when the new security system would be installed.

"Thomas said they'd be coming tomorrow." I folded up the empty bags of sugar and flour. "I'm sure we'll be fine here tonight. Especially since I'm keeping the security system armed from now on. It was foolish of me not to use it. I guess I learned that the hard way."

He pulled a card from his shirt pocket. "This is my number. If you need anything—like more pickles, or should you see anyone suspicious hanging around, give me a call."

"Thank you." I smiled and tried for a laugh. "If I see someone suspicious, were you planning on beating the crap out of them or, taking notes on their appearance, motivation, or possible accent for your next murder mystery book?"

"I can do both." Wyatt leaned in closer and studied my face. "I'm serious though. If you need something, Magnolia. Call me."

My heart fluttered, and my attraction to him caught me completely off guard. Wyatt Hastings *was* a nice-looking man. It sort of snuck up on you. I wasn't sure if it was the contrast of the pale blue eyes against the dark shaggy hair and short, neat beard, or if it was his quiet humor and intensity.

I found I had to moisten my lips before I could speak. "Thank you, Wyatt. I appreciate the gesture."

"You're welcome." He reached out and tugged on a lock of my hair that had fallen out of the clip. "I'll go, and let you get back to your cleaning."

While the gesture had been almost brotherly, his grin

had my heart stuttering in my chest. Silently, I walked him to the front door and stood on the porch, watching as he walked to his car. He gave me a friendly wave and backed his car out of the driveway. I went back inside and shut and locked the door behind me.

As I put away the grocery bags, I wondered if I'd misinterpreted his visit. Surely, he hadn't been flirting...had he? It surprised me that I sort of wished he had been. *Wyatt is a friend of Julian's,* I told myself, firmly. *He was merely being a good neighbor,*

Even though he lived three blocks over.

I blew out a breath and faced the truth: I was attracted to Wyatt Hastings.

***

By the next day the cottage had a new front door, an upgraded security system, and motion sensor lights in the landscaping surrounding it. Even though we were now equipped with a state-of-the-art system, I was surprised to realize that I still felt uneasy.

It was a sensation I'd experienced a lot growing up. The uncomfortable feeling that makes you glance over your shoulder, or double check the locks on all the doors and windows. Hard to put a pin in...but it was that gut hunch that insisted *something* was wrong on an energetic level.

I considered what my intuition was telling me as I loaded the dishwasher after supper. It didn't matter that

I hadn't practiced witchcraft in years. I still recognized bad energy when I felt it, and knew deep down, that some sort of protective wards were definitely needed around the cottage.

Every instinct I owned insisted it was the right move, and yet I still hesitated. I shut the dishwasher and straightened, only to discover that the cookbook was now out and on the counter.

I couldn't help but jump in reaction. I patted my hand to my heart and scanned the recipe on the pages. "*Witchy and Wild Blueberry Muffins,*" I read. "Designed to safeguard your home and protect your family from negative influences..."

I thought about Autumn's warning not to underestimate the book as I finished wiping off the counters. "Maybe whipping up a batch of those might not be such a bad idea...all things considered." As if in reaction to my words, the book scooted a tad closer to me.

I checked to make sure Willow was still in the living room. "I suppose I could go to the market and see if I can find any wild blueberries." And I seriously considered it for a few moments, but in the end I shut the book and put it back in the cabinet. "Damn. I'm not sure what to do," I muttered to myself. "I know I should do *something* to increase the protective energies. Protective wards still seem like the best way to go."

When I was a girl, I remembered, *Mama used to put crystal points on the window sills. Burn black candles, and set mirrors in the windows to reflect any evil sent our way—directly back to its sender.*

I shook my head over the memory. Truth be told, my mother had been so busy hexing anyone and everyone that she had a lot of reason to assume bad energy *was* coming back to her. However, I didn't have any sort of magickal supplies to do even the most basic of protection work.

I eyeballed the salt shaker that sat on the table. *Salt was good for cleansing spells...*but that clearly wasn't going to cut it. The cottage had been broken into and I needed to keep my daughter and I safe. As Willow romped around the living room, I began to wonder where I could find magickal supplies here in town.

My cell phone rang and Willow scooped it up. "I can answer it!" she shouted. "Maggie Parrish, event cord-in-nator," Willow said, trying her best to pronounce *coordinator.*

I held out my hand for the phone. "Thank you, darlin'. Give me the phone."

Willow ignored me and smiled into the phone. "Hi Autumn!" she said, excitedly.

"Um, hmm." Willow nodded at whatever Autumn had said. "Yeah, Mama's right here." She handed me the phone. "Autumn says we need to go shopping."

My heart gave a hard rap against my ribs. This was going to take some getting used to, having a psychic for a friend. "Hello, Autumn."

"Reluctant Witch or not, we need to get you stocked

up on supplies," she said without preamble.

"Yes, I literally was just thinking the same."

"I heard about the cottage being tossed. I wish you'd have called me Maggie, I would have come over to help. Hell, I would have rallied the troops. Lexie, Ivy and Holly would've been there in a hot second."

"I felt it best to keep things low-key," I said vaguely, as Willow was standing right there listening to every word coming out of my mouth.

"Plus, you didn't want to scare Willow," Autumn said. "I figured that was the case."

I tried to sound matter of fact. "Do you know somewhere that I could go to purchase a few essential items this evening? Discreetly?"

"You bet your ass." Autumn laughed. "I'll come and pick you up in five minutes."

"I'll have to br—"

"Bring Willow along," Autumn said, cutting me off. "It'll be fine. Trust me."

She ended the call and I stood there, blinking at the phone.

CHAPTER SEVEN

I hadn't known that the Bishop family owned a store. *Enchantments* was situated on Main Street, next door to the O'Connell's flower shop, and two doors down from Candice's bakery. I'd seen the store, of course, but had assumed it was a quaint, artsy boutique. I'd never even realized it was a magick shop.

We parked out front and I found myself checking out the store as we walked to the entrance. I could see Ivy working behind the counter through the windows and, thinking back to the words we'd exchanged at the bridal shower, wished it would have been anyone else. I told myself to suck it up. Things would only be awkward with my gothic cousin if I chose to make them so.

"Oh, pretty!" Willow breathed as we entered the store.

Enchantments truly was. Shelves filled with books ran along a far wall. The other walls were exposed brick, and the floors were done in gleaming old wood. A small tabletop fountain bubbled on a central display and surrounding it were numerous dishes of tumbled stones. The shop smelled pleasantly of herbs, incense, and candles.

"Hello," Ivy called cheerfully, moving out from behind the counter. She was wearing a long flowing dress in shades of purple and black, and heavy black boots. She looked exactly like she was, a modern, confident Witch.

"Ivy." I nodded.

Ivy smiled and purposefully directed her attention to Willow. "Hey munchkin, you want to come with me to *Charming Cakepops* before they close and see if Candice has any cookies left?"

"Yes!" Willow bounced up and down. "Can I, Mama? Please, can I?"

Ivy and Autumn had set it up so I could get the supplies I needed without Willow being any the wiser. "Sure," I said. "Behave yourself for your cousin Ivy."

Ivy took Willow's hand. "Maggie, I selected a few items I thought you might find useful." Ivy tipped her head toward a basket resting on the counter.

"Thank you," I inclined my head in acknowledgement.

"Be back in fifteen," Ivy said, and with a smile she and Willow headed a few doors down the street to the bakery.

Autumn went directly to the basket. "Let's see what Ivy pulled for you."

I joined her at the counter and eyeballed the contents

of the basket. Most of which I recognized. "I see several chunks of black tourmaline crystal." There were small packages of dried herbs. "Hyssop and angelica," I said, reading the labels.

"Both are very protective herbs." Autumn held up a third plastic bag. "Sea salt. This comes in handy for cleansing."

I nodded. "I remember."

Autumn lifted up a package of incense. "Dragon's blood resin. Good choice for self-defense."

I pursed my lips as I thought it over. "Agreed, but if y'all don't mind, I'd prefer sandalwood, actually."

Autumn went directly to a display of incenses. "Stick or cone type?"

"I favor the stick variety."

"Do you have an incense burner?" Autumn asked.

"No," I admitted. "Autumn, I haven't practiced since I was a teenager. I have literally *no* magickal supplies in my house."

Autumn selected a simple wooden burner decorated with a sun and moon. "How's this?"

"That's fine." I nodded, going back to the shopping basket Ivy had started. I pulled a handful of small black candles out and set them on the counter. "I'd rather not use black candles. They remind me too much of the magick my mother used to do."

"Don't tell me, let me guess. Patricia only used black candles?"

I grimaced. "That would be correct."

Autumn rolled her eyes. "That is *so* 1980's."

"Well, that literally was the time period, darlin'," I said, straight faced.

Autumn snorted out a laugh, motioning me over to a large display of mini tapers. "You can use purple candles for protection instead. Or you can use gray to neutralize negativity."

I joined her and considered the display of different colored candles. "I don't know. I need to be subtle around Willow. She sees an awful lot for a four-year-old."

Autumn grinned. "She's an intuitive. Like you are."

"You think so? I' haven't noticed anything overt as of yet."

"Trust me." Autumn gave me a friendly elbow jab.

"I do trust you," I said softly. "Otherwise I wouldn't be here."

Autumn gave me a one-armed hug. "That's the nicest thing you could've said to me."

Her words immediately made me feel ungracious. "I should apologize to y'all."

Autumn shrugged. "Whatever for?"

"It's just that," I began, "I swore to put the dark arts firmly behind me. And yet here I am buying occult supplies, and gearing up to practice again." I sighed, feeling defeated.

"First off," Autumn said. "You need to stop referring to magick as the 'dark arts.' Magick is a beautiful, joyous thing."

"How can I make you understand?" I said. "In the house where I grew up it *was* the dark arts. There was nothing positive or joyous about it."

"But it was for you." Autumn's words hit me like a ton of bricks.

"Well, I—"

"You're so hard on yourself, Maggie. It hurts my heart knowing what it was like for you as a child. But yet, you've become a successful business woman, a good mother, and a loyal friend."

"How do you know that I'm loyal?"

Autumn selected a large package of white tea light candles. "Because you've kept Julian and Holly's secret." Autumn held out the package. "I saw your memories of spotting them in the gardens, when I read you."

I took the package of candles. "Do you have any candle holders for tea lights?" I asked, attempting to change the subject.

"See?" Autumn raised her brow. "Loyalty. You won't even confirm that I spoke about it."

I silently perused a display of scented votive candles. I chose a creamy white, found it to be vanilla scented, and picked up another.

Autumn cleared her throat. "Look, to my knowledge no one in my family knows about their relationship. Holly isn't even aware that *I* know."

I eyeballed her. "And how did you discover it?"

"Duncan and I accidentally walked in on them in the

atrium at the Drake mansion last November."

I picked up another votive in soft purple and sniffed it. "Lilac," I said. "This is a good scent for protection, isn't it?"

"It is." Autumn nodded. "Looks like some basic correspondences are starting to come back to you."

I blew out a long breath and went to the counter, placing the candles in the basket with the crystals, herbs, and incense. "If I'm honest, they've never left me. I've simply tried to ignore them for a very long time."

Autumn held up a few glass votive holders. "These would work for the tea lights and the votives."

"I like those," I said. "They're pretty."

"No reason your magickal accessories can't be attractive," Autumn pointed out.

I ended up purchasing the plain tea lights, the scented votives, and the candle holders as well as the incense and holder, the crystals, the herbs and salt.

While Autumn rang me up, I'd had another idea pop in my head for reinforcing the energetic wards I was about to erect at the cottage. It was old-school, and entrenched in so much Southern folklore most folks wouldn't think twice about seeing it hanging above the front door in the cottage. *Now all I had to do was find one...*

Autumn was packing everything in a sturdy handled brown paper bag when Ivy and Willow came back.

Willow held up a small bag of cookies. "Look,

Mama!" she said. "I brought you one too."

"Thanks, sugar pie," I said distractedly, and wondered if I'd be able to find what I was looking for at the local antique shop. *Were they even open on a weeknight?*

"Until seven o'clock," Ivy said, seemingly out of the blue.

I frowned at her. "I beg your pardon?"

"The antique store is open until seven," Ivy said with a grin.

"Oh," I managed to smile in return. "Thank you, Ivy. I hope they'll have what I'm looking for."

"Oh, are we on the hunt for more mag—" Autumn caught herself. "More items for your home? Because I love a good quest!" Autumn rubbed her hands together, making me chuckle.

"Are we going hunting for an old horseshoe, Mama?" Willow asked from around a mouthful of cookie.

"How did you..." I trailed off, studying my daughter who smiled innocently up at me with her unique blue and brown eyes.

"Told ya," Autumn said, smugly, as she came from around the counter. It took me a moment to reply to her.

"Yes, Autumn, you certainly did," I said calmly, and took Willow's hand.

"Have fun antiquing!" Ivy waved.

Autumn held open the shop door and the three of us trooped down the block to the antique shop.

That evening, as soon as I put Willow to bed, I got to work. To my surprise, I found that my magick came back to me easily. I created magickal wards around the interior of the cottage first. Using a mixture of water, the herbs and sea salt, I marked protective pentagrams over every doorway, on each window and mirror in the cottage.

To seal the spell, I blessed and empowered the iron horseshoe, and nailed it open end up on the doorframe around the inside of the front door. That way all the protection and good luck would be held safely within the home.

As I tapped the final nail in place I felt the wards lock down. It made the hair rise on the back of my neck. I walked through the cottage, feeling and testing for any weak spots in my protection, but I found none. Lastly, I took the remainder of the herbed water and tossed it over the front porch to wash away evil, and to keep trouble from our door.

***

April sped by, and before I knew it, the month of May had begun and Autumn and Duncan's wedding was here. The rehearsal and following dinner was to be held in the ballroom at the Drake mansion, which was smart. We—I meant the Drakes—had plenty of space for the rehearsal and lots of room to set up not only a bar, but tables for the dinner on the opposite side of the ballroom.

In the days leading up to the wedding, I'd worked my tail off. Then again, so had Candice, Violet, and Nina. In addition to managing the Drake household, Nina was cooking a gorgeous meal to serve to the wedding party for the rehearsal dinner. The morning of the rehearsal I'd dropped off Willow at preschool and had personally supervised the placing of the rental tables, chairs in the ballroom, and the set-up of all the rehearsal table décor.

My sneakers were silent as I zipped around the ballroom. Today I had my hair in a high ponytail and had dressed for comfort with denim capris and a blue t-shirt my former boss, Annie, had given me. It read: *Bridal Consultant. Only because... full time multi-tasking NINJA is not an actual job title.* On stressful days like this, I needed all the reasons to smile that I could get.

Violet had outdone herself with the floral centerpieces. Each container was a rustic metal watering can in different shapes and sizes. Flowers in a rainbow of colors: peach, yellow, pink, blue and even a touch of lavender and green were accented by dusty silver foliage. The plan was to re-use the centerpieces for the food table at the reception tomorrow.

The Drake's staff was more than up to the task of handling a dinner party for twenty-five guests, and I left them to it. I had a final meeting to go over the details of the wedding reception with the caterer and his waitstaff.

I also wanted to get out to the site and check to see that the reception tents were being put up in place and the tables and chairs were being delivered.

They wouldn't be set and dressed until the morning of the wedding, of course. But I'd rather not have any unwelcome surprises. I wanted the main pieces in place, and I was leaving the mansion to head to the event site when Autumn suddenly appeared from around a corner, bumping into me.

I steadied her automatically. "Autumn," I said, laughing. "You're supposed to be on your way to the salon with the wedding party for your manicure."

"I know." She shrugged. "I only wanted to see how everything was looking..."

I turned her around and steered her right on out. "Honey, I promise you, everything is going exactly to plan, and is right on schedule."

"Well, I—"

"Trust me. I do this for a living." I said soothingly. "Now, all you have to do is go relax and be pampered. I'm here to sweat the details and all the small stuff."

"What about the tents and tables being set up in the gardens at the park?" Autumn fretted. "What if someone messes with them tonight?"

"They won't." I forced cheer into my voice. "I hired security."

"You did?" Autumn blinked. "I didn't know that."

"Of course I did," I said. "I'm leaving nothing to chance."

She tried to smile but it wilted around the edges. "At least the forecast is clear tomorrow."

I rubbed a hand over her back. "Everything will be wonderful. Trust me."

Lexie and Ivy met us in the back foyer. "There you are." Lexie glared at Autumn. "Come on, we're going to be late if we don't leave right now!"

"Maggie busted me," Autumn grumbled. "She wouldn't even let me get a peek at what's going on for the rehearsal dinner."

"Hey there, Lexie. Hey, Ivy." I passed the bride off to her attendants, nodding to each of them. "Can I trust y'all to keep our bride out of trouble for the rest of the day?"

"I'll cuff her and toss her in a squad car if necessary," Lexie said straight-faced.

I patted Lexie's shoulder. "I knew I could depend on you."

Lexie began to haul a laughing Autumn out, but Ivy remained behind, studying me carefully.

Impatiently, I checked my watch. I had to get moving to make my own appointments. "Something on your mind?"

"Nice shirt," Ivy said, soberly.

"Thank you," I said, and scooted her out the door as well. "It makes people laugh and relax a bit. And on a day like today, I can use every weapon at my fingertips."

"I like you. Didn't expect to," Ivy said. "I figured I'd

have to be polite—seeing as how you're a relative and all."

"Well, bless your heart," I drawled.

"Ha!" Ivy's eyes gleamed. "That's Southern for *kiss my ass*, if I ever heard it."

I simply tightened my ponytail and smiled.

"You people wrangle better than anyone I've ever seen," Ivy said.

I smiled. "Sugar, you ain't seen nothin' yet."

Ivy bit her lip. "Are you really going to make Bran wear pastel colored socks with his tux?"

"Yes," I said, taking her arm and moving her along. "He'll get a kick out of it. Trust me."

"Catch you later, bridal ninja." Ivy sketched a mock bow and rushed to catch up with Lexie and the bride.

I smiled after her. *I'll be damned if I hadn't ended up liking her as well...* I shook off the sentiment and took off at a dead run in the opposite direction toward my cottage so I could get to my next appointment.

I skidded to a halt when I reached my car. There, on the hood, was a dead songbird. It had been mauled, and I didn't want to leave the poor thing there, so I took a minute, hustled inside and grabbed a plastic grocery bag. Using that, I picked up the bird and carried it to the garbage cans.

"Stray cat got you, I suppose," I said, dropping the bird in the can. I shut the lid, ran back inside to wash my hands, and rushed to the car, hoping to still make my meeting on time.

***

The wedding rehearsal itself went as I expected, a few fits and starts, but I had the wedding party run through the processional, ceremony, and recessional, a second time and everything fell into place.

Now the dinner had been served and enthusiastically consumed, and the bar was open. Everyone was milling about, laughing and chatting. Ivy was on the move with her camera, taking candid shots for the bride and groom as the party wound down. The bride and groom were walking arm and arm around the ballroom, chatting up their wedding party. I checked for Thomas, saw that he was in deep conversation with the officiant, and then I spotted Julian. He was sitting alone at the bar, sipping on a drink.

Casually, I turned my head, and saw Holly sitting at a table and talking to the Jacobs family. It didn't seem fair to me that a couple were forced to keep their relationship a secret.

I studied my cousin as he sat there, outwardly calm and unruffled, in another one of his gorgeous tailored suits. To most folks he'd seem aloof, perhaps even slightly bored...but I knew him now. His back was tight and his shoulders were held stiff.

I snuck a quick peek at Holly. She was watching him, but trying not to. Most people wouldn't have caught that...however it struck me as unbearably sad.

Willow was occupied sitting and talking with Morgan and Lexie, so I decided to join Julian.

"Hey, there," I said, sliding on to the empty barstool next to him.

"Maggie." Julian lifted his glass in a slight toast.

"You looked lonely," I said. "Mind if I join you?"

"Not at all." Julian gave me a little smile.

The bartender appeared. "Shot of Jameson," I said.

Julian cocked a brow at the order.

I flashed him a sweet smile, and when the shot was poured I picked it up, toasted my cousin, and downed the whiskey. "That sure as hell hit the spot," I said, slapping the empty shot glass back on the bar.

Julian cleared his throat. "Magnolia, you're a woman of hidden talents and skills."

I tilted my head. "Sugar, you have *no* idea."

Julian threw back his head and laughed.

Faye Bishop strutted up to the bar on the arm of an older gentleman. Autumn had introduced me to him earlier, as Dr. Hal Meyer. He was Autumn's boss at the university and Faye Bishop's—boyfriend. I suppose would be the most accurate thing to call him. I didn't want to think of him as her lover.

"I believe the bride has a few questions for you, Magnolia. That is..." she glanced meaningfully at the shot glass. "If you can find any spare time while you're *working*."

I swiveled on the bar stool and met the woman's glare head-on. The rehearsal was all but over. She knew it and so did I. "Why thank you, darlin'," I said in my most exaggerated drawl. "I'll just mosey over yonder and see what she needs."

I moved directly to the bride and groom and, of course, they didn't need a thing. In fact, they both thanked me for all the hard work, and told me to relax and enjoy the rest of the party.

That old bitch, I thought as Faye sashayed across the room as if she owned the place. She might have been the most elegant older woman I'd ever met, but on the inside she was mean as a snake. I caught my negative thoughts and decided to take a break and step outside for a few moments so I could rein my temper back in.

I went to Thomas, asked him to keep an eye on Willow, and told him I'd be back in a few. Using Nina's kitchen for my escape, I ducked out the back door, pulled out the one emergency cigarette I had in my purse, and lit up. Huddling in the dark outside the kitchen, I indulged my frayed nerves. I probably should have felt guilty for skipping out on a family function, but that first drag and slow exhale released some of the tension I'd been carrying around for the past twenty-four hours.

No one would look for me here. The party had been a smashing success as far as I could see. The engaged couple were blissfully in love, and pretty much everyone else seemed happy... and for some reason that made me feel like an outsider, more than ever before.

I heard the padding of feet and a large black dog

appeared in the courtyard of the Drake's property. To my knowledge Thomas didn't own guard dogs. The dog was a distance away and while I could see he was a powerful breed, I couldn't have said what sort of dog it was. The dog gave a small *woof* and trotted off.

I heard the kitchen door handle turn. Quickly, I eased a bit further around the corner of the house, leaning into the lush ivy that grew along the stone walls. I didn't move quite fast enough, though. I'd been seen. It was a man who'd stepped outside, and my hiss of impatience from having my solitude interrupted, caught his attention.

"Hello?" The husky voice identified the owner as Wyatt Hastings.

Resigned, I leaned forward slightly and into his line of sight. "Mr. Hastings." I nodded.

"Magnolia?" He frowned, stepping a bit closer.

"The one and only," I said and lifted the cigarette to my lips.

"I didn't know you smoked."

"Just took it up," I shot back, and blew a stream of smoke towards the sky.

His lips twitched. "I see." He tucked his hands in his pockets and appeared content to simply stand there.

I could feel his silent disapproval, which for some reason annoyed me, even though I told myself that I didn't give two figs for his opinion. After a few moments of silence there was a definite hitch between my shoulder blades. I wanted him gone so I could brood in private.

"I suppose you'd prefer to be left alone," he said, "to enjoy your emergency cigarette."

I scowled at him. There was no point in wondering how he'd known that...the man was too clever, and far too observant for his own good. "Why thank you, sugar," I drawled. "Now go run along and leave me be."

His lips quirked into a wry smile. "I'm afraid you'll have to put up with some company, Magnolia. You're not the only person looking for a quick place to hide."

I raised my eyebrows. "Why on earth would *you* need to hide?"

"I have a problem with a fan...A local woman. She's been hounding me, texting me at all hours, she even followed me tonight."

"A big, strong man like you can't defend yourself from a fan?" I rolled my eyes.

"She's damn near becoming a stalker," he said, and swiped his shaggy hair out of his eyes.

"Well then, get a restraining order."

"I'm in the process of it, but she showed up here tonight anyway. I almost called the police, but didn't want to do anything to spoil the night for the bride and groom."

"On that point we agree," I said. "If it makes you feel any better we do have security at the wedding and reception tomorrow."

"I sincerely hope it won't come to that."

"Well, if she does try and crash the wedding, you

point her out to me." I smiled. "I'd be delighted to remove her."

Wyatt grinned at that, crossed his arms against his chest, and leaned against the stone of the house.

Since he showed no signs of leaving, I decided to go back inside. Dropping the cigarette on the pavers, I tamped it out. I scooped it up immediately—I couldn't stand it when folks left those lying on the ground. I carried the cigarette butt to a nearby trashcan and dropped it in.

A movement in the dark, had me spinning in surprise.

"There you are." An unknown woman rushed across the pavers of the courtyard, and straight to Wyatt's side. "I wondered where you'd run off to." She immediately latched onto him.

"Miss Darbyshire." Wyatt straightened, and removed her hand from his arm. "This is private property. You shouldn't be here."

"Awww," she said reaching for him again. "You're shy. I love that about you."

Wyatt held up a hand to ward her off. "I've told you before, that I'm not interested in you romantically." His voice was polite but firm. "Please, leave."

"And I've told you," she purred, "to call me Audrey."

I stood across the span of pavers and watched, fascinated, as Wyatt tried to discourage the woman. He obviously hadn't been kidding about his over-exuberant fan. I was fixin' to walk away and let him handle it, but apparently, the more polite he was...the more determined she was to put the moves on him.

Now she had herself plastered against his side, and Wyatt was trying to keep her hands from grabbing ahold of his backside. I rolled my eyes. *Clearly the man needed rescuing.*

This woman was very determined, and her actions could be considered stalker-ish, if not outright sexual harassment. While I agreed with Wyatt, that calling the police would ruin the evening for the bride and groom...there might be another way to get the woman to back off. When the idea bloomed, I started to smile. Tossing my hair back, I straightened my shoulders, and went for it.

"Hey!" I said, dropping the lid on the garbage can. It landed with a loud bang and I stalked towards the couple.

"I can take care of this..." Wyatt began.

"I can see how well that's going for you," I snarked, as I grabbed the woman by the arm and hauled her off him.

"Who the hell are you?" Audrey demanded.

Going for a 'soap opera diva' feel, I curled my lip at her. "I'm his *wife!*" I cried dramatically. "Who the hell are you?"

I wasn't sure who was more surprised, Wyatt or Audrey. But while Audrey gaped at me, Wyatt jumped right in. "Now, Petunia," he said, playing along.

I almost laughed, but managed to scowl instead. I slapped my hands on my hips and got up in his personal space, "I leave you alone for five minutes and you're out here catting around with another woman?"

He shrugged. "It wasn't *my* fault."

"But, I..." Audrey looked from Wyatt to me. "But I love him. He answered my fan mail, we're meant to be together, forever..."

I rounded on her, and amped up the drama. "Back off, bitch!"

"Well, I..." Audrey cowered away.

Caught up in the ridiculousness of it all, I grabbed ahold of both sides of Wyatt's suit lapels and then deliberately made eye contact with the other woman. "He belongs to me!" I declared, dramatically. *Joan Collins couldn't have done it any better,* I decided.

"Now, honey," Wyatt's voice trembled on a laugh.

Before Wyatt started laughing and blew the game, I tugged him close and planted one on him.

I don't know what possessed me. Maybe it was stress, maybe it was that shot of Jameson, or more likely it was that I simply got caught up in it all. The kiss didn't last long, and when I lifted my mouth from his, it made a cheerfully loud smacking sound.

"Well!" Audrey huffed. She drew herself up and stomped off, disappearing around the corner.

Wyatt and I stood there in each other's arms and watched her leave. When I realized his hands were resting on my hips, I let go of his suit and stepped back immediately.

"And, you're welcome." I told him, brushing off my hands. "There's one problem solved."

"Wow," Wyatt's voice trembled on a laugh.

I was slightly offended by the laugh, so I gave him a polite nod and started to walk away. "Enjoy the rest of your evening, Mr. Hastings."

I almost made it to the door when he snagged my elbow. "Magnolia, hold up."

"What?" I paused.

"Let's try that again," he said, and before I could blink, he pulled me into his arms and kissed me.

A *real* kiss this time. The last thing I'd expected was Wyatt Hastings to have such smooth moves. Being firmly held against him, I became aware that he was solid as a rock. What I'd mistaken for thinness was actually all lean muscle.

His beard was soft as it brushed against my face. I'd never been kissed by a man with a beard. It was different. When he ended the kiss with the smallest of nips to my bottom lip, every hormone I owned leapt up and cheered.

Damn-near eye to eye with him in my heels, we stood only a few inches apart and stared at each other. The power of speech had somehow eluded me. I blinked and was trying to figure out what to say next, when he tugged me close again. I went willingly.

Wrapping my arms around his neck, I held on. When our tongues touched for the first time, my brain all but started leaking out of my ears.

I felt him tangle one of his hands in my long hair and he gave a gentle tug, tipping my head back to change the angle of the kiss. My heart raced, my stomach flipped, and I felt my knees start to tremble. *This man could be trouble, Maggie,* I thought as the kiss went on.

We pulled apart after a few moments and both of us were breathing heavily. Silently, we measured each other.

He broke the silence first. "I've been wanting to do that since the first day I met you."

"You did?" As soon as the words left my mouth I regretted them. I was no ingénue. I'd known I was attracted to him since the day he'd brought me groceries after the break in. I cleared my throat and straightened my shoulders. "I should go back inside. Tomorrow is a big day, and I need to get Willow home."

"How early are you starting?"

"I'll be on site at the wedding venue at five in the morning."

He took one of my hands. "The ceremony starts at 10:30. That's a little early, isn't it?"

"I have to make sure the ceremony area is set and the reception tables are dressed and ready to go," I explained automatically. "Weddings like this don't simply *happen.* They have to be organized and controlled to go off smoothly. There's a lot of moving pieces to keep track of."

He smiled at me. "Like what?"

"Well, for example: there's the four piece ensemble to play at the ceremony, the DJ for the reception, the caterer, the florist has to set up, the dessert to be delivered and displayed..." I trailed off when Wyatt gave my hand a squeeze.

"I can't wait to see you in action," he said.

"It's my job. I'm damn good at it."

Wyatt nodded. "I have no doubt. See you in the morning at the park."

"Be sure and have the groom there by eight o'clock." I reminded him. "The photographer is starting at 8:30."

"I remember." Wyatt let go and slipped his hands in his pockets.

I reached for the kitchen door and opened it. "See you tomorrow." I did my best to sound composed as I began to step back in the house.

"Save a dance for me at the reception, Magnolia." Wyatt's voice stopped me mid-stride.

"I'll be working the event, Wyatt," I reminded him. "I'm not a guest."

"You actually believe that?" Wyatt measured me with those crystal blue eyes.

I shrugged. "I was hired to coordinate their wedding. The fact that I'm distantly related to the bride and groom doesn't change the fact that their wedding is in fact, my job."

Wyatt continued to study me. Finally he nodded. "Good night, Magnolia."

Damn. I found that I really wanted to kiss him again. *But there wasn't any time for that,* I realized. *Not right now.* So instead, I nodded. "Goodnight, Wyatt."

CHAPTER EIGHT

To my infinite relief the schedule for the day of the wedding went like clockwork. All my careful preparation had more than paid off. The weather cooperated, and the day had dawned with white puffy clouds floating across the sky and mild temperatures in the seventies.

A huge, white event tent sprawled across the lush emerald green grass of the reserved section of the park. The reception tables were dressed, and huge paper globes hung from the interior of the tent in an assortment of sherbet colors. The floral centerpieces popped against snowy linen and were in a variety of rustic containers. From old watering cans to blue glass jars and ceramic pitchers, the décor was a little boho, absolutely enchanting, and magazine photo shoot worthy.

Rows of rental chairs were arranged along either side of a paver pathway in the gardens of the park, and satin ribbons in a rainbow of colors were attached to the back of each chair. At the end of the path, a curved arbor stood before a large garden filled with perennials. The arbor had been expertly decorated by Violet and her mother, Cora, with lush greenery and fresh flowers in a kaleidoscope of colors.

The pre-ceremony photography was done and the guests were arriving. I'd been surprised to discover I'd been sentimental witnessing the first look photos for the bride and groom. I did remember to mention to the photographer about the men's socks...and as I figured, she'd snapped a hilarious picture of all the groomsmen sitting on a stone wall in the park with their rainbow of different colored socks showing.

Now, the string quartet was playing as the last of the guests took their seats. I checked my watch, the bride and groom were scheduled to exchange their handfasting vows in less than five minutes. I took one final peek at the guests and checked on Willow. She was happily sitting in the front row on the groom's side with Thomas and the Vasquez family. She turned, saw me, and gave a happy wave.

I went to the wedding party, who'd been tucked out of sight in the back of the reception tent, to direct the groom and his men to take their places. "It's time, y'all," I said.

Duncan gave Autumn a light kiss. "See you out there," he said, and went to join the groomsmen.

While the event staff did the finishing touches and lit the candles on the reception tables, I sent the bridesmaids down the garden path in order, straightening hems, flowers, or hair, as the case may be.

First, Candice in her pink chiffon dress went down the aisle. Violet in the lilac gown followed. The bouquets she'd crafted for the bridesmaids were a mass of spring flowers: blue hydrangeas, soft purple roses, yellow carnations, pale pink peonies and the soft silvery-green foliage of dusty miller added a bit of shimmer. Each bouquet had a coordinating satin colored ribbon to match the attendant's specific dress.

I smoothed a long cable of Holly's strawberry-blonde hair back from her face. "You look lovely, Holly," I whispered, and sent her off next in her sky blue dress. Ivy stepped up, tossed me a wink, and I shifted her bouquet so the matching mint green ribbon would show.

Lexie stood in her butter yellow dress, holding Morgan's hand. "I'll see you at the end of the aisle," she said to her son. "Behave yourself, Morgan John." She gave him a steely-eyed look, and then flashed me a smile and went down the aisle proudly as the matron of honor.

"Okay you three," I whispered to Morgan, Chloe and Sophia, the ring bearer and flower girls. "Here we go."

"I have to take the rings to Mommy." Morgan bit his lip. He was adorable in a white shirt, gray slacks and suspenders.

Chloe and Sophia stepped up behind him. The little girls were pretty as a picture in floral crowns and white dresses with tulle skirts. I sent the three of them off, and the girls made the most out of throwing their flower petals around.

Finally it was the bride's turn. I took a moment, gave the back of Autumn's gown some final fluffing. "Keep that bouquet at waist level," I reminded her.

"Okay, thanks," she whispered, lowering her bridal bouquet. It was a beautiful arrangement with pink veronica, clusters of baby roses in pale yellow and pink, peach peonies, blue hydrangeas, large white roses, and more of the dusty miller.

I gave the quartet their cue to start up the bride's processional music. "You look absolutely enchanting," I told Autumn, and it was true.

Her long brown hair was held back and fastened behind her head with a comb decorated in the rainbow of colored flowers she favored. The illusion neckline of her bridal gown had the tiniest bit of sparkle, and the long tulle skirt flowed. Her satin, pale blue shoes peeped out from the hem of the gown.

Autumn blinked her eyes several times. I could see she was struggling not to cry at the compliment, and also adjusting to the contact lenses she was wearing. "Thanks for everything, Maggie."

"It's my honor and pleasure." I shifted my attention to her Aunt Faye, who was escorting the bride down the aisle. "Your suit dress and hat are stunning, Faye."

Faye ignored my compliment and brushed at the pearl gray sleeve of her jacket instead. A moment later, she smiled fondly at Autumn. "Be happy," she said, and pressed her cheek to the bride's.

The music was nearing the point for the bride's entrance. And I let the anticipation of seeing the bride build a bit longer. "Okay," I said to Autumn and her great-aunt. "Off you go."

Faye nodded. I could see the sentimental tears in her eyes as I sent the two of them down the aisle. Once they had taken their places. I slipped discreetly in the back row where I could watch the ceremony and still be nearby, if needed.

After the ceremony ended and the bride and groom exchanged a kiss, the guests all clapped and cheered. The recessional began, and I was there waiting for them to help set up the receiving line. I stood at the end and directed guests to head to the tent, as the mimosa bar was open. Once the guests had all moved through the receiving line, I let the photographer take charge of the wedding party and herd them off for a few more group photos.

I made my way to the tent and saw that the cocktail hour was going nicely. The staff was moving the chairs to the reception tables smoothly. The DJ had some cheerful instrumental music playing in the background, and while guests sipped at mimosas, I stood at the entrance waiting patiently for the bridal party. Once they were announced and introduced by the DJ, I was able to slip into the background to see if any extra help was needed for the brunch set-up.

The wedding party had been seated, and a few more photos were taken. Thomas made a lovely speech welcoming the guests. Finally it was time to start the buffet. The bride and groom had insisted on the informality and fun of a brunch buffet and I got them going, and then began dismissing the guests table by table for their turn.

After the toasts and the bride and groom's first dance, the wedding party and family joined them out on the floor. Thomas danced politely with Faye. Julian, as the best man, danced with Lexie the matron of honor. Bran partnered up with Ivy, Holly was with Wyatt, Violet danced with Marshall, and Candice and Xander Hastings rounded out the group.

The photographer steered the bride and groom to the dessert table afterward and took photos while the bride and groom fed each other a cake pop. Once that was finished, the guests descended on the desserts with enthusiasm. I stood nearby, passing out dessert plates and or napkins to the wedding guests as needed.

The children certainly enjoyed the desserts, and I let Willow go and skip off with the ring bearer, flower girls, and Charlie Bell. I'd dressed my daughter purposefully in a bright pink dress today so she would be easy to spot in the crowd.

The DJ had the music pumping now, and I could start to relax a bit. The bartender handed me a bottled water and I stood off to the side subtly guarding the gift and card table, while keeping my eye out for potential problems, and watching everyone else dance and have fun.

The music changed to a slow song, and now, Lexie and Bran were dancing together, as were several other couples. Faye was dancing with Dr. Meyer. Candice was standing at the bar, flirting with the handsome bartender, and Violet and Matthew Bell swayed in time to the music.

I felt a tug on my jacket and found Charlie Bell smiling up at me.

"Hello, Miss Charlie," I said.

"Hi! I remember you from my birthday party."

"Are you enjoying yourself?"

"Yeah." She nodded, and Chloe, Sophia, and Willow all joined her. I was surrounded by the four little girls.

Charlie gazed up in my eyes and gave me a sweet smile. "Is it okay if we all go have more cake pops?"

I felt the strongest emotional pull from her, and it hit me in the vicinity of my heart. *She's such an adorable child,* I thought. *Who'd ever say no to her?* "Sure," I said. "Let me go get y'all a few more..."

"Charlie!" The sharp voice came from Cora O'Connell. "What have we said about you asking *really hard* for things?"

I blinked as if suddenly coming out of a daze. Cora dropped a hand on my shoulder. "I apologize, Maggie," she said.

I had no idea what she was apologizing for, but even as I rubbed the heel of my hand over my heart, I gave her my best professional smile. "The dessert table is open. The children are welcome to help themselves to another cakepop if they want."

Cora thanked me and steered Charlie over to the dessert table.

Sophia Jacobs shrugged, "Well it was worth a try," she said, mysteriously. Her sister and fellow flower girl Chloe followed Charlie to the dessert table. Willow was right behind them.

"Are you having fun, honey?" I asked her, straightening the satin bow I'd tied in her hair.

"Yeah!" Willow grinned at me. "Charlie is teaching me tricks!"

"That's nice," I smiled and watched fondly as Willow joined the other girls. *It had been the right decision to move here. Willow was very happy and making new friends.* I watched as the girls all ate their cakepops, giggled with each other, and trooped off to the dance floor.

I shifted my focus to Violet and her partner Matthew Bell as they danced together. *I'd be shocked if those two weren't engaged within six months,* I thought. I shifted to check the reception area, scanning again for any possible problems, and my gaze lighted on Julian. He was standing off to the side sipping at a glass of champagne. I followed his line of sight, and found Holly.

Holly was also standing alone and looking fairly miserable, as she pretended not to watch him from over on the opposite side of the reception area.

"We'll just see about that," I muttered. Taking a swig of my water, I set it aside and marched over to Julian. "Come with me," I said, taking ahold of his arm and firmly pulling him along.

"What are you up to?" he smiled, good-naturedly.

I leaned back speaking close to his ear, as not to be overheard. "You should go dance with Holly."

Julian stopped dead. "That wouldn't be wise."

"Why on earth not?"

"She works for me. People would talk," Julian said.

"I can't see how anyone would, so long as you behave yourself on the dance floor." I scowled at him. "A polite slow dance with a fellow member of the wedding party is hardly scandalous behavior. It's actually considered socially acceptable. *And* it's something a gentleman would do if he saw a bridesmaid standing alone and looking miserable."

Julian sighed.

I narrowed my eyes at him. "Unless your daddy didn't raise you right, and you're not a gentleman..."

"Maggie, I—"

"Or unless you're afraid." There. I'd practically double-dog dared him.

"Damn it, Magnolia." Julian glared at me for a second. "I had no idea you were so bossy."

I crossed my arms and sized up my opponent. "I prefer the term, 'strong willed'."

Julian gave me a withering look.

"Go on." I nudged him in her general direction. "Go dance with her."

He handed me his glass, and I watched as my cousin made his way around the perimeter of the dance floor to ask Holly for a dance.

The look on Holly's face was everything as he offered her his hand. Surprise, pleasure, and hope all combined into one. Smoothly, Julian led her to the dance floor and the couple began to slow dance with the rest of the guests.

I watched over them for a bit, and subtly checked for any response from the crowd, but no one reacted or seemed horrified by this new development. As a matter of fact, Autumn gave me a 'thumbs up' from over Duncan's shoulder. She'd seen the whole thing.

I lifted the glass in toast to the bride and winked at her. Another slow song started and Julian and Holly continued to dance.

Wyatt appeared at my side. "You look lovely today," he said.

I glanced down at the sky blue jacket and black skirt that I wore. It was a practical 'work outfit' and while stylish, it was hardly lovely. "This old thing?" I smiled as I said it. "I've worn it before while working other weddings." The skirt hit right above my knees and was secretly stretchy, which allowed me to move. I'd added my Grandma Taylor's pearls, with a silky white camisole underneath the blazer. Due to the grass, instead of my typical heels, I wore black flats.

"You look very professional *and* beautiful."

I nodded. "Thank you."

"Dance with me." His voice was low and sent a shiver down my spine.

"Thank you, but I'm working."

Julian and Holly waltzed past us. "Come and dance, Maggie," Holly called over Julian's shoulder.

Autumn and Duncan slow danced past me. "Go and dance," Duncan said. "Enjoy yourself."

Aw hell, I decided. *I supposed a single dance wouldn't hurt anything.* I set the champagne glass down I'd been holding for Julian. "Alright, I'd love to."

The man danced well, and I found myself smiling up in his face as we slow danced around the large, raised wooden dance floor. It was a perfectly polite slow dance, but secretly I yearned for more. If I'd have been anywhere else—as in not working—instead of a well-mannered hand on his shoulder and the other held formally in his, I'd have wrapped my arms around his neck and pressed close to him.

But I *was* working, so I smiled and made small talk. "How do you like your sky blue socks?" I teased him.

"They're very stylish, and it could have been worse."

"It was supposed to be for fun," I countered.

"At least I didn't have to wear the pink socks," Wyatt said loudly enough so that Xander, who was dancing nearby with his date, could hear him.

The other couple danced closer. "Real men are not

intimidated by wearing pink," Xander said to his brother.

"You're such a stud, Xander." Wyatt said dryly.

"Y'all behave now," I warned them as Xander and his date moved father away.

"What are you doing this evening?" Wyatt asked me.

"Well I have to help clean everything up after the reception ends, and make sure the gifts get taken care of —"

"No," Wyatt interrupted me gently. "I meant what are you doing tonight? You've worked your ass off today, I thought you'd like to go out to dinner. With me."

"That's a lovely offer, but honestly I'm going to be wiped out. The only thing I had planned was to put on my pajamas, eat pizza, and crash on the couch."

Wyatt tugged me slightly closer. "How do you feel about Chinese takeout?"

"That sounds like heaven." I said even as my stomach growled.

Wyatt frowned over the noise. "Haven't you eaten today?"

"Early this morning."

"You didn't eat with the wedding guests, did you?"

"Why would I do that?" I frowned at him. "I'm working this event. I'm *not* a guest."

"Magnolia," Wyatt said softly. "Autumn and Duncan would be horrified to hear you say that."

"For heaven sakes, I *am* here to work. Thomas is

paying me extremely well to make sure today goes off without a hitch."

"Well someone has to make sure you eat today." Wyatt tilted his head to one side. "Why don't I come over around six o'clock tonight—with supper?"

"Make that steamed shrimp and mixed veggies and you've got yourself a date."

"What should I pick up for Willow?" he leaned closer to my face as he spoke.

I stared up into those crystalline blue eyes and felt my heart start to speed up. *Wait, what had we been talking about?* I scrambled to remember. *Oh, we were talking about food!* "Willow can share mine."

For a second I thought he was going to lean in and kiss me, but the song ended, and regretfully, I stepped back from Wyatt. "Thank you for the dance," I said with a smile, making my way off the dance floor.

I checked in with the caterer who was packing up, and the bartender to see how his supplies were holding. I picked up a couple of water bottles and took them over to the two security officers, who more than appreciated the gesture. Slowly, I made the circuit around the reception again, checking to see how the dessert table was fairing. The cakepops were almost gone, so I shifted the remaining ones to the front of the display.

Willow giggled, and turning, I saw her dancing out on the floor with the flower girls and their parents. The gift and card table was fine, and I didn't imagine anyone would try anything with a police officer and security present. I worked my way around the reception tables again, picking up empty glasses and reminded folks to be sure and sign the guest book.

I'd just handed the empties to the bartender when a couple who were about to leave passed me a card for the newlyweds. I assured them I would see that the bride and groom received it. Walking over to the gift table, I dropped the card in the big decorated birdcage. Violet had decorated it in silk flowers and white organza ribbon, and it was almost filled with cards.

"This turned out to be a charming day, even if their wedding theme and décor is horribly tacky." The snide voice was female, low, and husky.

A striking brunette stood beside me. She wore a short, chic, black dress, killer heels, and a matching cambric cloche style hat. I didn't recognize her, and my instincts screamed that this young woman was *not* an invited guest. "Can I help you, ma'am?"

"Oh lord, that accent." She rolled her eyes. "How utterly white-trash you sound. I'd heard some poor little Southern cousin had arrived in William's Ford, and moved in with the Drakes...you *must* be Magnolia."

"That's right." I smiled politely even as my stomach tightened.

"So tell me," she continued. "How does it feel to have the family treat you like hired help? But then again, you'd be used to working in the service industry, wouldn't you?"

Her insults didn't faze me. I studied her carefully, and wondered where she'd come from. For some reason I'd felt like I'd seen her before. She was definitely new to the reception, because I would have spotted the big black hat and designer dress immediately among the guests. Her haute couture outfit stuck out like a sore thumb in a sea of pretty and casual spring colors and pastels. My gut said *wedding crasher*, but there was something familiar about her...

"Let me offer some friendly advice," the woman said. "You're going to want to leave William's Ford. Things aren't working out for you here."

"On the contrary." I folded my arms across my chest. "Things are going wonderfully."

"I'll only warn you this one time," she said. "Pack up that brat in your trashy car, and get out while you still can."

Before I could respond, Wyatt walked up holding out a fresh bottle of water. "Magnolia, I brought you..." he trailed off as he focused on the young woman in the hat. "Leilah." His voice was flat and hostile. "What the hell are you doing here?"

She flashed a sly smile at Wyatt. "I simply had to see this fiasco for myself."

"You aren't wanted here." His voice was tough as nails.

"Oh." The woman's mouth moved into a faux pout. She managed to hold it for a moment, but started to laugh. "I have to say, I was very disappointed not to have been invited to cousin Duncan's wedding."

Wyatt's whole body language had changed. I'd seen enough drama at weddings to know when a nasty scene was about to cut loose. "This is a private event." I stepped smoothly between Wyatt and the woman. "Since you've admitted that you weren't invited, ma'am, I'm going to have to ask you to leave." Taking her firmly by the elbow, I looked for the security personnel. Catching their eye, I motioned for them to come over.

The woman threw back her head and laughed. The husky sound cut through the reception and several people stopped, looking over toward us at the same time. *Oh no you don't,* I thought, and began to steer her out, even as security hustled forward.

She dug in her heels and began to struggle. "Let go of my arm or I'll put you on your ass." Her voice was low and mean.

I had no doubt she'd try to do as she threatened. What she wanted was to make as big of a scene as possible, and I was determined not to give it to her. I wrapped my left arm tight around her shoulders, and pulled her snug against my side as if we were close friends. "Aren't you precious?" I flashed a smile that was all teeth and no mercy, even as I kept her moving.

I felt her muscles tighten and had no doubt she was about to pull an epic stunt, but Diego Vasquez stepped in and took her other arm. "Don't even think about it, Leilah," he said.

The woman gasped and was silent. I wasn't sure what Diego had done, maybe hit a pressure point on her arm or something, but it worked.

Security caught up to us a moment later and we passed her off to their capable hands. The two men moved to either side of her. Each taking one arm, they lifted, and hauled her out. Her feet weren't even touching the ground.

Diego and I followed them, and once they were clear of the reception tent, I directed security to remove the woman from the reserved area.

"You're going to regret this!" As she struggled, her hat fell off. She swore at the security, but the team was unfazed and kept on moving.

I checked over my shoulder. Wyatt, bless him, had gone to the DJ and requested that the dollar dance begin. Drama forgotten, folks enthusiastically began to line up to dance with the bride and groom, cash in hand.

I met his eyes and mouthed, *thank you.*

Wyatt tipped his head in response, and I gave him a thumb's up for thinking of the distraction. With a sigh of relief that an ugly scene had been averted, I went over to pick up the young woman's fallen hat. As I expected, it too was designer, and I wondered why a young woman of obvious wealth would pull such a mean-spirited stunt.

"I've seen a lot of crazy things at weddings, ya'll," I said to Diego, "but that was new."

"I'm glad I was nearby to help," Diego said quietly.

"She shouldn't be here."

"So you know her?"

Diego nodded.

"She said that she was a relative...Wyatt *knew* her. He called her Leilah." I glanced up from the hat I held to Diego's dark eyes. "Who the hell was that?"

Diego didn't answer immediately. Instead he stood there looking handsome in his suit and tie, watching as the security team carried the woman out, and over to a parking lot well past the reserved section of the gardens.

"Diego?" I prompted.

"That was Leilah Martin Drake," he said. "She's Julian's half-sister and Thomas's daughter."

I bobbled the hat. "Holy shit!"

Diego studied my face. "You didn't know." It was a statement not a question.

"No, I sure as hell didn't know!" I caught myself and immediately lowered my voice. "Not one of ya'll saw fit to tell me."

Diego dipped his hands in his pockets. "There's some bad blood between Leilah and Holly Bishop. Thomas disowned Leilah last year. I'll admit I was very surprised to see her here, but you handled it well. Hardly anyone noticed."

"Did the bride or groom see her?"

"No." Diego slung an arm companionably around my shoulder. "Neither did Thomas. Julian did, but he kept his father distracted."

"I don't understand any of this," I said. "I need to find out what in the world—"

Diego cut me off. "I'm going to give you some advice. Don't mention this to Thomas until after the wedding is over. Give him today."

I yanked back on my impatience to get answers immediately. This wasn't the time or the place. I had a wedding reception to finish and the bride and groom deserved my undivided attention. "Alright." I bit back my frustration, but still managed to smile at Diego. "Thank you for the help."

"*De nada.*" He smiled in return. "Let's go back inside."

Walking back into the reception tent with Diego, I stuffed the designer hat into a nearby garbage can, without breaking stride. I went directly to the edge of the dance floor, where the lines had formed with guests waiting to dance with the bride and groom.

Willow was standing in line holding Thomas' hand. When their turn came, Thomas gave Willow a few dollars, and she handed it off to Lexie and then my girl went to dance with Duncan. Duncan scooped Willow up and danced with her, making her laugh.

Thomas handed Wyatt a crisp bill and began to dance a smooth, formal waltz with the bride. They went slowly around the dance floor and, fortunately, Autumn didn't trip.

"Welcome to the family," he told her as they danced past where I stood.

Autumn was positively glowing at his words, and she gave the man an affectionate hug and kiss on the cheek.

I eased over to Wyatt's side. "Thank you for the distraction."

"You bet," he said.

"Wyatt," I said under my breath, "I'm going to want to talk to you tonight about...everything."

Wyatt kept his attention on the line of guests waiting to dance with Autumn. "That can be arranged," he said smoothly.

I wasn't sure if I admired his suddenly suave attitude, or if it annoyed me. I made sure to continue to keep my voice low. "I'm going to want some answers."

"Of course." He smiled and held up his hand, silently telling Oliver Jacobs that he'd have to wait a bit longer for his turn to dance with the bride.

"My money is good," Oliver laughed, holding up a twenty-dollar bill.

"The gentleman before you was a bit more generous," Wyatt said and flashed the one hundred dollar bill Thomas had given him. This caused a laughing reaction from the line of people waiting to dance with Autumn, as they all realized they'd have to continue to wait.

Chloe and Sophia were hopping up and down waving five-dollar bills, and Lexie motioned for them to come up and take a turn with the groom. Duncan solved the problem of who would go first, by taking each of the girls' hands and dancing with them, together.

I'd been told about it, but I had to say that this 'Dollar Dance' was a new wedding tradition for me. But it soon became apparent that the more you "paid" the longer you were allowed to dance with the bride or groom. It was adorable. The extra cash they received from the guests was intended for use on the couple's honeymoon.

I retreated into the background. Lexie and Wyatt had things under control, but I still had work to do.

"Mama!" Willow ran over to me. "I danced with the groom!" she said proudly.

Wyatt tapped Thomas on the shoulder and Thomas surrendered the bride. Oliver Jacobs swooped in and began an enthusiastic jig with the bride that had her howling with laughter.

Thomas came over to stand with us. "You did a beautiful job with the wedding, Maggie."

"Thank you." I smiled at him even as my stomach churned with dread. *He was so happy,* I thought. *I didn't want to do or say anything to spoil the day for him, or the bride and groom.*

As he stood there smiling at me, I could see over his shoulder that Ivy had slapped a twenty in Lexie's hand. She tapped the woman he'd been dancing with on the shoulder, and as soon as she stepped back, Ivy swooped in and began to lead Duncan around the dance floor. A moment later, Ivy managed to dip the groom, and the guests roared with laughter.

Julian joined us with three glasses of champagne. "To the bride and groom," he said.

Since the wedding was all but over I went ahead and shared a celebratory drink with—I caught myself. I'd mentally been thinking of them as *my family* for the past few months, but now I wasn't so sure.

Family didn't keep secrets. Not secrets like this.

As I tapped my glass to Julian's I could see a bit of resemblance between him and Leilah. Truth be told, both of Thomas' children favored him, and I had to wonder if the problems with the dis-owned Leilah had influenced how the older man had swooped into the rescue for Willow and me last year.

Discovering they'd all kept things from me had made me start to question their motives.

Which in turn, made me feel ungrateful.

"To family." Thomas made the toast and my smile felt strained as I did my best to act as if nothing was amiss. Thomas Drake had been nothing but kind and generous to us, but now he seemed more like a stranger than ever before.

So, Thomas had a daughter. In the almost five months I'd been in William's Ford not one person had ever mentioned her existence to me. Julian caught my eye and gave me slight nod. Almost as if he knew where my thoughts lay. I looked at his unusual eyes, glanced down at Willow and reminded myself the proof of our family bond was right there. Stamped in

Willow's blue and brown eyes as surely as they were in Julian's.

And if Julian was a magickal practitioner, I realized suddenly, *or had any sort of intuition like I had, maybe he* did *know my thoughts.*

Telling myself to remain calm, I inclined my head in acknowledgement to whatever he was trying to tell me. *Perhaps he was simply silently thanking me for suggesting that he dance with Holly.* It could be that simple. I tried to uncoil the muscles that were tight in my shoulders, sipped my champagne, and made a real effort to enjoy this moment with my...family.

And I considered as we all stood there smiling so calmly at each other...what other secrets had I yet to learn about the Drakes?

What else weren't they telling me?

CHAPTER NINE

By the time I'd arrived home from breaking down the wedding reception, I was wiped out. I started to pull in the driveway, but found it blocked by an alarmingly large dog standing at the bottom of the drive. I gave the horn a quick toot, hoping it would scare the animal away. He didn't budge. Annoyed, I shoved open the car door, stood, and faced down the stray.

"Shoo!" I waved my arms at the hound.

The dog resembled a Rottweiler, and yet he didn't leave. Instead he sat down in the center of my driveway and watched me.

I walked around my car door to try again. "Get," I said. "Go on home!"

That got me no reaction either. "Well, shit." I muttered, and started to walk closer. "Are you lost, boy?"

The dog growled. I scrambled away from it as fast as I could and hopped back in my car.

My heart pounding, I shut the door and checked to

see if the dog had chased me, but I couldn't see him anymore. I put the car back in gear and eased forward in the driveway, pulling up until I was even with the front porch.

I sat waiting for a few minutes, but there was no sign of the stray. With a shrug, I got out and scooped up Willow who'd fallen asleep in the car. I let myself inside, laid her down on her own bed, and covered her with a light blanket.

I went back to my car, watching for the animal, but the dog was gone. *Guess he ran off,* I decided, scanning the surrounding area. "I hope the poor dog finds his way home," I said, retrieving my work tote bag and purse.

I brought those inside and locked the front door behind me, making sure to re-engage the alarm system.

The cottage was calm and blessedly quiet. It was like a soothing balm after several hours of music, laughter and high energy. I rolled my shoulders and headed straight for the shower. Stripping out of my suit, I let it drop to the bathroom floor. Turning up the spray to full blast, I stepped in, tipped my face up, and let the water rinse away the stress I'd been carrying all damn day.

After I toweled off and dried my hair, I slipped into a pair of soft floral yoga pants, and a thin pink t-shirt. I wiggled my bare toes, comfortable and content, and caught sight of myself in the bedroom mirror. "Aw, hell," I said. The fabric of the shirt was far too sheer to wear without a bra—especially as Wyatt was coming over in a couple of hours.

I fished a pretty lace bra out of the drawer and tidied up the bathroom. My stomach rumbled, and I padded off to the kitchen to make a light snack to hold me over until dinner. Sitting at the drop leaf table in the kitchen with my apple and cheese, I considered everything that had happened at the wedding reception.

Why had Leilah told me to leave town? What was her issue?

On a hunch, I picked up my laptop and booted it up, doing an internet search on Leilah Martin Drake. I found an article on her being involved with a theatre group at the university, saw a few pictures of her from the society page from some fancy fundraiser held the year before. But other than that, there was nothing else. Her social media accounts were all set to private. I could see that it was in fact her, but other than that, zero.

I sat back drumming my fingernails against the tabletop. *Why did Leilah seem so damn familiar to me?* The harder I concentrated on her, the more difficult it was to remember where I'd seen her before...

I shook it off. Diego had mentioned that there was some bad blood between Holly and Leilah. Maybe I need to look elsewhere for information. Nodding to myself, I began a search for any local news involving Holly Bishop.

I discovered that Holly had once been the victim of a robbery while working at the local antique store. I scanned the newspaper article and saw that significant damage to the stock had been reported and a jewelry theft had also occurred at the store. Holly had been attacked, ending up in the hospital. I followed up on that robbery story, changing my search parameters and saw another article dated a few months later. It reported that the perpetrator had never been caught, but that an anonymous source had returned some of the stolen items to the police.

I tried a search on the Drake family, scrolled through several society mentions in the local paper, and my jaw hit the table when I read that Duncan's mother, Rebecca Drake-Quinn, had died a few years prior in a fire at the Drake mansion.

"Good lord!" I read the newspaper article and saw that the fire was believed to have been started by lightning striking the roof. I also saw that Faye Bishop had been injured during the fire and so had Duncan. While Duncan had been treated at the local hospital and released, Faye had been admitted.

"What in the hell was Faye doing at the mansion?" I muttered as I scrolled through the article and accompanying photos.

By accident, I stumbled across yet another article from the same day, mentioning that a police officer had been seriously injured during a home invasion. That officer had been none other than Lexie Bishop, and her attacker had been Rebecca Drake-Quinn.

Now all the stiffness and weird energy I'd felt from

Bran and Lexie around the Drakes made a horrible sort of sense.

As my stomach churned with dread, I continued to search and found an article dated six months later, also from the local paper. It was entitled "Historic Drake Home Being Rebuilt". There were pictures of the Drake mansion with a section of the roof missing after the fire, and then another photo of the progress made while the house was undergoing repairs and restoration. The article went on to say that the entire third floor was being rebuilt.

I tried a new search and eventually came across an obituary for Rebecca Drake-Quinn. Unsurprisingly, it was a perfunctory one at best. Nowhere did it say 'loving mother' or 'dear sister.' It simply listed her birth and death dates, and stated that she'd been preceded in death by her father and husband.

My stomach churned. No one had mentioned *any* of this to me. Nothing about Duncan's mother, or the fact that she'd actually perished at the mansion. I'd been all over the mansion for the three weeks after my accident. I'd rambled through the third floor a couple of times. It, like the rest of the home, was gorgeous but I'd seen no evidence there'd ever been a fire...

"Mama?" Willow's voice had me jumping.

Feeling nervous after my discoveries, and slightly guilty for snooping, I shut the laptop down. "Hi baby."

Willow came in carrying her favorite babydoll and dragging her blanket behind her. "I'm hungry."

I stood. "Would you like a snack?"

"Can I have a cookie?"

"No, darlin'," I said, even as she pouted. "You had plenty of sweets already today." I could see in her eyes that she was on the verge of pitchin' a fit. "How about a cheese stick and apple," I said, and when that got me nothing, I went for the big distraction. "Or, you can take a shower."

"I want a shower!" she said. Showers were her new favorite thing. Willow had decided a few weeks ago that baths were for babies.

I checked the clock while I followed her to the bathroom. I had an hour before Wyatt was due, and enough time to put a face back on after Willow had her bath.

At six o'clock on the dot, Wyatt knocked on the front door of the cottage. Willow beat me to the door and was standing by my side when I opened it. "Hi Wyatt!" she said.

Wyatt flashed a smile that had my heart melting. "Hi Willow." He raised his eyes and met mine. "Magnolia."

He stood there wearing a button down chambray shirt, khakis, and scuffed trainers. He was holding a large paper bag filled with Chinese food, and I wasn't sure what I was craving more. Dinner, or another taste of him.

He paused in the doorway for a moment. "You know," he said. "I keep wondering if I'll ever see you looking less than gorgeous. But no matter what the circumstances, you always are stunning."

"I think you need to get out a little more," I said dryly.

"I think you need to learn how to take a sincere compliment," he replied, stepping inside.

We ended up on the sofa, sitting side-by-side, and eating off the coffee table. I poured Wyatt and I each a glass of wine, and Willow perched on a couple of pillows on the floor and sat across the table from us with her juice.

I waited to see how Wyatt would react to eating dinner with a rambunctious four-year-old. But he enjoyed himself. Once dinner was over, Willow decided she wanted to sit between the two of us and climbed right over Wyatt's lap in order to do so.

As she did, the cuff on his shirtsleeve slid up, revealing more of the burn scars than I'd ever seen before.

"What's that?" Willow asked pointing to the back of his hand and wrist.

"Willow," I said. "Don't be rude."

Willow raised her unique brown and blue eyes to me and shifted to regard Wyatt. "Do you have an ouchie?"

"When I was ten years old, I hurt my arm," Wyatt said matter-of-factly.

"How?" Willow wanted to know.

"There was a fire."

"Let me see," Willow said tugging on his cuff.

"I'm sorry, Wyatt," I began, feeling embarrassed.

"It's alright," he waved my apology away, and calmly rolled up his long sleeve. For the first time I saw what he'd kept hidden. The burn scar began at the back of his hand and rolled up his forearm, stopping just above the elbow.

Willow reached out and ran her fingers over the scars. "Does it still hurt?"

"No." Wyatt said, sitting there cool as a cucumber. "It happened a long time ago."

Meanwhile I was silently sweating bullets, wondering what—if anything—I should do.

"Mama always kisses my ouchies," Willow said, and with that she bent over and dropped a kiss to Wyatt's arm. "There, all better."

Wyatt had gone completely still. I watched as he took a steadying breath before he spoke. "Thank you, Willow."

"Do you feel better now?" she wanted to know.

"Yes." Wyatt nodded. "Thanks."

Willow began to yawn. "Mama, I'm sleepy."

"It was a big day," I said. "Let's get you into bed."

"Okay." She agreed without an argument, which only proved how tired she was.

I glanced over at Wyatt. "This will take me a couple of minutes."

He picked up his wine glass and stretched out and crossed his feet on the coffee table. "That's fine. I'll sit here and relax."

"'Night, Wyatt," Willow said around a huge yawn.

"Goodnight, Willow." He smiled as she climbed off the couch and began to shuffle towards her room.

To my surprise, Willow climbed straight into bed. Obviously all the excitement of the wedding and the rehearsal dinner the night before had caught up with her. I tucked her in, dropped a kiss on her forehead, switched on her nightlight, and left her door cracked open.

When I returned to the living room, Wyatt was sitting on the couch waiting for me. "Is she all settled?"

I sat down next to him trying to figure out where to begin. "Yeah, she was worn out." I picked up a throw pillow and put it in my lap. "I have some questions. But, I confess it feels a might odd to ask you—I don't want to put you in an uncomfortable position."

"That's alright." Wyatt nodded.

"Today, when security carted Leilah out, Diego suggested I not say anything to Thomas. So he could have the day without Leilah ruining the wedding for him." I checked Wyatt's expression, he appeared at ease so I continued. "That being said, I find myself hesitant to bring any of this up to Thomas, or to Julian."

"I understand." He nodded. "Go ahead."

"My first question is about Leilah Martin Drake." I hugged the pillow for comfort. "I didn't even know Thomas had a daughter."

"That didn't come out publically until a few years ago," Wyatt said in a matter-of-fact tone.

"I'm guessing he and Leilah's mother weren't

married?"

"No." Wyatt's crystal blue eyes regarded me calmly.

"I've noticed in town, folks get very nervous when anyone mentions the Drake family name."

Wyatt shrugged. "Small town gossip. It can be nasty."

"No one speaks of Julian's mother, that's sort of odd, don't you think?"

"Yvonne." Wyatt said. "She and Thomas divorced when Julian was very young."

"Is she a part of Julian's life now?" I asked.

"No." Wyatt said. "Not that I'm aware of."

I thought back to the article I'd read online. "How did Duncan's mother really die?"

Wyatt blinked. "In a fire at the mansion."

"Again, none of y'all have ever mentioned that either." I thought about Rebecca attacking Lexie, decided to leave that for the moment and blew out a long breath. "All these secrets. They make me uncomfortable, and it has me questioning Thomas' motives for inviting me to move to William's Ford."

"How do you mean?"

"Well, think about it. He disowned his daughter, and his sister perished in a fire. Does he expect Willow and I to somehow replace them?"

"No, he'd never do that," Wyatt insisted. "I can tell you that it was Thomas who dragged Duncan from the house that night. If not for him, Duncan would have died as well." Wyatt's voice was quiet.

"The article I read said that Duncan and Faye Bishop were both injured. What happened to Duncan's mother that night? Was she trapped?"

Wyatt flinched at my words and I immediately apologized.

"I'm very sorry, Wyatt," I said, feeling like the world's most insensitive clod. "I wasn't thinking. I didn't mean to bring up any bad memories of your own past."

His brows rose, disappearing under that mop of hair. "I take it someone mentioned that my own parents died in a fire at my childhood home?"

"Thomas told me," I said. "He explained you managed to save your younger brother, but that you yourself had been injured. That was an incredibly brave thing for a young boy to do."

"I don't know how brave it was. Xander wouldn't jump, so I ended up basically throwing him off the roof." The side of Wyatt's mouth curled up.

"You *threw* your brother off the roof?"

"Xander was only six. He was too afraid to drop over the edge," Wyatt explained. "So I gave him a shove and he landed in the snow covered yew bushes. They broke his fall...mostly."

"Yet you were burned anyway." I nodded towards his arm.

"At first I tried to get to my parent's room, but I couldn't. I ran to get Xander and somehow the sleeve of my pajamas caught on fire."

I took his hand, gave it a squeeze. "You're a hero."

"I didn't feel that way at the time," Wyatt said softly. "I dropped down after Xander, but wasn't so lucky with my landing. I managed to break my ankle in the fall. The firefighters hadn't arrived yet. I could hear the sirens coming closer, and I crawled across the bushes to get to Xander. We huddled together in the snow and watched our house burn." He took a sip of wine. "The next thing I knew someone was picking the both of us up and carrying us to a car."

"A neighbor had come to help?" I asked, scooching a bit closer.

"It was Thomas," Wyatt said. "He rescued us both."

Involuntarily I squeezed his hand. "He did?"

"Thomas had seen the flames and came to try and help," Wyatt said. "He bundled Xander in his coat, and pulled the sweater off his own back, and wrapped me up in it as best he could."

"He did that?" I blinked.

"He didn't tell you about that part of the story?"

I shook my head. "No, he didn't."

"It was Thomas who stayed with Xander and I at the hospital until my grandparents could get to William's Ford. Thomas had been friends with my parents, and he refused to leave Xander and I alone until our grandparents arrived the next day." Wyatt leaned forward and took my hand. "Thomas Drake is many things. He's powerful, shrewd, a hell of a businessman, and he can be intimidating. However he is also one of the kindest men I've ever known. He's simply discreet about it."

"So he has a habit of rescuing people in one way or another," I said

Wyatt nodded. "I found out years later from my grandparents, that Thomas had covered the funeral expenses for my parents, and he'd also set up a college fund for both Xander and me. That fund paid for my degree, and covered almost all of Xander's firefighter training."

"I thought your brother was an EMT?"

"He's both, actually," Wyatt said proudly.

"I've enjoyed getting to know Xander over the course of the wedding," I said. "You two have similar coloring, his eyes are a deeper blue, but you're taller and thinner."

"My brother outweighs me by a good fifty pounds." Wyatt brushed the hair out of his eyes. "It's all the weight training. Xander does CrossFit."

With my free hand, I poked a playful finger in Wyatt's ribs, making him twitch. "You're no slouch there, honey. That's all lean muscle."

Wyatt grinned at me. "You think so?"

"I know so," I nodded. "I felt it when you held me on the dance floor. Makes me wonder if you do some sort of Yoga or something to stay in shape?" I'd meant for my comment to lighten the mood after such a serious conversation. But I saw that his eyes had changed. In fact his entire posture had.

Oh my. I thought, repressing a shiver. *Things were about to get very interesting.*

Slowly, Wyatt leaned in, pressing closer beside me on the couch. He waited, watching me carefully. "I've been thinking about kissing you again since last night."

I smiled. "Well sugar, maybe you should stop thinking and start with the doing."

"Aw hell, you called me sugar," he groaned. "Haven't you figured out what that does to me?"

"What does it do to you?" I asked softly.

"Let me show you," he said, and in one smooth move, I found myself pressed under him on the couch.

I tipped my face up as his mouth came down and met his kiss with my own. The kiss started out soft and testing. After a few minutes Wyatt lifted his head and gazed down in my eyes.

"Wyatt," I whispered, and reaching up I sank my hands in his hair and tugged him back down to me.

His reaction was explosive. Now our kiss was open-mouthed, and we strained to touch each other. He swept his hands gently over my breasts, causing me to shudder. In turn, I passed my hands over his chambray-covered chest. I slipped a hand inside his shirt, felt all that lean muscle, and purred in appreciation.

Wyatt suddenly paused, and gave my bottom lip the smallest of nips. "I want you," he said.

My heart slammed hard against my ribs. "I'm not quite ready for this," I admitted, removing my hands from him.

"Magnolia." Wyatt shifted slightly and it left no doubt as to his desire for me.

"Oh god," I managed, as any good sense I had threatened to go straight out the window. I reached up for his face, as I started to tremble.

We stayed exactly like that for a few moments. Him staring down in my face, and me lying beneath him. My hands were tangled in his hair, while the both of us tried to catch our breath.

Eventually, Wyatt sighed and rested his forehead against mine. I was surprised when he dropped a chaste kiss on my mouth and lifted his weight from me. He leaned back on the far side of the sofa, out of arm's reach and calmly smiled.

"I didn't mean for things to go quite so far tonight." Wyatt's voice was a low rumble.

I pulled my long hair over one shoulder. "The truth is, it *can't* go any farther. We aren't alone, and I'm not exactly prepared, or ready for such an event."

Wyatt's lips twitched. "Event?"

I tipped my head to one side and sent him a considering look. "Wyatt, I've only ever been with one man, and I married him. Since my divorce I haven't been with anyone else because I am very cautious. It's not my style to casually jump into bed with a man, even if I am attracted to him."

"I appreciate your honesty," Wyatt said soberly. "But to be clear, I've never thought of you as the 'quick tussle in the sheets' type, Magnolia."

My eyes ran over his partially naked chest and I told myself to be practical, to be smart, and *not* to pounce on the man. "Do me a favor will you?"

"What?"

"Button up your shirt." I said. "It's distracting having you sit there like that, when I'm trying to be sensible."

At my words, a slow smile spread across his face. It made my stomach jump. *Lord almighty,* I thought. *Seeing him like that, all that lean muscle, made me want to drag him to the bedroom, lock the door, and go crazy with him. And to hell with sensibility.*

"What are you thinking?" Wyatt asked, jolting me from my wayward thoughts. "You have this look on your face, Magnolia."

I tried for a laugh. "I'd tell you...but I wouldn't want to scare you."

He threw his head back and laughed. "I write murder mysteries for a living. You can't frighten me."

"Maybe *I* scare me," I said. "I didn't expect things to move so quickly between us. I'd feel more comfortable if we took our time, getting to know one another."

Wyatt nodded. "I can handle that."

I blew out a long breath in relief. "Okay." I nodded. "Good."

Wyatt suddenly stood and began buttoning his shirt. "I think it's time I head home." He started for the door.

"Wyatt."

He stopped with his hand on the doorknob.

"Thank you for dinner and the talk," I said.

"Thanks for the wine." He held open the door. "I'll call you tomorrow."

I rose to my feet and walked over to him. I went up on my toes to give him a soft kiss on the lips. "Goodnight, Wyatt."

"Magnolia." He kissed me again, nodded, and left.

I locked the door after him and remembered to engage the security system. I went around the room, turning off the lights one by one. I headed for bed, but sleep eluded me. I lay staring at the ceiling for a long time wondering about Wyatt Hastings.

I hadn't come to William's Ford looking for a romance, and yet I found myself teetering on the brink of one anyway.

***

After careful consideration I decided *not* to talk to Thomas about Leilah crashing the wedding reception at all. I did seek out Julian the next day and found him in his home office. I wasn't at all surprised to see that he was once again dressed impeccably.

While Willow was occupied romping around the new herb gardens with Nina, I shared everything I'd learned with my cousin. Julian, in turn, proceeded to fill in the gaps on what I didn't know. He explained some of the more 'colorful' Drake history with me...and it sounded damn-near medieval.

Seemed like my mama had inherited her penchant for dark magick from her daddy's side of the family. According to Julian, his grandfather, Silas Drake had been a very ruthless man. His determination to keep the male-dominated side of the magickal family tree going had consumed him. He'd practically forced a young Thomas into an arranged marriage with what he'd considered a suitable bride, and after she'd produced a male heir, Silas considered her unnecessary. The marriage fell apart and Thomas was left to raise Julian on his own.

Silas Drake had ignored his own daughter, Rebecca, and when she'd married a mundane he'd overlooked it because his only concern had been the unbroken line of power that had passed from father to son. But when Rebecca had a son of her own—Duncan—and when he'd shown talent, *then* Silas had been interested...in his grandson...but not his daughter.

His callous treatment of Rebecca had caused more damage than anyone knew, and it had driven the woman power-mad. In her pursuit of a grimoire, she'd manipulated Julian, until he'd broken. When Julian explained to me how bad it had been, and what he'd been forced into doing while under her magickal influence, it made me cry for him.

"Save your sympathy," he said. "Aunt Rebecca played on my weakness and my vanity. It was a hard lesson for me to learn. But it was a vital one."

"I'm beginning to understand what Nina meant when

she'd said that you'd walked a long dark road to find yourself again."

"I got off easy," Julian insisted.

"How's that?" I asked.

"Rebecca literally murdered other Witches and mundanes who'd been in her way." Julian folded his hands on his desk. "Including her husband—Duncan's father. It was all in her pursuit of a dark magickal object: The Blood Moon Grimoire."

"God almighty!" I gasped over the revelation.

He proceeded to explain that while he'd been away recovering from all the psychic damage his aunt had inflicted—hence the 'rehab' story to cover it up—she'd next turned her maleficence onto her own son. She'd stripped Duncan of his free will, practically making him a puppet. The woman had become unstable and deadly dangerous in her pursuit of power.

"Is that 'pursuit of power' why she attacked Lexie Bishop?" I asked. "I saw an article online from the local paper."

"Rebecca had gone after the grimoire," Julian explained. "Parts of it had been hidden in the Bishop house, and she broke in and stole them. Lexie defended herself and Morgan, who was an infant at the time." Julian paused, sitting back in his chair. "Truthfully, there was only one person who could have stopped my aunt, really."

"Who?" I demanded, on the edge of my seat. "Who stopped her?"

"Faye Bishop did her best, and it cost her."

"Oh my god." *The article I'd read,* I recalled. *It'd said that Faye had been hospitalized the night of the fire.*

"Next, Autumn burst in to the mansion. Recklessly, trying to help." Julian shook his head. "It was brave but foolish."

"Autumn took Rebecca on?" The thought of Autumn facing down that sort of evil made my blood run cold.

"Autumn tried," Julian said. "She attempted to rescue Faye and when she realized she was outgunned, Autumn did the next best thing. She stalled and waited for help."

"So what happened?"

Julian sighed over the memory. "Autumn blasted Rebecca with everything she had, *and* what energy Faye lent her. It bought her a few moments. She tried to get herself and her great-aunt to safety, but in the end she was outgunned. She had her ass handed to her."

"Oh no."

"Then my father walked in."

I swallowed hard. I truly didn't want to imagine that the man I'd come to care about... who'd gallantly shown up in Louisiana out of the blue when I'd needed him the most...the man who'd saved a young Wyatt and his brother from further injury on the night they'd lost their parents...watching quietly over them as they grew up; had magicked his own sister to death.

I sat silently, as Julian recounted how the battle had

gone down. Explaining that Rebecca had fallen by her own hand, and that he'd been the one who helped get Autumn and Faye outside, while Thomas had pulled Duncan from the burning third floor at the last second.

I sat silently for a few moments and let it all sink in. Suddenly all the gossip in town and nervousness about the Drake family made a horrible sort of sense. "No wonder no one talks about Rebecca...or any of this. It's ghastly."

"Our family has fought hard to be strong, healthy and whole since that day, Maggie." Julian paused, straightening his tie slightly. "We—Duncan, myself, and Dad—had made great strides too. That is until Leilah came to live with us."

I blinked. "There's more?"

"Yes. Leilah has caused all sorts of problems." Julian nodded. "The worst had to do with Holly Bishop."

"What happened?" I asked, reaching for his hand across the desk. "What did Leilah do?"

He took my offered hand and held it. "Leilah was spoiled by her mother and she has an inflated sense of entitlement. In the simplest of terms, she uses her magick to bully her way through life."

"I could see that after meeting her yesterday." I nodded. "She told me to leave town."

Julian rolled his eyes. "She's just jealous."

"Of what?"

"Your place here with the family."

"Hmmm," I thought about how she'd acted toward

me. "So Leilah's a mean girl—when it comes to magick?"

"Basically, yes. She and Holly have a long history." Julian told me the story of how, when Holly was still in high school, she'd used magick to take on Leilah. "But Holly lost her temper, and her magick spun horribly out of control," he explained. "After that episode, Holly abjured her powers for years."

"I can completely understand her decision," I said, feeling sympathy for my cousin. While I'd never personally lost control of my magick, I knew all too well how destructive of a force it could be...Which was why, in order to live a normal life, I'd cut myself off from it.

Julian continued with his story. "Leilah decided that after Holly came back to William's Ford, the time had come to take her revenge."

The newspaper article about Holly, I recalled as my stomach rolled over. "Would that revenge have anything to do with Holly being attacked at the antique store?"

"You heard about that?" He wanted to know.

I nodded. "After Leilah crashed the wedding, Diego made a comment to me about there being bad blood between Holly and Leilah. On a hunch I did an internet search yesterday, and read the newspaper article about Holly being injured during a robbery at the local store."

"It was Leilah," Julian said, letting go of my hand. "Holly refused to use her magick to stop Leilah, and my half-sister took full and brutal advantage of that."

"God almighty," I managed.

Julian rubbed his hand across his forehead. "I was the one who broke things up before it got any worse."

"You were there?"

"Maybe it was fate," Julian mused. "I was basically in the right place at the right time. I pulled Leilah off of Holly, threw her out of the antique store, and called for an ambulance."

"Poor Holly," I said. "How badly was she injured?"

"She had cuts, bruised ribs, and a concussion." Julian's voice was grim. "You may have noticed a small scar along her left eye."

I got this sudden cognitive pop in my mind—an inner knowing. My solar plexus tightened, confirming the information. "That's when you two began to fall in love with each other, wasn't it? When you rescued her from Leilah."

Julian didn't even flinch. He steepled his fingers and blandly stared at me, neither confirming or denying my question.

CHAPTER TEN

I put my hands in my lap and sat back in my chair. "I accidentally saw y'all in the gardens together, on the night of the bridal shower."

"I see." The tiniest of smiles hovered on Julian's lips. "So that's why you goaded me into asking her to dance at the wedding yesterday."

"I prefer the term *encouraged*." I smiled and tossed my hair over one shoulder.

Julian shook his head. "I'm sure you do."

"So long as we're being honest with each other," I began, "I did mention to Nina that I'd seen you two together. She told me that your relationship was secret."

"I see."

"I've kept quiet about that," I said. "Although, frankly, Julian, I can't see what business it is of anyone's, who you're involved with..."

"Her family would never approve of the two of us together. I don't imagine my father would either."

"Why?" I demanded. "Autumn is a Bishop, and

Thomas approves of her and Duncan being together."

"That's different," Julian said. "Plus, Holly and I work together. She's my assistant. If our relationship became public knowledge there would be backlash at the museum."

"*Pfft.*" I rolled my eyes. "People who work together, date, and fall in love all the time."

"Stop and consider everything I've told you about the family and our history with the Bishops."

I opened my mouth to argue, but I stopped and considered what he'd said. "Alright." I nodded. "Maybe, I can see the reason for keeping your relationship quiet, but secrets have a way of coming out. Whether we want them to or not."

"We've been discreet," Julian insisted.

"Maybe not as much as y'all thought. Because Autumn and Duncan know."

"What?" Julian frowned.

"They've known for a while and have stayed silent." I reached out and took his hand again, giving it a friendly squeeze. "I think, Julian, that you and Holly have more allies than you realize."

"Perhaps." Julian gave my fingers a squeeze in return. "So," he said in a totally different tone of voice. "How did your date with Wyatt go last night?"

I withdrew my hand from his, and scowled. "How did you know?"

"Oh...so we can discuss my love life but not yours?" He teased. "Fine, fine...I see how it is."

"It wasn't a formal date," I insisted. "He brought dinner over to the cottage, and we spent some time together."

"Aaaaand?" Julian drug out the word.

"And that's it." I folded my arms. "We're in the 'getting to know each other' stage. I think it's best to take things slow."

"How did Wyatt feel about that?"

I frowned. "He was fine with it."

Julian smiled. "Wyatt's a good man."

I raised my brows. "Is that your way of telling me you approve, sugar?"

"Uh-oh." Julian started to laugh. "You called me, *sugar*. I'm in big trouble now."

"Oh, shove it Julian." I said, with a laugh.

He stood up from his desk. "Come on, cousin, let's go see what Willow is up to."

"Hell's bells!" Guiltily, I jumped to my feet. I'd been so engrossed in our conversation that I'd forgotten. "I hadn't meant to leave Willow with Nina for so long. I hope Nina isn't angry."

"She won't be," Julian predicted.

I hustled out of his office and down the stairs, and Julian fell in step with me.

"I promised Willow we'd go out for lunch today," I said. "Maybe I'll ask Nina to bring Isabel, and we can make it a girl's outing."

"Would you have room for one more?" Julian gave me an elbow nudge, making me laugh.

"Of course," I said. "If you're feeling brave enough to go out with two women, a four-year-old, and a baby?"

"Sounds like fun to me," Julian said with a smile.

The two of us moved directly outside and around to the herb gardens. Nina knelt at the edge of the flowerbed, contentedly adding yarrow plants, and Willow was busy pushing a gurgling Isabel around in her stroller.

Nina tipped her face up to us. "Did you two have a nice talk?" She was all smiles.

"I'm sorry I was gone so long," I apologized.

"Don't be. Willow kept Isabel happy and I got a lot of planting done."

"Hi Mama! Hi Julian!" Willow waved and steered Isabel over to us.

Isabel spotted Julian, and the baby let out a happy squeal.

"How do you feel about going out for lunch?" Julian said to Nina, before I could.

"I feel very happy about that. It'd be nice to eat someone else's cooking." Nina said, gathering up the empty pots. "Give me five minutes to wash up and change Isabel, and we'll be ready to roll."

"Can I have french fries?" Willow wanted to know.

"Of course you can." Julian passed his hand over Willow's hair.

"Hooray!" Willow shouted.

I considered Julian's clothes, and wondered about

whether my casual cotton shirt and jeans were appropriate. "Should I change? Is this a formal restaurant?"

"No. It's family style." Julian grinned. "Trust me. I know the perfect place to take all my best girls out to lunch."

I smiled at his cheerful words. As he stood there talking to Willow, I began to understand that Julian Drake was as hungry for family connections as I'd been. Maybe even more so, considering everything he and his father had been through.

***

The week after the family wedding, things began to settle down. My schedule loosened up allowing me a bit more free time. I met with a few prospective brides and grooms. As expected they'd been recommended to me by guests from Autumn and Duncan's wedding, and one of the couples was interested in having a barn reception at a local farm/wedding venue within the next four weeks.

With her wedding looming so quickly, the bride, Caroline, had begun to panic and had decided she needed professional help to organize her rustic style wedding. While I quite understood her nervousness, I was still a might surprised at how last minute they'd decided to hire an event coordinator. The bride was about to graduate from the university with her Master's degree, and her fiancé was a science teacher at the local high school. The wedding was scheduled for two weeks after she received her degree.

With the timeline so short, I wasted no time in driving out to the McBriar family farm to meet with the owner and to inspect the setup on my own. The farm was picturesque, and the barn had been cleverly decorated with a mixture of rustic and antique pieces. I could see why Caroline and Lee were interested in the venue, but *before* they signed a contract I wanted to check the space out for myself.

After speaking to the owner, Diane McBriar, she'd disclosed that their wedding bookings had been down for the past year or so. This was the first time in months anyone had even been interested in booking their venue.

I found that surprising as rustic weddings were very much en vogue at present. Diane began to subtly ask if *I* felt their décor, and the packages they offered their wedding clients, were up to snuff. She was obviously very concerned that they were either overcharging *or* not offering the sorts of amenities that brides were currently expecting.

Basically the woman wanted a *free* assessment of her venue, and it wouldn't be the first time I'd had that happen to me. With a smile, I politely informed Diane that if she wanted to hire me as a consultant for her venue that we could sit down and work up a contract.

She blinked in surprise, and I steered the

conversation back to the plans for Caroline and Lee's big day and decided that the venue bore close watching.

After the meeting, I had a couple of hours to kill before picking up Willow from preschool. I drove down to the adjacent McBriar farm stand and checked out the perennials and annuals they had for sale.

It might be nice to plant up a strawberry pot full of herbs for myself, I decided, as I considered the plants. If I placed it on the sunny back porch of the cottage, I'd have culinary herbs close to hand for cooking.

With that thought in mind, I picked out a large pot, loaded it in the cart and began to select my herbs. A man's voice drifted over to me as I shopped.

"Are you serious?" His voice carried clearly. "You asked the snooty Southern wedding coordinator for her advice and she actually said that you'd have to offer her a contract to be a consultant *before* she'd discuss it?"

My back stiffened. I straightened up from where I'd been perusing through the culinary herbs and focused on the person who was speaking.

A rugged man stood about twenty feet from me. Clearly he had no idea that his voice was carrying as far as it was. I gave him a swift assessment as he snarled into his cell phone. He appeared to be in his late twenties. He wore jeans, sturdy boots and an embroidered ball cap that said, *McBriar Farms.*

I stood there, continuing to listen. *He might have been attractive, if not for the sneer on his face,* I thought.

"For god sake's, Mom," he said. "We've taken a huge hit on the wedding venue ever since that business with Holly Bishop." He took off his cap and scrubbed a hand through his blonde hair. "Don't tell me to calm down! I bet you she and her family are behind this somehow...You know they are. They probably hexed us or something."

I set the herbs I'd been about to purchase back down. I couldn't believe the man—who I surmised was Diane's son—was standing there out in the open and bashing both my cousin and me.

I'd be damned if I'd give them any of my business, I decided. *There were other garden centers in town.* I left the cart where it was and walked away.

"Excuse me, Miss?" The man's voice called out to me.

I stopped and slowly turned to face him. I spotted a nametag attached to his polo shirt. It read: Erik McBriar. *Bingo,* I thought.

"Can I help you find anything?" Erik had ended his call and was slipping the phone in his back pocket.

I looked down my nose at him. "Why, no thank you. I've decided to take my business elsewhere."

His eyebrows raised at my accent. I could practically watch the wheels turn in his head, and saw the precise moment when he figured out who I was. "You overheard me."

I nodded. "I sure as hell did, sugar."

"People who eavesdrop may not like what they

hear," was his comeback.

I popped a hand on one hip. "I wasn't eavesdropping, Mr. McBriar. You were *shouting* into the phone." I tossed my head and headed for my car.

"Wait a damn second," he said, rushing forward.

I spared him a glance from over my shoulder. "By the way, you can tell your mama that the 'snooty Southern wedding coordinator' will do her level best to try and find a *different* venue for the bride and groom who hired her."

His nervous expression was most satisfying. I walked to my car, started it up and left the rude Mr. McBriar standing there with a look of shock on his face.

"There are other places in town that might work for the rustic theme Caroline and Lee are after," I said, thinking out loud as I drove. "I'll head back in to town, grab a coffee and brainstorm at the coffee house."

Caroline and Lee only had eighty wedding guests, that smaller guest list would allow me more options. I blew out a long aggravated breath. I simply had to find the perfect venue...today.

I replayed the whole scene in my mind as I drove back to town. My temper was on a nice rolling boil as I thought back over the outrageous things Erik McBriar had said about my cousin...and then it hit me.

I'd automatically thought of Holly as my cousin...and had reacted protectively. It was a hell of a jolt to realize that I'd begun thinking of the Bishop girls as my family. Not relatives, but *family*.

With the import of my discovery sinking in, I parked in front of the coffee shop and walked in. I was pleased to see that the line was short, and I ordered a cappuccino and took my seat.

Janelle, the manager brought it to me a few moments later. "How goes everything?" she asked.

"Hey, Janelle." I smiled when I saw she'd added a biscotti to the saucer of the oversized cup. "It's going." I considered her as she stood there. "You seem to have your finger on the pulse of this town. I was wondering...would you know of a local venue for a small wedding for under one hundred guests, that would have a rustic or vintage feel?"

She raised her brows. "Besides the McBriar Farm Wedding barn?"

I resisted the urge to curl my lip. "Exactly."

"Ooooh." Her eyes lit up and she took the seat across form me. "I smell gossip. Gimme."

I cleared my throat against a chuckle and struggled to keep a neutral tone of voice. "I recently viewed the McBriar barn..."

"And?"

"And I'm not sure it has the right, *atmosphere* that my bride and groom are looking for."

"Did you speak with Diane McBriar? She runs the wedding part of the business."

I nodded. "She was one of the people I spoke to."

"You must have run into Erik." Janelle's eyes

narrowed. "He's a real piece of work, and he *hates* the Bishop family."

"Why on earth would he?"

The bells over the coffee shop door tinkled. "Here's the person who can best answer that for you." Janelle said, smiling at someone over my shoulder. "Hey, Holly."

I shifted in my chair and saw Holly standing in a beam of light. The bright sunshine backlit her hair, and the long strawberry-blonde curls shimmered around her shoulders. "Hey there, Janelle." She shifted her eyes to me. "Good morning, Maggie."

Janelle stood and held out her chair. "Have a seat. Maggie has something to ask you."

Holly smiled, passing Janelle a list of coffee orders. "For the office at the museum," she explained.

With a nod, Janelle accepted the list. "I'm on it," she said, moving behind the counter.

"What's up?" Holly asked, smoothing the skirt of her long pink dress as she sat with me.

"Do you have a few moments?"

She brushed her curls away from her face. "Sure, I'm out making the coffee run for the office at the museum."

"I went to view the McBriar wedding barn today for some clients of mine..." I trailed off as Holly's shoulders stiffened.

"How'd that go?" she asked casually.

"Not well," I said. "I had a run-in with the owner's

son."

"Erik." Holly blew out a long breath.

"He was less than pleasant, and he appears to hold a grudge. Particularly where you are concerned."

"Erik hates me." Holly's voice was soft and sad. "And that hatred has made him bitter."

"Ah, I see. You must have broken his poor heart." I tucked my tongue in my cheek. "A man scorned, is he?"

Holly snorted. "Me? Break Erik McBriar's heart? I don't think he even has one. Ivy calls him Erik McDouchebag."

"That sounds like Ivy." I chuckled, leaning forward. "Tell me, Holly. I'll admit that I'm mighty intrigued."

"Okay," Holly said. "It started when I went to work at the antique shop…"

I sat and listened while Holly explained to me her past association with the McBriar family. When she finished I was simmering mad. "Let me get this straight," I began, "the antique store you were attacked in was owned by Erik's sister?"

"Yes." Holly nodded.

"And because of..." I made sure to lower my voice. "Leilah Martin Drake, they sustained a huge loss to their inventory."

"Correct."

"God almighty," I breathed. "Julian told me about this, but I didn't know it'd had such serious repercussions."

"As far as the McBriar family is concerned; even

though the majority of the jewelry was returned, the *culprit*," Holly said, "was never apprehended."

"So afterward, while you were recovering, Erik encouraged you to quit because he was uncomfortable about the gossip concerning the Bishop family's...shall we say...hobbies?"

"Yes." Holly nodded.

"Julian told me that you didn't use magick to defend yourself from Leilah."

Holly shook her head. "No, I didn't. because I'd already done much worse to her years before."

"He told me." On impulse, I covered her hand with mine. A warmth grew between where our hands were joined, and I felt a real bond with her. "Holly, I understand what it is to walk away from power that you can't control, or are afraid might end up controlling you."

Holly's aquamarine eyes searched mine, and she nodded. "Autumn told me about your life when you were young. I'm sorry for what you went through with your mother."

I gave her hand a pat. "I'm sorry for what you went through with Leilah."

"Yes, well, she got what she wanted," Holly said. "The robbery was never solved, and because I wasn't able to identify my attacker to the police...I fell under suspicion, which caused the fallout between me and the McBriar family."

"What a mess."

Holly sat back in her chair. "When Erik McBriar urged me to quit, I told him I'd rather speak to his sister —the owner of the store. Erik however, wanted me to stay away from them. He insinuated that he was worried for his sister and her children's safety. His exact words were. '*To each his own. It's nothing personal*'."

"That son of a bitch!" I hissed. "He was just being ugly."

"Ugly?" Holly tilted her head.

"Being mean," I explained.

"What he didn't count on, was that he said all of that *in public*. Right here, in the coffee shop." Holly tapped her fingers on the table. "Several people overheard him, and what he'd said to me spread through town like wildfire."

"So their antique store felt the backlash."

"For a while," Holly explained. "The older families boycott them, and the wedding venue as well. The tourists are the ones who basically keep the antique store going. But the wedding venue relies on word-of-mouth from the locals, and as you can imagine...it took the brunt of it."

"Well that's his own fault." I caught myself and lowered my voice to avoid any more gossip being spread. "Erik McBriar had no right to blame you back then, or to be publicly claiming that you've hexed him, now."

"Erik became bitter after he and his fiancée broke

up. It was messy, very public, and Raelynn had been manipulating him with magick," Holly said. "Magick that she paid for."

"Paid for?" My stomach rolled over. "I know first-hand how vicious spells can be when done to manipulate and control another. It had been a specialty of my mother's. The karmic backlash is typically severe on both the person who paid for the magick *and* on the caster."

"That's true," Holly agreed, sadly.

I shook my head over the old memories. "My mama habitually claimed she was under attack from jealous Witches. Even though she'd been the root cause of all her own problems..." Pushing the old memories away, I focused on Holly. "Who did his fiancée pay for the spells?"

Holly grimaced. "Erik's fiancée paid Leilah to manipulate him with magick, so he would do whatever she wanted."

"Leilah Martin Drake. Again," I blew out a long breath.

"When Erik became aware of what Raelynn had been doing, it changed him. The whole experience made him bitter," Holly said. "Now Erik hates anything to do with magick, and especially those who practice it. Like me."

"Well, bless his heart, he picked a hell of a town to live and run a business in, all things considered." I smiled. "Maybe he should consider moving."

Holly burst out laughing. "I love the way you say that."

"What?"

"Bless his heart." Holly tried to mimic my accent.

I tossed my hair over one shoulder. "Well darlin', you know what they say: Only a Southern woman can offer up an insult sweet enough that you'd think it was a compliment."

Holly grinned at that. "You know, Maggie, I think I might have a possible venue idea for your bride and groom."

"Oh?"

"Yeah." Holly said, tapping a finger to her lips. "Let me go pay for the coffees and I'll take you to meet Sharon Waterman."

I stood when she did. "Who's she?"

"Sharon is a member of the chamber of commerce. She and her husband have this historic, wooden carriage house on their property. It's huge. They actually used it for one of their niece's wedding reception last year."

"Oh?" My ears practically perked up. "Here in town? Why that could be perfect for Caroline and Lee."

"You're going to love it," Holly predicted. "The Waterman family decorates their carriage house for Yuletide every year as a part of the Holiday Light Walk. It's gorgeous."

I followed her to the counter. "Do you think she'd be up to speaking to me about the possibility of renting it out?"

"I'm sure she would. Mrs. Waterman mentioned to me at Autumn and Duncan's wedding how impressed she was with the work you'd done. She made some noise about getting you signed up with the local business association." Holly smiled. "She's the chairperson."

"In that case," I said, excited at the idea, "I'm buying all the coffees for your office."

***

The tip from Holly saved the day. I met with Sharon Waterman, and she loved the idea of renting out the carriage house for the upcoming reception. After a quick tour of the property, I also found myself with an application to join the local business association.

I thanked her, and Sharon had given me an air kiss. She told me to take all the photos I wanted to send to the bride and groom. Taking her up on her offer, I took several photos and immediately texted them to Caroline and Lee.

As expected, the bride was over the moon at having a venue in town. That way they could move from the chapel on campus and go only a few miles to the Waterman's carriage house for their reception.

The next weeks passed quickly. Wyatt invited Willow and I over to his house for a casual dinner one evening, and I was very interested in seeing his home. I was also curious about his workspace. What did the office of a mystery writer look like anyway?

I chose my outfit that evening with care. Casual navy slacks paired with a pretty yellow blouse that featured fluttery cap sleeves. I left my hair down and added my fun turquoise necklace to jazz things up. Willow wore her favorite blue dress, and I told myself not to be nervous.

Applying my lipstick, I gave myself a good, firm talking to in the bedroom mirror. "All right, Maggie," I said. "This is a casual dinner date. It's your chance to get to know the man better, and you did ask for the time to do that. Besides, it's not like anything is going to happen tonight...not with Willow there."

It was my wisest course of action to slowly get to know Wyatt, I decided. Even if I was more than a little obsessed with that long, lean body of his. I'd lost several nights' sleep wondering over it. "Stop that," I told my reflection.

The last time I'd been this fascinated with a man I'd been in college. I'd jumped right in to the physical aspect of the relationship with Beau and it had been exciting and reckless...and of course, I'd been so dazzled by the sex that I'd been stupid enough to marry him.

I stopped in my mental chastisement of the younger me, and deliberately capped the lipstick. I was an adult now, and a mother. I had my daughter to think of, after all. It wouldn't do my reputation any good, to be playing fast and loose with the first man I dated in William's Ford. *I needed to be cautious and smart, and take the time to get to know Wyatt Hastings,* I reminded myself.

That whole, 'Be smart. Take my time,' line was damn near becoming a personal mantra... I made a face at myself in the mirror and reminded myself there was no rush. I would know when it was the right time to take the next step.

A few minutes before six, I parked at the curb in front of his house as he'd suggested. For a few moments, I indulged myself by simply enjoying the view. The historic house had been built in the Greek Italianate Revival style. The brick was painted a warm cream, and the columns on the porch were bright white. The shutters and trim had been done in a smoky blue-gray. The house was charming with neatly trimmed shrubs in the front. As we walked down his pathway and began climbing the porch steps, I saw a big dog in the backyard.

Willow noticed it too. "Mama, does Wyatt have a dog?"

"I guess so," I glanced over for another look, but the dog had moved out of sight.

Wyatt answered the door and greeted us with a smile. "Welcome," he said holding the door open.

I stepped over the threshold and looked around in delight. The old home had wide archways, old pine floors and had been tastefully decorated with historic colors, but modern comfortable furniture. "This is a lovely home," I said.

"What's your dog's name?" Willow asked. "Can I play with him?"

Wyatt smiled down at Willow. "I don't have a dog."

"Oh." I frowned. "I could've sworn I saw one in your backyard..." I shrugged it off and focused instead on Wyatt as he ushered us back to the kitchen.

Wyatt was a wonderful host and we had a great time at his house. His office, it ended up, was on the third floor. Duncan had done a marvelous job remodeling it, and now the space featured a long custom desk, lots of shelving and yet it still maintained the vintage quality of the home.

Willow exclaimed over all of Wyatt's cover art from his novels. They actually filled up an entire wall. I noted there was a fire escape on the third floor too, and an ornate wrought iron, spiral staircase that led to the ground floor.

After supper, Willow raced around his back yard, and Wyatt and I sat on the back porch enjoying the pretty late May night. When the evening was over he walked us to my car, and while Willow was preoccupied climbing into her booster seat, he snuck a kiss.

"Goodnight, Magnolia." His voice was low, and I struggled to maintain my composure even after the briefest of kisses.

"Goodnight, Wyatt." I smiled and climbed in the car.

I was so distracted from that sneaky kiss that I actually got lost on my way home. It took me a few minutes to figure out where I'd taken the wrong turn, and it made me laugh at myself.

***

The next week, we managed a date night, and ended the evening by taking a moonlit walk at the riverside park. We sat on a park bench under an old tree, talking and kissing for a long time. Wyatt didn't pressure me for more, and it both relieved and frustrated me.

The Sunday before Caroline and Lee's wedding, we attended the town picnic together with the Drakes and the Vasquez families. The picnic was held at the same charming park where Duncan and Autumn had their wedding reception.

Wyatt, Willow and I walked slowly along the merchant's row. Wyatt carried a picnic basket for me, and Willow was excited to see everything. Candice Jacobs had a booth where she was selling cupcakes and cakepops. Judging by the line of people, she was doing very well.

We stopped to speak to Xander, Wyatt's brother. He was out with the local firefighters, and the fire truck was on display for the children to see. I snapped a few pictures of Willow as she posed by the fire truck.

We made our way to the pavilion where Thomas had managed to claim a picnic table. "Hey, y'all!" I waved to the family.

The newlyweds were back from their honeymoon, and Autumn greeted me with a big hug. Willow began chattering to Autumn, wanting to know all about the cruise they'd been on.

Wyatt was talking to Duncan, and I helped Nina unpack the chicken and potato salad that she'd made up for the families. While Duncan arranged the paper plates on the table, Wyatt set out plastic utensils. Diego jiggled Isabel on his knee, Autumn was pointing out the flowers to Willow, and Thomas and Julian handed out the drinks to everyone.

While we sat and ate, I saw several people that I knew. Sharon Waterman introduced me to her husband. Caroline and Lee strolled by and were cheerful and excited about their impending wedding. Violet, Matthew Bell, and his daughter Charlie stopped and said hello.

Violet showed us all her brand new amethyst and diamond engagement ring, which had Autumn cheering and leaping to her feet.

While Autumn hugged her friend, I congratulated the couple.

"We need to talk soon, Maggie," Violet said to me. "I want to hire you as our wedding coordinator."

"Do you have a date in mind?" I asked the couple.

"Soon," Matthew said, with a wink to his bride.

"December, maybe," Violet agreed. "Sixth months is all I want to wait."

"What sort of wedding were you thinking of?" I smiled at the couple. "Large and splashy or smaller and intimate?"

"Elegant, and intimate," Violet said. "I figure we can realistically pull that off in six months time."

I promised to call Violet soon so we could sit down and hash out the details, and as we finished our conversation, Holly and Ivy came over with their own picnic dinner and ended up joining us.

Once Violet, Matthew and Charlie moved on, I subtly watched Julian and Holly. They'd ended up sitting together at the picnic table, and were so casually polite to each other you'd never have reason to guess there was more to their relationship other than being co-workers.

Ivy distracted me from my thoughts when she announced that she was helping to shoot the wedding at the carriage house.

"I had no idea you were apprenticing with a local wedding photographer," I said. Although I remembered seeing her take candid shots at the rehearsal dinner, I hadn't put it all together.

"I'm hoping to work my way up to shooting smaller weddings solo within a year, and then after that, to start a photography business of my own," Ivy said.

"I'd love to see your work sometime," I said to her. "Do you have a portfolio?"

"I do." Her whole face lit up. "You're really interested in seeing it?"

"Of course." I smiled. "I understand what it's like to work your way up the ladder. I did that when I first started as a wedding coordinator."

"I'm good." Ivy said, sipping her soda. "Trust me."

"Ivy did the engagement photos for Duncan and me," Autumn announced from across the picnic table.

"Well, well...I've seen them displayed at the mansion. They're excellent," I said, pulling out the basket I'd brought. I lifted up a big pan of frosted brownies I'd made. "Who wants dessert?"

"You brought dessert?" Duncan asked.

"Homemade brownies." I set the pan on the table with a flourish. "It's an old family recipe."

Duncan snatched his hand back as soon as the pan hit the table. "Old family recipe, you say?"

"Where exactly did you get the recipe?" Autumn asked suspiciously. "It's not from Irene's cookbook, is it?"

I bit my lip to keep from laughing. "No, it's not. The recipe is from my Grandma Taylor. She won three blue ribbons with this recipe." I took out a spatula and began to serve.

After the meal, Ivy left to go get some shots of the picnic for the local paper, and baby Isabel decide to wow the crowd by taking her first steps on the park grass.

Once the sun went down, a local band began to play at the nearby gazebo, and I sat in the grass on a blanket cozily next to Wyatt with Willow cuddled in my lap and listened to the music.

When he took my hand it all seemed absolutely wonderful. I rested my head on his shoulder, smiled up at the waxing moon, and thought to myself that my life was damn near perfect.

I had no reason to ever suspect that a few days later, my world would implode.

CHAPTER ELEVEN

June had arrived, and the days were sliding over from spring to summer. In merely a few days Caroline and Lee's wedding would happen, and I woke early, a couple of hours before Willow, to go over my schedule for their wedding day.

I was comfortable in the cozy dark before the sun came up, wearing a pair of gym shorts, my old purple LSU t-shirt, and with my hair clipped sloppily on top of my head. I had risen to refill my coffee when something banged against the window over the kitchen sink. I jumped in reaction, almost dropping the mug, and hot coffee sloshed over my hand.

I swung my head toward the noise that had come from the rear of the cottage. My first thought was that something had been thrown against the house, and I headed directly to the back door. Twitching the shade aside to look, I saw nothing amiss. Slowly, I opened the back door, half-expecting to see a ball or something, but instead discovered a bird that lay twitching on the porch.

"Oh, did you fly into the window?" I knelt down to get a closer look, and it broke my heart when I realized that the bird wasn't merely dazed, it was dying. "Poor bird," I murmured. Even as I reminded myself that a bird flying against a window was a common occurrence, I still felt uneasy. Rising to my feet, I studied the property behind the cottage. Nothing was out of place, and yet I held completely still, listening to the pre-dawn noises.

I waited, and when nothing else happened, I went back into the kitchen and retrieved a plastic grocery bag. By the time I got back to the porch, the bird had died.

Thankful that Willow was still sleeping and wouldn't have to see the bird, I picked it up with the bag, and carried it directly to the outdoor garbage cans. I was turning to walk back inside when I spotted a shimmer on the ground. *What would make that sort of reflection?* I wondered, pausing in mid-step. I bent over for a closer look, and saw that something had been drawn in a bare patch of lawn along the edge of the sidewalk.

The hair rose on the back of my neck, and my stomach tightened painfully as I studied the symbol. "That's not something Willow would have done playing," I said, shining the light from my cell phone on the ground. "That's a rune."

Thurisaz, a Norse rune that symbolized a 'thorn' had been carved into the soft dirt. Thanks to my mother's proclivities, I knew that this particular rune could be used for cursing and hexing. And in fact, this rune had been drawn reversed. Meaning the intentions were to lure out the negative qualities of the symbol, namely: evil, malice and hatred.

Slowly and carefully, I made my way down the rest of the driveway, searching for any other symbols. I found the second rune, *Nauthiz,* drawn on the stonework used as decorative trim at the corner of the cottage. It too was reversed. With a sinking feeling in my stomach, I snapped a quick photo with my phone.

While runes were considered generally positive, like any magickal system they could be twisted into serving darker purposes. The reversed *Nauthiz* rune could invoke: distress, confusion, and poverty. I blew out a shaky breath as I considered the second symbol. It had been inscribed with chalk, meaning it hadn't been there very long. A week at most, considering we hadn't had any rain in the past few days.

"God damn it," I hissed, and went back to get a picture of the first rune I'd found.

As the sun rose, I walked around the cottage searching for anything else that didn't belong. I found three more occult symbols, including an inverted pentagram, and while I wasn't particularly afraid after my discoveries...I was starting to become downright *pissed.*

It would take a little time and effort, but I could counteract any of the maleficence directed toward us.

After all, I had recently stocked up on protection magick supplies at *Enchantments*.

I was finishing up my second pass around the cottage when I saw a flash of color in the bushes. Using a fallen branch from the magnolia tree in the yard, I knelt, reaching up inside the bush with the stick, and pulled something out. It plopped onto the grass, rolling toward me, and my anger turned to horror.

I'd found another fashion doll. The doll had been originally intended to be a 'younger sister' to her famous Malibu style sibling. What had me gulping back fear was that the doll had been made over to look exactly like Willow.

I sat back on my butt, staring at the poppet resting in the grass. "Lord almighty," I whispered. *On the first night we'd moved in Willow had found a doll,* I remembered, and I'd burned the nasty thing in the fireplace. I'd even gone as far as to break my own long-standing 'no magick' rule by working a quick banishing spell over it.

While that first doll had its hair all tied in knots, the hair of this doll was styled in two long brown pigtails. The same way Willow preferred to wear her hair. It had on a blue floral dress too. Again, similar to the one my daughter favored. The difference between this doll and the other was that this doll had been bound in intricate knots of twine and string, and lastly a black ribbon had been stapled across its mouth.

The evil emanating from it made me want to vomit.

My phone chimed, alerting me of a text, and I recoiled at the sound. I glanced down and saw that it was a message from Holly.

Good morning. How goes the preparation for the wedding reception at the carriage house?

There was no such thing as coincidence. If Holly was contacting me this early, I needed to reach out to her first, before I did anything else.

I need your help. Serious magickal problem. I texted back. *From what I can tell the outside of my cottage has had hexes laid all around it.* I hit send and followed up my text with the photos of every symbol that I'd found.

I sat in the grass waiting for her to read the message, look over the photos, and hopefully, respond.

I got the photos. I'm on my way. Holly texted back a few minutes later. *I'm walking out the door right now.*

There's more. I texted back to Holly. *It's much worse than the others.*

The text had barely been delivered when my phone rang. The read out showed that it was Holly. I hit 'accept'.

"Tell me." Holly's voice was urgent. "What else did you find, Maggie?"

"A sort of poppet," I said. "It's made from a fashion doll, and it looks exactly like Willow."

"Shit! Don't touch it!" I could hear that Holly was running. "I'm at my car. I'll be at your place in less than five minutes."

"I didn't touch it," I said. "I'm sitting in the back, behind the cottage. I want to keep searching and make sure there isn't anything more."

"I'm on my way. Wait for me." Holly said, and she hung up.

Feeling numb, I went inside for another garbage bag, and I sat on my back porch step and waited. I heard Holly pull her car in the driveway, and then her door open and shut. She wasn't running when she appeared from around the side of the cottage, but she looked like an avenging angel—albeit one in a black maxi dress.

I'd never seen her wearing anything remotely witchy before, and it came as a bit of a surprise. Or perhaps I was in a slight state of shock, since it was easier to focus on her outfit instead of the reality of what I'd discovered.

I stood as she approached. It was everything I had not to take a step back from her. The energy crackling off Holly was palatable.

"Show me," she said.

I walked her over to the poppet. "I found it tucked in the bushes."

"You're sure, you didn't come into contact with it?" she asked as she studied it.

"No. I used a stick to pull it out." I shook my head. "Holly, I've never seen work like this before."

"God damn it." Holly's voice was grim. "I have."

"You know who did this?"

Holly knelt in the grass, holding her hands out, and

sensing the energy from the poppet. "Yes, I know."

"Who?" I asked, kneeling down beside her. "Who would try and use magick to harm Willow?

"Leilah Martin Drake," Holly said. "She absolutely would, and this *is* her work. I've seen it before and I know exactly the sort of damage it can do."

I blinked in surprise. "What could possibly be Leilah's motive?"

Holly placed a hand on my arm. "At a guess I'd say she's jealous of your and Willow's place in the Drake family."

After everything I'd heard about Leilah, it all made a horrible kind of sense. My horror was slowly being replaced by anger, and with that came a sudden realization. "She's messing with Willow because she knows nothing would hurt me more."

"Exactly." Holly nodded.

My stomach roiled. "I grew up watching my mother wield dark magick, Holly. But even she *never* went after a child!"

Holly went to retrieve the garbage bag. Efficiently she used the stick to roll the poppet inside the bag. "Have you ever found anything else like this since you moved in the cottage?"

"The first night," I said, and quickly told her how I'd destroyed it and worked a banishing.

"It's a damn good thing you listened to your instincts, back in January."

"I did put a warding in place after the cottage was

broken into and trashed," I said. "Autumn took me to your family's store and I loaded up on supplies."

"That probably bought you some time." Holly folded her arms. "Has anything else been happening? Anything weird?"

"Shit!" It hit me hard, and I slapped a hand to my forehead. *The dead birds,* I realized. *The creepy black dog...I'd seen a black dog in the middle of the road right before my car accident too. It was the reason I had stomped on my brakes...* "Oh my god," I said, shutting my eyes against my own stupidity. "Yes, there has been. I just never put it all together before now."

"Hey, don't be so hard on yourself." Holly slipped her arm around my shoulders and steered me back to the bistro table and chairs on the back porch.

"God damn it! If anyone should have put this together—it should have been me!" I caught myself. I'd almost been shouting, and I didn't want to wake Willow. With an effort, I lowered my voice. "I was raised on this style of magick, Holly. I can't believe I was so blind to it."

"Have you considered that perhaps you were purposefully blinded?" Holly's soft voice had me considering her.

"How do you mean?"

"Perhaps a reluctance was used against you."

"I'm not familiar with that term."

"A *reluctance*," Holly explained. "Can be used to disguise something, make it seem less desirable, or to even cloak another practitioner's actions."

"That actually makes a sick sort of sense." I nodded. "I think someone's been watching us since we moved in. I've been seeing this black dog at the oddest times. Willow's seen him too. Then there's the dead birds."

"Tell me about that," Holly said. "Whatever you can remember that's stuck in your memory as odd, or anything strange that made you uncomfortable."

"Let's go inside," I suggested. "Where we can be assured of privacy."

With a nod Holly followed me in. She calmly placed the wrapped poppet on the kitchen counter, picked up my salt shaker, unscrewed the top and poured all of the salt over the bag.

"Smart," I said, nodding at the salt.

Holly went to the sink to wash her hands. "Would you get me some paper and a pen? I think it's a good idea to take notes on your experiences, and create a sort of timeline."

I joined her at the sink, washing my hands as well. "You bet. First I want to check on Willow. Once I get her breakfast and take her to school we can get into all of this and come up with a game plan."

"Perfect." Holly nodded. "I'm going to start us some tea," she said, making herself at home in the kitchen.

"Okay. Be right back." I walked to Willow's room determined to be cheerful and not to let my daughter know I was worried. I took a deep breath, put a smile on my face and opened the door. "Morning, sleepyhead!" I sang, turning on her lights.

My smile faded when I focused on her bed. It was empty.

"Willow?" I went to the hall bathroom, and opened the door. "Baby are you in there?"

Nothing.

I hurried into my room, yanked my covers back, in case she had burrowed in my bed. It too was empty. My heart slammed in my throat. "Willow!" I called her name again and shoved open the door to the bath off the master suite.

"Maggie?" Holly's voice came from the kitchen. "What's wrong?"

I ran to the living room. "Willow's not in her bed!" I said. "She's not here."

"Maybe she's hiding," Holly said, and pulled open the coat closet door in the living room.

It took only moments to check the cottage, and she wasn't there.

"I'm going to check outside," Holly said. "Maybe she walked over to the main house. I'll call Julian."

I nodded and raced back in Willow's room, checking under her bed again. My heart was pounding as I sat back up, noticing for the first time that her bedroom window was open slightly. It hadn't been open when I'd put her to bed last night.

"Willow?" I rushed to it and pulled up short. Her favorite babydoll was lying face down under the window and on the floor.

I picked up her doll and saw a smear of blood. It trailed over the windowsill and to the outside of the cottage.

And I knew. Someone had taken my baby. *Willow was gone.*

I dropped to my knees and screamed.

***

I don't remember too much of the hours that followed. It was Julian who'd held me when I'd first fallen apart. It had been Holly who comforted me later as I cried. Diego, Nina and the entire staff had torn the grounds and the mansion apart on the off chance that Willow was either sleepwalking or hiding.

She wasn't.

One of the responding officers to our 911 call was Lexie Bishop. I sat numbly on the couch in the library of the Drake mansion, holding Willow's favorite babydoll, and answering the same questions over and over again.

When was the last time you saw your daughter?

What had she been wearing?

Could her father have anything to do with her disappearance?

Did you leave the door unlocked when you went outside in the morning?

"I got ahold of Dad," Julian's quiet voice had me focusing on him for the first time in hours. "He is chartering a private plane. He, Duncan and Autumn will all be home in less than two hours."

I nodded, remembering that they'd all gone to a big home improvement show in Chicago. "Tell him, thank you," I said, my voice raspy from crying.

"They're all coming home as fast as they can," Julian said, giving my shoulder a bolstering squeeze.

I nodded, not trusting myself. I was afraid if I opened my mouth I'd start screaming. It was brutally hard to sit and wait while the police did their jobs. What I wanted to do was get up and run, or drive around looking all over William's Ford until I found my daughter.

Forensics had taken over the cottage, and the poppet had been bagged as evidence. We'd all been relocated to the main house and kept out of the way.

At the moment, Ivy Bishop was standing at the teacart that one of the Drake's staff had kindly brought in and was making a cup of tea. Holly sat beside me on the couch, with her arm tight around my shoulders. Diego and Wyatt were standing, speaking in low voices to yet another detective across the room.

Lexie Bishop pulled a chair up across from me. "Maggie," she said. "I know it's hard, but I want you to go over everything with me, one more time."

Silently, I nodded my head.

"When was the last time you saw Willow?" Lexie's voice was brisk, business like.

I clutched the babydoll closer to my chest. "When I

went to bed the night before."

"What time was that, Maggie?" Lexie asked.

"Ten-thirty maybe…eleven," I said.

"You didn't see her this morning when you got up?"

"No," I said. "I let her sleep so I could get some work done." I covered my eyes with my hand. "I didn't check on her when I got up...What kind of mother doesn't check on her own child when she gets up?"

"Maggie," Lexie pulled my hand away from my face. "Stop that."

"Oh my god. This is my fault." I whispered, my voice breaking. "I was trying to get some work done." I heard my own voice as if from far, far away. "I didn't check on her when I got up, Lexie."

"That's not unusual." Lexie said, briskly. "I creep past Morgan John's room all the time, hoping he'll sleep in."

"I thought she was still sleeping," I said. "Oh, god. This is all my fault."

"No, it's not." Lexie's voice was tough. "Maggie, the other detective is finally out of the room. I need you to tell me more about the runes, and how you found that poppet of Willow."

"I took pictures of them all," I said, passing Lexie my phone.

"That was when I'd called her," Holly said, telling Lexie about her part of being at the cottage that morning.

I held Willow's doll closer to me. It helped

somehow, making everything feel far away, or foggy. I was having trouble focusing on Lexie's questions. Deep inside my intuition screamed at me to figure it out...but I couldn't.

Lexie rested her hand on mine, "Maggie," I heard her say. "Maggie, can you hear me?"

All I could do was stare at her.

I flinched when Ivy jerked Willow's babydoll from me. She pulled it out of my arms, tossed it to the floor, and promptly shoved a mug of tea under my nose. "Drink this," she said brusquely.

"Oh. Thank you, Ivy," I said, but couldn't do anything other than sit there, holding the mug.

"Maggie." Ivy bent down until she was at eye level. She snapped her fingers in front of my face, and I didn't even react.

"Julian, are you seeing this?" Holly's voice sounded alarmed.

"Maggie?" Julian knelt down in front of me. "Maggie can you hear me?"

I could but it seemed like too much trouble to answer.

"Hey!" Ivy was suddenly back in my line of vision, putting the mug to my lips. "Drink your god-damn tea, Maggie, or I'll pour it down your throat!"

Shocked at her harsh tone, I automatically took a sip. As soon as I swallowed, I felt the warmth, and it wasn't from the liquid. It was *magick*. "What have you done?" I asked.

"Keep going," Ivy said between her teeth.

"Julian," Holly said. "Help her."

I felt Julian mercilessly grab the back of my head, while Ivy tipped the mug to my mouth.

"Drink all of the potion," Ivy said to me. "We need you to snap out of it. Willow needs you."

I had no choice other than to swallow. I started to struggle and suddenly realized that Ivy was using her magick to force my compliance—and it was either drink the potion, or choke on it.

Only after I'd chugged the entire contents did they release me. "Damn it!" I swore and the mug dropped to the carpeted floor. "What are you playing at?" I coughed. "My daughter is missing. This is no time to be using magick on me against my will!"

Ivy retrieved the mug. "You didn't give us much of a choice."

Julian stayed kneeling down in front of me. "Maggie." He gave my hands a brisk squeeze. "If you want to find your daughter quickly, then I suggest that you snap out of this fog you're in and help us find Willow."

"What in the hell are you talking about?" I said.

"I'm talking about you using the talents you were born with and putting them to work." He stood and crossed his arms. "Stop acting like a victim, Magnolia, and start thinking like a Witch."

I'd have been less shocked if he would have slapped me. "What did you say to me?"

"You heard me." Julian cocked an eyebrow. "It's time to stop feeling sorry for yourself, and face the truth."

"Which is?"

"Perhaps, Maggie, if you'd been more diligent in your practice none of this would have happened."

"*What*?" I asked, incredulously. "Are you crazy?"

"Not one bit. I've been tested." Julian tossed me a mock salute as I sputtered. "You on the other hand have been running from magick most of your adult life. You turned your back on your talents and have tried to pretend you were a mundane for fifteen years."

"But you don't understand—" I began.

"Oh, I understand," Julian interrupted. "You only used magick when you felt you had no choice. It's left you weak, and out of shape as a practitioner."

"Don't push me," I warned, rising to my feet. "You have *no* idea what you're playing with, Julian."

"Ha!" Julian snorted. "Try it! I dare you."

I clenched my fists at my sides literally shaking with anger, and the effort it took to rein my powers in. "Stop it."

"Julian..." Holly's voice was beseeching. "There has to be another way."

Julian ignored Holly and got up in my face. "Poor Magnolia Sutton...Embarrassed by your mother, so you abjured the Craft—trying to hide from it by playing the mundane in the mortal world."

His words were painful, and I averted my face.

Julian kept right on going. "Eventually Magnolia, magick was bound to find you, and Willow unfortunately is the one paying the price for your cowardice."

My head snapped around at being called a coward. "You son of a bitch," I hissed, and the library door slammed shut.

Everyone in the room jumped, except me. I stood there, panting, and fighting like hell against my temper while the magick itched to be set loose.

Julian simply sneered. "The truth hurts? Doesn't it, sugar?"

My blood was pounding in my ears and suddenly, I felt a *snap*. I pushed out with one hand and Julian went shooting across the room. He landed hard in the lounge chair several feet away from where he'd been standing.

While everyone else scrambled back, Julian simply laughed. "Oh, come on Maggie, you can do better than that!" He rose to his feet, straightened the cuff of his shirt, and shot me a contentious look. "Or was that merely a lucky shot?"

With an inarticulate shout of anger, I bunched my right hand together and yanked my fist upward. In response, Julian was pulled off his feet and left to dangle in mid-air, directly in front of Diego, Nina, the baby, and Wyatt.

"You condescending asshole," I snarled. "Don't you speak to me that way. Not *ever*!"

Even as he swayed in mid-air, Julian deliberately

yawned. "You should really try and put some effort into it, Maggie."

"Don't hurt him, Maggie!" Holly said.

"Nina," I said, through my teeth. "Take the baby from the room."

"No," Nina said calmly, as Isabel squealed and clapped. "We're all staying."

"Shit." I heard Lexie's voice from behind me. "I'm going to be pissed if I have to taser somebody."

Julian began to laugh again, and the sound had me seeing red. I stalked over to stand directly underneath him. "*Shut your damn mouth!*" I snarled, even as Julian went closer to the high ceiling.

"And...there you are." Julian sounded immensely satisfied as he smirked down at me. "So all those stories I heard about Magnolia Sutton were true after—" his words were cut off by my will.

"Not another word." I gritted out. "Do you want me to completely lose control?"

"I'm *trying* to get you to tap into what powers you have." Julian managed to say, even as his face began to turn purple.

"Maggie." Holly's hand on my arm was gentle. "Let him go. He's only trying to help you."

"Back off!" I warned her.

"This is totally bad-ass," Ivy cheered. "You go girl!"

"Shut up, Ivy!" Lexie shouted.

"You do understand what he's trying to do, don't you, Maggie?" Holly said, reasonably. "Hurting him won't help a thing."

Ivy chuckled. "It sure is satisfying to watch, though."

I felt the anger begin to recede and my magick slipped a tiny bit. Julian began to drop down from the ceiling inch by inch.

"Holy mother of god..." Wyatt's voice came from across the library. It was soft, a little fearful, and it snapped me back.

What the hell was I doing? I wondered, glancing around the room. Julian's feet were still dangling a few inches above the floor, and my handsome cousin was an alarming shade of purple. Nina and Diego stood holding their baby and their faces were set and watchful. Lexie was at attention waiting to see if she'd have to intervene. Ivy and Holly stood next to me, trying to talk me down, and Wyatt had backed away from me as far as he could get.

"My god," I breathed, and the red haze that I'd seen vanished just as quickly as it had appeared.

Purposefully, I opened my hand and Julian dropped down to the floor. He landed with a graceless thud.

"Julian!" Holly rushed to his side.

"I'm so sorry, Julian," I said, staggering toward the sofa. "I've never in my life done something that violent before..."

"I pushed you," Julian rasped as he regained his feet. "Guess I had it coming for goading you into it."

"You took an awful risk, Julian," Holly chided, and

had to steady him when he wobbled.

"It worked," Julian pointed out, and managed to grin.

"It's not a game!" I said gripping the back of the couch for support. "I could have killed you!"

"I don't think so. There's no real cruelty in you," Julian said, examining his shirtsleeve. "You did however tear my shirt. Damn, it was Burberry."

"I think I'd like a drink." Wyatt walked directly to the brandy Thomas kept by the fireplace. He was sickly pale, as he pulled out a decanter, poured himself a glass, and downed it.

"Speaking of drinks..." Ivy's voice was bright and cheerful. "How'd you like that tea I gave you, Maggie?"

"That wasn't tea!" I said to her. "I can still feel it roaring through me."

"Chamomile," Ivy said, blithely. "Works like a charm."

"Chamomile, my ass!" I hissed. "You used magick on me!"

"I had some help," Ivy tipped her head towards Nina, who stood with Isabel still on her hip.

"Ah," Nina shrugged. "What can I say? My *avo's* potions never miss a trick."

"Nina!" I gasped. "How could you!"

Diego took Isabel from her mother's arms. "You're up, Nina," he said and wisely moved himself out of the range of fire.

Nina walked over, planted her hands on her hips, and went toe-to-toe with me. "It was either spell you out of it, or I could have slapped you out of it."

"Personally, I was down for the slapping," Ivy chimed in.

"I don't understand," I said rubbing my hands over my face. "This isn't a game, what were all of you thinking?"

Ivy reached out, giving my shoulder's a brisk shake. "Don't you understand, Maggie? We think you were spelled!"

"Specifically the doll you've been clutching for the past few hours," Nina explained.

"The doll was spelled?" I shook my head, as the last of the potion rushed through my system like wildfire. "Aw hell, I think I'm going to throw up," I said.

"No you won't," Nina said, gripping my shoulder. "Ride it out, my friend."

Whatever they'd given me was working because once the roaring in my ears subsided, everything was suddenly, horribly clear.

I blinked several times and saw the room around me with absolute clarity. Yes, I was terrified, and *yes*, I was still heartbroken. However, the horrible debilitating fog that had descended over me when I'd seen that smear of Willow's blood, had lifted.

I had an enemy and I knew *exactly* who it was.

"Where's Leilah?" I asked them all.

"We don't know." Lexie said.

"Well, you better hope to whatever god is listening that you find her before I do," I shot back.

"A BOLO has been issued," Lexie said calmly.

I turned to regard Ivy and Nina. "Thank you both. I don't know what you used on me, but I'm thinking clearly again."

"You're welcome," they said together.

"Julian," I called to him and waited until he looked my way. "Thank you."

"Of course." He nodded.

"I'm going to take Wyatt down to the family kitchen," Diego said, and passed Isabel to Ivy's waiting arms. "I think he needs a break from all of this." Wyatt went along with Diego without saying a word. He kept his face averted, never even looking at me.

"I guess I'd better go with them," Julian said. "Wyatt has never seen magick like that before. He'll surely have some questions."

Slowly I walked around the sofa and sat my butt down. With a shuddering breath, I leaned my head back against the cushions. "Good god. Wyatt." I shut my eyes against the reality of him witnessing my magick. "He's never going to look at me the same way again, will he?"

"Personally, you impressed the hell out of me," Ivy said.

I opened my eyes. "Will any of you ever look at me the same way?"

Before anyone could comment, Isabel began to fuss.

Nina took her daughter from Ivy, saying that she needed to go feed the baby. She too exited the room, and Ivy trailed along asking whether or not Nina would let her see her grandmother's spell book.

"Lexie?" Holly said to the blonde. "Do you think you could give Maggie and I a few moments alone?"

"Sure." Lexie nodded. "I'm going to head back over to the cottage. See if the team has any new information."

I waited until it was only the two of us, and I raised my eyes slowly to Holly. "I'm very sorry," I began.

Holly nodded. "I know you are."

"What the hell do we do now?" I asked her.

Holly started to sit beside me, and as she did, she accidentally brushed against Willow's babydoll. Her color drained away, and I thought for a moment she would faint.

"Holly!" I called her name in alarm.

Holly dropped beside me and was shaking, hard. "Wait," she said through her teeth. "I'm seeing something..."

As I watched, my cousin kept contact with the doll. She purposefully leaned her leg against the doll and focused. The effort it took her to be in contact with the doll was visible. She began to tremble and sweat popped out on her lip. With a ragged gasp, she pulled away from the doll, and started to pitch forward on the sofa.

"Hey!" I caught her before she face planted.

"I had a psychic vision." Holly shuddered.

"What did you see?" I demanded.

"Willow." Holly gulped in air. "I saw and *felt* Willow."

As I gripped Holly's shoulders, I looked deep into her eyes and in a flash—her vision became mine.

In a jumble of emotions and a quick flash of images, it passed. When it was over, I shook my head and found that Holly was gripping my arms every bit as hard as I'd latched onto hers.

"I know where she is," I said.

Holly nodded. "Leilah took Willow to the barn on the McBriar property."

I jumped to my feet. "I'm going, right now," I said, running for the door. "I'm not waiting for the cops. I'm going to go get my daughter."

"Wait!" Holly hissed, running after me.

"I won't wait!" I whispered furiously. "Don't you dare try and stop me!"

"I'm not," Holly said, urgently. "I'm coming with you." She grabbed my hand. "You may need backup."

Without another word the two of us slipped down the hall, and I led the way out a side door. Once we cleared the house we went running through the dusky light, heading for the family garage.

"Take Julian's car," Holly suggested. "He leaves the keys in the glove box."

"Good idea." I ran toward the black Mustang. Holly shoved open the garage door and I started up the car.

The engine rolled over with a powerful purr. I shifted the car into gear and rolled forward, pausing only long enough for Holly to hop inside.

"Let's go," she said, buckling herself in.

I nodded and steered the car to the end of the driveway. I pulled onto the street and kept to the speed limit, as to not draw any undue attention to ourselves. Once we cleared the neighborhood, I stomped on the accelerator.

CHAPTER TWELVE

Julian's sports car hugged the roads and allowed me to drive much, much faster than I normally would have dared. With a summer storm brewing to the west, I drove like a woman on a mission...and I was.

Holly had been silent during the trip until we reached the entrance to the McBriar Wedding barn. That's when we both saw that the fancy, decorative gate for the wedding barn was closed. I tightened my grip on the steering wheel, punched the gas anyway, and drove right through the wooden gate.

"God damn!" Holly's breath exploded out much the way the gate had.

Gravel shot out from beneath the tires of the car as I raced to the top of the drive. The car came skidding to a stop, spinning to the side like a stunt in some cop movie, and I barely took the time to put it in park before jumping out and running full steam toward the closed barn doors.

Willow was inside. *I knew it!* I grabbed the metal

decorative handle on the door and got a nasty burn. "Shit!" I jumped back and shook out my hand. "What was that?"

Holly went forward with her palms up and out in front of her. Sensing the exterior of the door from a few inches above the surface. "It's another spell," she said. "A barrier spell, and it's designed to keep people out."

I'd never run across anything like that before. I shook out my hand again, suddenly noticing that what I'd thought had been a burn on my hand, wasn't a burn at all. I'd cut myself, and blood was dripping from my fingers and into my palm.

"Now this, I can use," I said, half to myself.

"What are you thinking?" Holly asked.

"That this is no time to be squeamish," I said. My stomach lurched as I considered my options. *While blood magick was a line I had never wanted to cross, it would practically guarantee my success in getting past the barrier.*

I told Holly to stand clear, took a few precious seconds and dug down deep. Chanting under my breath, I began to raise power. I lifted my bloody hand and pit my magick against the barrier spell. "By my will, by my blood; this barrier will fall. By my will, by my blood; this barrier will fall!" I chanted.

Pressing the palm of my hand squarely against the center of the barn door, I repeated the spell for the third time. I pushed my magick against Leilah's, using all the love I felt for my daughter, and the barn door suddenly went flying back.

The implosion from the displacement of the spell's energy hit me right in my solar plexus. I staggered back, and the barn door shot off to one side, landing with a thud.

Holly and I jumped forward together, and as soon as we stepped inside the barn, all the decorative lights strung across the rafters of the reception space exploded with loud pops. Sparks shot and rained down and I ducked automatically. Whatever enchantment had been placed on the barn, I'd just blown past it.

"Willow!" I called out racing through the main level, but saw no sign of my little girl. Holly and I ran around for a few moments checking bathrooms, closets, and the office, but we found nothing.

"The balcony?" Holly said, pointing to the back stairs.

I spotted the staircase to the second floor and ran directly toward it. I clattered up the stairs, and there I found Willow lying on her back, off to one side of the balcony. "Willow!" I screamed, running straight to her.

I reached for my girl and she was stiff and cold to the touch. For a horrible second I imagined the worst. "No!" I gasped, and quickly pressed my ear to her chest. Thankfully, I heard a heartbeat.

"Let me see." Holly dropped beside me.

"Baby?" My voice broke as I took her small face in my hands. "Honey, can you hear me?"

"Her heartbeat is strong, but her breathing is wrong."

Holly said with her hands on Willow's chest. "It's too rapid and shallow."

"We need to get her to a hospital," I said.

"Well, well..." Leilah Martin Drake's voice echoed across the loft. "If it isn't my lucky day? I've got two birds with one stone." Her high heels clicked against the wooden floor, and the long dark skirt of her dress swished as she strutted out from the far corner.

I angled myself protectively in front of Willow. "What have you done to my daughter?"

"It's only a spell. Not that I'd expect you to understand." Leilah grinned.

"Release her!"

"Not until you and I have a chat," she said, casually brushing at her short hair. "By the way, Holly, you've leveled up. I'm almost impressed with you getting past the spells I had on this place."

"Go to hell, Leilah!" Holly snapped.

I reached back blindly for Holly's hand. When I found it I gripped it hard. "Stay with Willow."

"I think I can undo her magick, but I need some time." Holly's voice was low. "Try and stall her as long as you can."

I squeezed Holly's fingers in recognition of her words, and stood to face my adversary.

"Cousin Maggie from Louisiana," Leilah purred. "I've been wanting to find a way to have a heart-to-heart with you."

I took a few steps closer. "Well, sugar, here I am."

"In all your glory." Leilah rolled her eyes. "Seriously, you went out of the house wearing an old college t-shirt and those shorts?"

"I'm a simple woman," I said. "I didn't dress for the occasion as carefully as you obviously have." I stood with my feet planted, and my heart was pounding as my magick began to build and roll inside of me, once again.

Leilah tapped her finger to her cheek. "You know, I can't decide if you're either the bravest mundane I've ever met, or an idiot. Most mundanes would have run screaming for the hills by now."

"What do you want, Leilah?" I asked. "Why did you take Willow?"

"Oh my god. How *stupid* are you?" Leilah tossed up her hands. "You brought this all on yourself! I told you weeks ago to leave town. But did you listen? No. Instead, you stayed." Leilah began to pace back and forth as she shouted. "You've been living in the cottage my father promised to me! You think you can replace me? Take *my* inheritance, *my* birthright? Thomas is *my* father, the Drakes are *my* family—not yours!"

While Leilah had been on her rant I'd been silently continuing to build energy. Feeling my power rise up within me, I fought hard to keep it under control...

Until I needed to let it go.

I crossed my arms, trying to hide that I was practically vibrating with magick. Once she wound down from her tirade, I tipped my head as if considering her. "So you're jealous, is that it?"

"Jealous?" Leilah was shaking with rage.

Good, I thought. *Lose control. It will only make it easier to turn your own magick against you...* "Oh, I see," I said, "you're simply feeling threatened."

"Threatened?' Leilah threw back her head and laughed. "Of you? A mundane like you wouldn't stand a chance against a Witch like me!"

Unfazed by her theatrics I got right up in her face. "Release my daughter. Now."

"I'd step back if I were you," Leilah said. "Don't make me break out the darker magicks...because I will."

"You wanna see *darker* magicks, sugar?" I asked. "You sure as hell came to the right place." I smiled, and with a flick of my fingers; I sent Leilah flying. She bounced off the far wall of the balcony with a bang and fell in a crumble to the loft floor.

Leilah pushed herself upright, shook her head, and spat out blood. She stared at me with very large eyes. "How did you..."

"It wasn't Holly who broke through your barrier spell," I said, softly. "It was me."

"You?" Leilah blinked. "I don't understand."

"You need another demonstration, sugar?" I pointed to the opposite side of the barn and she went screaming through the air again. This time I kept her pinned to the wall and let her think about the precariousness of her current situation.

"I trust you are starting to put it all together." I called over to her, watching as her eyes bugged out in fear. "It sure would hurt an awful lot if I let you fall this time, Leilah." I smiled when she glanced down and gasped. "That's a good two story drop to the dance floor. Potentially fatal," I added.

"I'm sorry!" she shrieked. "I made a mistake."

"Oh well, shoot," I said, mildly. "Ain't that a cryin' shame?" I pointed to the ceiling next and Leilah shot upward to be pinned to the rafters. I left her dangling there, face down.

"I didn't realize you were a Witch!" Leilah screamed.

"And now that you know?" I asked coolly.

"Shit, I'm *sorry*!" Leilah began to cry. "It's a simple spell, I can wake her up. Please don't kill me! It was supposed to be a joke."

"A joke?" I repeated. "I sure as hell ain't laughing." I was however, starting to shake from the effort of holding her in place, and against gravity. Before I lost control, I pointed to the balcony floor at my feet, and sent Leilah airborne again. She hit the floor hard in a tangle of skirts, and skidded for several feet. "Get up, Leilah," I said, coldly.

Leilah was slower gaining her knees this time. "I can fix it," she said, holding up her hands, pleading. "I promise. She'll be fine!"

"Remove the spell, now!" I said stalking toward her.

Leilah scrambled over toward Willow on her knees. "It was all supposed to be a joke, ya know? I just meant to scare you. She's only under a thrall. I promise you, the kid is—"

I focused on Leilah's face and watched as she grabbed at her own throat. "No more excuses," I warned. "Release her. Before I lose my temper."

Leilah nodded and I allowed the pressure to lessen. She sucked in a huge gulp of air, knelt beside Willow, and lifted her hands.

Holly snagged Leilah by the wrist. "Don't you physically touch her! If I sense *anything* I don't like, I'll kick your ass," Holly warned Leilah.

Leilah nodded, and immediately passed her hands in the air several inches above Willow, as she lay unmoving and cold on the floor.

"Holly?" I asked.

"Willow's moving, Maggie!" Holly said, excitedly. "She's starting to wake up."

Only once I saw that Willow was indeed moving, did I allow the rest of the pressure on Leilah's throat to ease up.

She sucked in air loudly. "There. You see?" Leilah rasped. "No worries. I fixed it for you." She reached for Willow's shoulder. "The kid will be fine."

"Don't you touch her!" Holly blocked the touch and pushed out with both of her hands. Her magick sent Leilah sliding away and across the balcony floor. Leilah came to a stop when first her backside, and then her head thumped loudly against the balcony railing.

"Hey, I said I was *sorry*!" Leilah whined, wiping the back of her hand nervously over her mouth.

"It's too late for apologies, Leilah," I said, adding my own magick to keep her pinned in place. "The damage has already been done."

Leilah began to struggle against the magickal restraints. "I had *no idea* you were a practitioner," she said.

"Well, now you do," I said, walking toward her.

Leilah cringed away from me. "Please, Maggie." Her voice took on a placating tone. "This has all been a big misunderstanding."

"Understand this," I said, pulling up power that had Leilah shooting upright and leaving her toes barely brushing the floor. "You fucked with the wrong Witch."

"I'm so sorry," she managed to sputter.

"Release her from the thrall, completely," I said. "I want to see my daughter awake and healthy."

"Okay, okay..." Leilah said, and started to chant quietly.

I watched Leilah's face, never taking my eyes from her. "Holly?" I called over.

"Willow's warmer now, Maggie," Holly said. "Her breathing is stronger, and she's waking up!"

"See?" Leilah said after a moment. "I told you, the kid will be fine."

I allowed Leilah's feet to settle back to the floor. "For your sake," I said, "you better pray that she is."

Leilah staggered a bit. "I promise, She'll be fine. No harm done."

"No harm?" I asked incredulously. "Leilah Martin

Drake." My voice echoed with power as I called her by her full name. "Blood daughter of Thomas Drake, half-sister to Julian. I bind you *and* your powers."

Leilah's eyes went wide. She tried to back away, but came up short against the railing.

"I make this vow before the old Gods." I reached over and yanked a lock of her hair out.

"*Ow!*" Leilah screamed.

I held the hair aloft. "Leilah Martin Drake, you will *never* use magick to harm or to terrorize anyone, ever again. If you're foolish enough to try; your magick will turn immediately against you."

Leilah pressed a hand to the side of her head in shock. "You pulled out my hair!"

"I have your hair *and* your flesh, now," I said, looking at the tiny patch of scalp that had torn free. "You like to play with dark magick? Oh, honey, let me demonstrate how this shit *really* works." I squeezed the hair and skin tight in my own hand and watched as she dropped to her knees, screaming painfully in reaction.

Horror clear on her face, Leilah tried to stand, but ended up leaning heavily against the railing. "You shouldn't be able to do that!"

"I just did." I leaned in close to her. "I own you now, Leilah. Try and come after me, my child, my family, or *anyone* in this town, and the retribution will be brutal and swift."

"I'll find a way," Leilah swore defiantly, as she drew herself upright. "No matter what! I'll take all of you down. You, your stupid kid, my father, *all* of you!"

"Then you will fall by your own hand." The words had barely left my mouth when I heard a loud crack. Before I could blink, the railing behind Leilah gave way, and she fell backward screaming.

I did not try and save her.

The thud Leilah's body made hitting the barn floor below was punctuated by a roll of thunder. As rain began to fall on the barn roof, I took a deep breath, and let any residual magick drain from me. Tucking the swatch of hair and skin in my short's pocket, I stepped closer to the edge of the balcony to look.

Holly raced to my side and peered down with me. "Is she dead?"

I studied the young woman lying so still on the barn floor. She was flat on her back, arms akimbo, and one of her legs was bent at a hideous angle. "No," I said, after a moment. "She seems to still be breathing." As we watched Leilah twitched and moaned.

"Well, here's hoping she keeps breathing. Because I'm sure as hell not giving that bitch, mouth-to-mouth." Holly's voice was dry as toast.

"Mama?" Willow called out in a shaky voice.

"I whipped my head around. "Baby?"

Willow sat up rubbing her eyes. "Where are we?"

"Willow!" I ran to my daughter, gathered her up in my arms, and held on.

"S'ok, mama." Willow's teeth were chattering. "Did I sleepwalk again?"

"I love you baby," I said, holding her chilly body to me tightly. "I love you so much."

"Love you too, Mama." Willow burrowed against me. "I'm cold."

"I can help with that," Holly came over and rested the palm of her hand against Willow's head. In seconds, Willow's teeth stopped chattering.

"I'm hungry." Willow's complaint had Holly chuckling.

As for me, after hearing her words *and* the normalcy in them, I dropped my head to my daughter's shoulder and wept in relief.

***

Holly called the police from the office in the barn, and when help arrived Leilah Martin Drake was still alive. Once the authorities and emergency services descended, I refused to allow Willow back down the stairs of the barn's balcony until Leilah was removed.

No one argued that point with me.

Of course, both Holly and I were interviewed by the police. Fortunately, because Holly and my stories matched, and since Leilah appeared to have fallen on her own, the investigation didn't go any farther. I'm not sure if Lexie Bishop had a hand in that, or perhaps it was due to the Drake family's influence with the locals...Either way I was relieved.

No one was very happy that I'd taken off on "a

hunch" to confront the kidnapper on my own. But they were thrilled with Willow being found unharmed. She rode to the hospital in an ambulance, and Holly and I accompanied her. The ride delighted Willow, and thoroughly stressed me out.

Sitting beside Willow, all I could think about was how much worse it could have been. It didn't matter that my girl was chattering up a streak, or that she was waving at Holly who was riding shotgun in the front with the driver. All my mind could do was circle with a thousand, *what ifs*?

Once we arrived at the hospital the family was waiting *en masse*. Julian walked right into the treatment room, ignored the nurses and doctor who were checking out Willow, and grabbed me up in a big hug. "God damn it, Maggie!"

"I'll pay for any damage to your car," I said.

"I couldn't care less about the damn car." His voice was shaking. "You scared me." Julian pulled back, holding me at arms length, and frowned down in my face. "Don't run off and play hero alone. Not ever again."

"I wasn't alone." I patted his arm. "I had back up."

"It was my idea to take your Mustang," Holly admitted with a small smile.

"Jesus, Holly," Julian reached out to tug one of her long red curls. "Why am I not surprised?"

Holly leaned over, tipping her face up to his. They were just about to kiss when Ivy waltzed right in.

"There you are!" she crowed, causing Holly and Julian to jump apart.

"Hey, Ivy—" I began only to be cut off when she pulled me into a hug that was so hard my breath whooshed out

"I can't wait to hear how you took down Leilah!" she whispered fiercely in my ear. "So fucking proud of you!" She stepped back. "I'm very glad you and Willow are safe," she said in a conversational tone. "There's my favorite munchkin!" she said, going over to drop a loud smacking kiss on Willow's cheek.

Willow giggled. "Hi Ivy! I rode in an ambulance!"

"Was it fun?" Ivy asked with a cheeky grin. "Did they turn on the siren for you?"

"Yeah!" Willow giggled. "It was *loud*!"

"Ms. Parrish," the doctor began, "I must insist that your family vacate the treatment room for a few moments..."

I shooed everyone out, and the ER doctor assured me a short time later that besides some scrapes and bruises, Willow was fine. He was happy to let her go home, and all things considered, she was bouncing back remarkably well.

Lexie Bishop and a representative from children's services did speak to Willow before she was discharged. I understood with an abduction that processing all the evidence wouldn't be quick or simple, however the police did their best to keep things easy and non-stressful for Willow.

Bottom line, while there wasn't any repercussion from law enforcement over the way things had gone down...that didn't mean there wouldn't be any in regards to how my family would feel about it all. I bit my lip fretting over what Thomas would say to me, but even though Julian told me he'd returned to William's Ford, Thomas never came and checked on us while we were in the ER.

A few hours later, after all the paperwork was finished and we'd been discharged, I scooped Willow up and started to carry her out of the ER department.

"Bye!" Willow said, waving to the nurses.

I walked around a corner looking for the exit, only to discover that Thomas was standing with his back to me across the hall. He was in the waiting room, speaking to both the police and the doctors about Leilah.

I stepped back where I could still hear them, but not be seen. Willow felt my tension and went silent.

I clearly heard the doctor tell Thomas that Leilah was still in surgery. She was stable, they said. I heard a police officer inform him that she would be charged with kidnapping. I took a quick peek and saw that Julian was now standing silently with his father, his hand on the man's back. Autumn and Duncan were there as well, lending Thomas their support.

Stuck, I eased farther away, and decided to go in the opposite direction. Holly and Ivy had already gone home, and I wondered if maybe a nurse could call us a cab. I'd taken about three steps before I bumped into

Lexie.

"Need a ride?" she asked before I could.

I accepted gladly. The police officer who drove us back to the cottage was actually Lexie's father. John Proctor informed me that he would be staying in the squad car, keeping an eye on the cottage, for the rest of the night.

"We look out for our own here in William's Ford," was his quiet reply as he opened the front door of the cottage for us.

His kind words had tears pricking my eyes. "Thank you, Officer Proctor." I said, carrying Willow inside.

"Try and rest," he advised. "I'll be parked at the bottom of the driveway if you need anything."

I locked the door and headed for the shower. Willow was thrilled with taking a shower together, and I couldn't stand the thought of her being out of my sight. So it was a win-win. Afterwards, she stood in her fresh pajamas as I dried her hair. I let her climb into my big bed and towel dried my own hair. Finally, I hopped in beside her.

"Come here, you," I said, holding out my arms.

She snuggled up close. "Is that bad girl all gone, Mama?"

I swallowed past a lump in my throat. "Yes, baby," I said.

Willow studied me solemnly with her unique blue and brown eyes. "Are you sure?"

"You don't have to worry." I pressed a kiss to my

daughter's hair. "I made her go away. She won't bother you, or anyone else, ever again. I took care of it."

"Good." Willow nodded.

"Try and sleep now," I said.

Willow fell asleep almost immediately, and I held her protectively close in my arms all night long.

I didn't expect to sleep, not with everything that had happened. I lay awake until dawn staring at the ceiling wondering about the repercussions of the magick I'd unleashed on Leilah.

Mostly, I was worried about Thomas and his reaction to the news of what Leilah had done. The consequences would be serious. She'd obviously do time in jail, and of course there were the injuries she'd sustained from her fall...I had no idea how severe they actually were. Either way, Thomas would be devastated.

I'd have to tell him everything. How I'd used magick against Leilah, that I'd bound her powers...all of it. Once he was aware that I'd unleashed dark magick against her...Well, I'd probably have to find a new place to live. I couldn't imagine Thomas wanting me to stay on the property, living so close by, after I'd maimed his only daughter.

Truth be told, I wasn't sure *I* wanted to live in the cottage anymore, not after everything that had happened here.

When dawn finally broke I got up, and retrieved the chunk of Leilah's hair from my shorts pocket. I put the tiny piece of scalp and attached strands of hair into a sealable freezer bag, dumping salt all over it. The salt had two purposes. It would stop any lingering negativity from Leilah, and it would help dry out and preserve the dime size section of flesh. I hid the bag in a safe place with the hopes that I would *never* have to use it again.

That unpleasant task completed, I washed my hands, crept back in my room, and selected a casual summer weight dress. While Willow slept, I ran a brush through my hair. After brushing my teeth, I went to the kitchen and started a pot of coffee, bracing myself for a very long day.

"Mama!" Willow came bouncing into the kitchen after the first rumble of the coffee pot. "Lexie's daddy stayed in our driveway all night long!"

"He did?" I asked around a yawn.

Willow ran to the living room window. "He's still there!" She waved wildly.

"He said he would stay and watch over us." Impressed, I pulled a mug down out of the cabinet. "Let's go take him a cup of coffee."

A couple of moments later I carried the mug down the driveway to John Proctor, with Willow skipping beside me. When he saw us coming he climbed out of the squad car and stretched. "Morning, ladies." He smiled.

"Thank you." I passed him the mug.

"Mama says you watched over us last night." Willow said.

He drank deeply and ruffled Willow's hair. "Well, after all your excitement I figured your Mom might sleep better if she knew you were both safe."

I flashed a smile but said nothing.

"But," John continued, "I can see she didn't sleep."

"Not a wink," I said.

"Give it some time," John said kindly. "After Lexie was hurt and in the hospital a few years ago...Neither her mother and I slept for days afterward. Didn't matter that she was grown, married, and with a baby of her own. Parents worry."

"Hey, Mama!" Willow chirped. "Thomas is here!" Willow's happy words had me jolting, even as she took off like a shot.

I shifted to watch as Thomas chuckled in obvious delight while Willow ran full-out toward him. "How's my best girl?" he asked, scooping her up and pressing a kiss to her forehead.

My stomach lurched, hard. I guessed the big confrontation would be this morning. *God,* I thought. *I didn't want to have to move to a different city, again.* Watching Willow with Thomas, I knew it would hurt her to be parted with the man she had come to think of as a grandfather.

"Have you spoken to Thomas yet?" John asked in a low voice. "About what happened?"

"No," I whispered. "He was with Leilah at the emergency department, and then waiting for her to come out of surgery last night." I took a careful breath.

"Did she survive the surgery?"

"She did." John rested a hand on my arm. "According to my information, she has a spinal injury and a severely broken leg."

God almighty, I thought. *Thomas will surely hate me.* Doing my best to keep my tone of voice neutral, I cleared my throat before speaking to Officer Proctor. "Will she walk again?"

"I don't know anything about that. All I *can* tell you officially is that the DA is going ahead and pressing charges for kidnapping."

"Good." My gaze swung uncertainly toward Thomas, and I jumped a foot up in the air when I felt a gentle hand on my arm from John Proctor.

"Give Thomas a chance, Maggie. He may surprise you." John passed me his almost empty mug and a business card. "If you need anything. Anything at all. Here's my number."

"Thank you," I murmured, slipping the card in my pocket. I sincerely hoped I wouldn't need to call.

John gave me a smile and strolled back to the squad car. With a wave he started it up and left as Willow and Thomas walked over hand-in-hand.

"Good morning, Thomas," I said, formally.

"Good morning." He stood there, in a fancy polo shirt, summer slacks, and shielding his emotions. Even I could tell that. With his silver hair waving in the breeze, the man seemed more remote to me than ever before.

I felt seriously outclassed, standing barefoot in the grass wearing an old summer dress and no makeup. "We should talk—"

"Can Thomas stay for breakfast?" Willow cut me off.

"Oh." I glanced quickly at him. He'd always been quiet and reserved, but today, his face gave absolutely nothing away. "He's probably busy..."

"No," he said, calmly. "I happen to have this morning free."

"Please, Mama?" Willow begged. "Can he stay?"

"Of course." I forced cheer into my voice but my smile was strained as I followed them both inside. *It was after all his house. How could I say no?*

I kept myself busy, scrambling some eggs, and toasting bread. Willow's non-stop chatter filled up what I'm sure would have been a very awkward silence. I scooped up the eggs onto plates, added the toast and served Thomas and Willow who were seated at the drop leaf table.

We were both so polite to each other that it made me a nervous wreck. I couldn't eat a thing. I merely pushed the eggs around on my plate instead of eating them. Finally Willow went to her room to change out of her pajamas, and I found myself alone with Thomas.

"I'm sorry," we said simultaneously.

"You have nothing to apologize for." Thomas said seriously. "I knew that Leilah was troubled, but I never would have guessed she'd take things to this level."

"You should know," I began. "I used magick against your daughter yesterday."

Thomas nodded. "Yes, I know. Holly told Julian, and he shared it with me."

"It was dark magick, Thomas," I said. "The type I learned from my mother. The kind of ruthless magick that I had sworn to put behind me for the rest of my life." I took a moment to steady myself. "But it was my only real option for making Leilah remove the thrall she had over Willow."

"I'm sure you did what you felt was necessary," he said gravely.

"I won't apologize for it." I said, folding my hands on the table and meeting his eyes. "And I'd do it in again in a heartbeat if it meant keeping my child safe."

"I would expect nothing less from you."

I did a double take at his words. He'd almost sounded proud.

"Yesterday, you stood up for your daughter, did what had to be done, and owned your power." Thomas placed one of his hands over mine. "I'm *very* proud of you, Maggie."

"Oh." Was about all I could manage, as I struggled not to cry.

"As to you continuing to live in the cottage," he said, "I find that unacceptable."

My heart sank, but before I could speak, Thomas was continuing.

"There's been far too many hexes and curses laid

against this cottage. It's been broken into twice, even after I had security updated. So it makes sense to me that you and Willow should move into the mansion, permanently. With the rest of the family, where you rightfully belong."

I blinked. "Where we belong?"

"Exactly," Thomas said, giving my hand a brisk pat. "I would certainly feel better, not to mention, sleep much easier, if I could keep an eye on the *both* of you, myself. Plus it would certainly be more convenient to continue your training there."

"My training?" I'd been reduced to parroting his words, I was so caught off guard by the turn of events.

"Absolutely, you have the makings of a fine magician, my dear. According to Julian, you have remarkable gifts." He paused and leaned forward. "Did you really send him up to the ceiling?"

"Yes, I did," I said. "He was goading me into to trying to lose control at the time,"

Thomas smiled. "I would have like to have seen that."

"It was the first time in fifteen years I let my magick off the chain," I admitted.

Thomas rubbed a hand over his chin. "I see...Tell me, Maggie, do you speak or read Latin?"

"Ah..." I tried to keep up with him. "Nope, no Latin."

"We'll work on that." Thomas gave me a wink. "You know your grandfather Phillip was an excellent magician, he taught me quite a bit."

"He did?"

"Yes," Thomas said, "I still have his journals. I'd love to share with you what he taught me."

Now I began to smile. "I think I'd like that."

"I'm back!" Willow shouted, sliding across the hardwood floor in her stocking feet. "What are we going to do today, Thomas?"

He scooped her up and set her on his knee. "You're going to pack up...Because you and your mother are moving into *my* house. Today."

"Can I bring all my dolls and toys?"

"Absolutely." Thomas nodded.

"Do I get my own bathroom?" Willow asked.

"Of course," Thomas said.

"Can it be pink?"

"Willow!" I warned her. "Maybe you should say *thank you* before you start wheedling to get the bathroom painted in your favorite color."

"Thank you." Willow leaned back and gave Thomas a winsome smile. "I'm gonna want W's on my towels."

"I'm sorry?" Thomas tipped his head in confusion.

"Monograms," I explained. "She wants a W for Willow."

Willow giggled. "That way everyone knows they're mine."

"Are you sure you're ready for all of this?" I asked Thomas. "Pink bathrooms, dolls, and monogrammed towels?"

"Honestly?" he said, "I'm looking forward to it."

"Hooray!" Willow jumped down. "I'm going to go get my stuff!"

CHAPTER THIRTEEN

The rest of our summer passed quietly into fall. Willow and I had indeed moved into the Drake mansion the day after Willow's abduction. It was lovely to settle in with the family and comforting to have them all so close. We were given a set of rooms in the family wing, on the opposite end of the hall from Julian's.

Thomas had invited us to make ourselves at home. So we did. My bedroom had a small attached sitting room, which allowed me to have a television and a love seat so Willow and I could have private time if we wanted it. I was also told to help myself to any guest room on the third floor, for use as an office for my bridal consultant business. I selected a small one and rearranged it to suit my needs.

I redecorated my bedroom in the casual farmhouse style that I preferred. Thomas and Julian hadn't grumbled too much when I asked them to help me haul in an old wrought iron bed from a guest room. Thomas even sat on the floor and helped me put it back together.

Nina, Diego, and I went antiquing with our girls and found a few more rustic, vintage pieces to add to my personal space. Diego and I hauled everything up the stairs, with a lot of good-natured swearing, and put things in place. My rooms do look completely different from the rest of the house's more formal style, but they are my own personal sanctuary...Which, I've come to discover, is vital when you live in a house with several other people, and staff.

Staff...I still am trying to get used to that. While Nina expertly runs the household and the kitchens, I do try and stay out of the way of the staff, as not to add too much to their duties. I was fussed at by one of the maids right after we first moved in. She got upset when she discovered me scrubbing the toilet in my own bathroom. After spending a half hour explaining that *no,* I was not unhappy or dissatisfied with her cleaning skills, I surrendered the toilet brush and promised to never take it upon myself to clean the bathroom again.

At least I let her think that. I still do my own laundry, and I have some cleaning supplies secretly stashed in the closet.

Willow did get her pink bathroom, complete with a set of hot pink monogrammed towels. Julian thought the towels were a riot, until one of the magenta washcloths was accidentally washed with his athletic socks and undershirts. It turned everything *pink*.

Nina had laughed until she cried, and told him it was what he deserved for not doing his own laundry. While the staff member in charge of the Drake's men laundry had apologized profusely, I went out and picked up new packages of undershirts and socks for my cousin.

Willow even gift-wrapped them for him. Julian laughed over his present and promised her that he didn't hold a grudge.

I wished that everyone felt that way.

I wondered how long Wyatt Hastings would hold a grudge. If that's what he was doing. Maybe he was scared, or maybe he was simply no longer interested. He was a quiet, private man, after all. One who'd probably prefer dating an *ordinary* woman—who didn't have so much drama in her life. I had no way to know. I hadn't seen or heard from him since that horrible day.

I was left to wonder, until a few weeks after the abduction. That was when Wyatt finally called and asked to see me. We'd ended up sitting in the family library, and at first it was very awkward.

"I thought it might be best to give you and Willow a few weeks to settle in, after everything that happened," he said as soon as we were seated.

"I see." I folded my hands in my lap and nervously began twisting my sapphire ring.

"I was also finishing a book. There was a tough deadline I was up against, and I tend to shut everything out until I get the book off my desk. Only after it's in the hands of my editor, do I relax and come out of my cave." He smiled slightly. "I wasn't ignoring you, I was simply working."

"If anyone understands schedules and contracts, it's me," I said.

"I heard you were back at work coordinating that carriage house wedding reception, only two days after Willow's return."

I nodded. "I had a contract to fulfill. It's my job. I take it seriously, and their wedding reception went off without a hitch."

He grinned. "I have no doubts that it did."

I considered him as he sat beside me on the couch. Figuring the truth was the best—scratch that—the only way to go, I took a deep breath, and put all my cards on the table telling him about my background. To his credit, he sat and listened to me carefully when I shared what my childhood had been like, and why I'd shunned magick for fifteen years afterward.

"Julian explained some of this to me," he said. "It's a fascinating tale."

"It better not end up in one of your books," I said, half-joking.

His crystal blue eyes were solemn when he took my hand. "Magnolia, I would never do that."

"I hope you're not afraid."

"Of what?" His brows disappeared beneath his mop of hair.

"Of me—because of well, everything."

"Why on earth would I be?" he scoffed. "I consider myself a feminist. I'm not threatened by a strong woman."

"To be fair though, you still don't have any real concept of what I'm truly capable of." I said, trying to explain. "I've been mortally afraid that I might have inherited a penchant for cruelty from my mother." I pressed a hand to my heart. "I still worry about that."

"Why?"

I looked down, unable to meet his eyes. "Because I don't have any sympathy for Leilah's injuries or for the time in prison that she faces. She got what she deserved."

"I happen to wholeheartedly agree with your sentiments," he said. "She spelled and abducted your daughter. She put Willow in harm's way, and there is no coming back from that." He took my hand from my lap and waited until I met his eyes. "I only wish I would have been there to see you take her down."

I shook my head. "You sound like Ivy."

"Look, in my mind, you are like a soldier with specialized combat training."

"How's that?" I asked.

"You wouldn't put an Army Ranger or a Navy SEAL in a situation where they felt they would have to defend themselves or a loved one...Because their training would take over. They are trained to react and to counter violence, or a threat, in a very specific way."

"I suppose that's one way to look at it."

"I thought it was a damn good analogy, myself." Wyatt grinned at me and tossed his dark hair out of his eyes. "Now, come over here for a minute, will you?"

"Why?" I asked.

He gave me a gentle tug. "Because I really want to kiss you, and I've missed seeing your face these past few weeks."

"I missed your face too," I said, leaning forward to meet his kiss halfway.

"Are we okay?" I asked after the kiss.

"You bet we are," he said.

After that conversation, Wyatt and I began seeing each other again. We worked around each other's schedules, my weddings and events, and his book deadlines as best we could for the rest of the summer. A free weekend is rare in the world of event coordinating/ bridal consulting, so we typically saw each other during the week. It worked for us, and Willow is absolutely crazy about him.

Besides a few nightmares, Willow didn't suffer any ill effects from her experience. When she spoke to me about it, she described it all as a bad dream. If she should need more help in the future, I'll get it for her.

Truth be told, Willow is happy as a clam living at the mansion. She loves having Julian close by and Thomas is wonderful with her. In fact, she recently took Thomas to preschool for Grandparent's day.

Technically he's not her grandfather, however he's the closest thing that she has. It made me misty watching them go off hand-in-hand. Plus, I would have paid good money to have seen Thomas sitting at a miniature table doing arts and crafts with all the children and grandparents. According to one of Willow's teachers, he was quite the hit with the other children.

Thomas Drake, it turned out, is a big old softy.

When the September temperatures began to change, swinging dramatically back and forth from hot—to cool —to hot again, Willow came down with an ear infection. I truly don't know who suffered more, Willow or Thomas. He insisted on going along to the pediatrician and I was damn tempted to send the nurses flowers as an apology afterward.

After Willow had been dosed with antibiotics and eardrops, Thomas worked a healing spell on her, which he promptly taught me how to do as well. He says that I am a natural with healing magick.

Thomas was good to his word about training me in magick. For myself, I've found it comforting to learn a magick that is healing and positive, as opposed to strictly defensive and protective. Julian rolled his eyes at me and said I'm an occult overachiever. But despite his teasing, he's always there to answer a question about a spell, or to help me if I need it.

I discussed it with Thomas first, but I ended up trying a recipe in Irene's cookbook. I chose the *Avalon Apple Pie* to invoke the wisdom of my ancestors, and had some wild dreams where I was sitting in the park chatting with my grandfather Phillip Drake.

He seems like he was a wonderful man. I wish I could have met him while he was alive.

I found myself smiling over that thought as I finished changing from my business clothes into casual jeans and a light sweater. I took my hair down from the clip I'd had it in for my meetings with an upcoming October bride and brushed it out to flow down my back.

We'd all been invited to Autumn and Duncan's bungalow to celebrate Autumn's birthday, and the equinox, with a family barbeque. I smiled at the sound of Willow's voice. I could clearly hear her in her room next door to mine. She was talking to her dolls, having a tea party.

I walked over and poked my head in the doorway. "Hey, sugar pie, are you ready to go to the party?"

"I like barbeque!" She jumped to her feet, wearing jeans and an orange sweatshirt featuring a black cat.

I held out my hand. "Me too."

"Mama, can we get a cat?" Willow wanted to know.

"Hmmm," I said. "We'll have to talk to Thomas about that."

"It can stay in my room. I'll take care of it," she said.

We started down the staircase, dodging a few toys. It was common to find dolls and toys on the grand staircase these days, not to mention the huge custom baby gate that was stationed at the bottom. It was placed there as a precaution since Isabel is toddling. Thomas made the staff baby-proof the entire house too. Even the antique tables in the library and living room have safety corners on them now.

We were halfway down the stairs when Julian

arrived home from the museum. He said hello to us as he swung a leg over the gate. He'd gone up a few risers and was in the act of unbuttoning the top buttons of his dress shirt as we passed each other.

"What's that?" I asked, pointing to the collar of the pink stained undershirt peeking out from beneath his fancy designer dress shirt.

He raised his eyebrows. "Sorry, what?"

"Don't play dumb with me," I said. "It doesn't suit that pretty face of yours."

"I don't have a pretty face. You do," he said tugging on a lock of my hair.

I rolled my eyes. "Bullshit." I poked him in the collarbone. "Why are you wearin' that old thing? You're the most fashion-conscious straight man I've ever known."

"Uh-oh, Mama said, *bullshit*," Willow announced with a laugh.

"Don't say that word, sweetie," I corrected automatically.

Julian brushed at an imaginary speck of lint from the sleeve of his tailored gray suit, but he didn't answer.

"Julian..." I rolled my eyes. "I bought you a package of new undershirts several *weeks* ago. Willow even gift wrapped them."

"With a pink ribbon," Willow added.

"I happen to like this undershirt." He shrugged. "It's very comfortable. Now if you'll excuse me, I need to change for the family barbeque."

Thomas stood smiling at the bottom of the stairs and watching our exchange. "Is everyone ready to go?"

"I am!" Willow sang.

"I'll be down in two minutes," Julian called, and hustled up the stairs.

I stood there trying not to laugh as my handsome cousin sauntered off, perfectly comfortable in his pink stained undershirt.

***

Autumn and Duncan's Craftsman style bungalow was absolutely charming. I stood in the cheerful red and white kitchen, helping put a salad together, while Ivy and Holly argued over the best way to assemble a fruit and cheese platter.

My great-aunt Faye wasn't with us today, and while I was secretly relieved that I wouldn't have to put up with her attitude, I did my best not to show it.

"Aunt Faye is off on a six month tour of Europe with Dr. Meyers," Holly told me.

"That's nice," I said, trying to sound like I meant it.

"I bet you five bucks they end up getting married," Ivy said.

Willow chased Morgan through the kitchen, and the two of them were happily screaming with laughter. At the noise and stampeding feet, Autumn's cat dove for cover.

Lexie stood with Belinda on her hip. "Outside, you

two!" She held open the backdoor. "You can scream all you want in the backyard."

Willow grabbed Morgan's hand and they went running right out the door.

Lexie let the screen door slam behind them. "By the goddess. I suppose I have that to look forward to when Belinda is big enough to chase her brother."

"Bye-bye," Belinda waved at her brother through the screen door.

Autumn's calico cat, Luna, came out cautiously from under the kitchen table. "Meow," she cried.

"Poor kitty." I bent and patted her head. "Does anyone know someone who has kittens for adoption? Willow's been pestering me for a cat."

Lexie tossed her head, sending her dark blonde ponytail swinging. "Do you think Thomas would go for that?"

Autumn glanced over from the vegetable tray she was unwrapping. "Please." She rolled her eyes. "He'd do anything for that little girl."

I placed the bowl of salad on the table. "She's right. He's a total sucker for kids."

"I heard he went to Grandparent's Day with Willow at the preschool," Lexie said.

"Awww," Holly sighed. "That's so sweet."

"He truly is wonderful with children," I told them.

Autumn grinned at me. "You know, he hides it pretty well, but the truth is, he's an old softy—" She immediately stopped talking when Thomas opened the backdoor and stepped into the kitchen.

"Ladies." He smiled at everyone. "Duncan says he needs more barbeque sauce."

"Okay." Autumn went to her pantry and came back out with a bottle.

Belinda chose that moment to try her fourteen-month-old wiles on Thomas. She smiled coyly and waved her fingers at him.

"Hello, Belinda," Thomas smiled in return. To everyone's shock, Belinda leaned out of Lexie's arms and reached for Thomas.

Without a blink Thomas took her and hitched the baby on his hip. "If it's alright, Belinda and I will take the sauce outside to Duncan." He waited for Lexie's permission.

"Sure thing." Lexie smiled and reopened the back door for them. "If she gets to be too much, just hand her off to Bran."

Thomas competently straightened the baby's stretchy headband. "We'll be fine, won't we Belinda?"

Belinda's reply was a happy bounce and squeal.

Autumn kept a straight face as she silently passed Thomas the barbeque sauce.

"Bye-bye, Mama," Belinda beamed over Thomas' shoulder as he carried her outside.

The door closed behind them and the kitchen was silent for five humming seconds.

"Told ya," Autumn said with a laugh.

Holly and Ivy collapsed into giggles, Lexie roared

with laughter, and I couldn't help but join in.

"If I wouldn't have seen it, I would have never believed it," Ivy said, wiping her eyes. "The biggest, baddest magician in town is putty in the hands of a blue-eyed baby Witch."

I peeped out the back window and saw that Thomas was currently sitting with Belinda on the glider in the shade. Wyatt sat companionably next to him while Willow and Morgan ran circles around them both. Julian was fishing cold beers out of the cooler and was carrying them over to Duncan and Bran who were working at the grill.

Duncan was turning the chicken, and I could hear Bran through the window. He was cheerfully debating the pros and cons of different types of barbeque sauce with Julian.

Duncan called over his shoulder. "Autumn! We'll be ready to go in five minutes."

"Okay!" she called back through the window.

A short time later, everyone was standing in line at the make-shift buffet, filling their plates. I helped Willow select a chicken leg, and she managed to grab a few carrot sticks to add to her plate. Eventually were all seated at the oversized picnic table in the back.

They were certainly a noisy bunch, I thought as multiple conversations went on around me. *But they were* my *family.* I couldn't honestly remember ever being happier.

Hours later, after the dishes had been washed and the

family sat out across the back lawn, I slipped inside Autumn's house and checked the messages on my cell phone. I had two from the bride I'd met with earlier in the day, she'd finally settled on her program style and font, so I took a few moments and messaged her back.

I tapped a quick note in my phone's calendar, reminding myself to stop by the printer's and get a mockup for the bride to approve. I was slipping my phone back in my pocket when I caught movement out of the corner of my eye. I bit back a startled scream.

The woman stood by the kitchen table, wearing a casual dark blue dress. Despite the lines around her eyes she was a striking. Her hair was silver and her eyes matched the color of her dress precisely. I recognized her from my mother's family albums. It was Irene Bishop, my maternal grandmother.

"Finally," she said. "I've been waiting for a chance to speak to you alone."

"Land sakes!" I pressed a hand to my galloping heart. "Hello, Irene," I managed.

"Don't be so formal!" she said with a laugh. "Come over here and let me get a good look at you."

She appeared corporeal, but as I moved closer I could see a slight shimmer around her. Before I could comment, she leaned forward and studied my features.

"Yes," she said, sounding very satisfied. "You do have my eyes. But you favor your grandfather, Phillip."

"I met him in a dream the other night," I said. "I worked the *Avalon Apple Pie* recipe."

"What did everyone think of it?" she wanted to know. "Did Willow enjoy it?"

"I wouldn't let anyone other than Thomas taste the pie," I explained. "I was worried what affect I it might have on them."

Irene rolled her eyes. "My stars, girl! I wouldn't have enchanted the cookbook for you to find that particular recipe if I thought for one minute it would cause harm to my great-granddaughter."

"Autumn told me that she had a few magickal snafus with your recipes last year," I said. "I thought it best to be cautious."

"Well at least you finally started flexing your magickal muscles a bit."

"Thomas has been training me," I told her.

"That's good." Irene nodded. "After all, your grandfather taught *him*."

"Yes, he told me." I smiled. "Thomas gave me a few of Phillip's grimoires to study."

Irene smiled. "I always knew Thomas would come around someday. Between your grandfather's magick and mine, you'll be a very well-rounded practitioner."

The pride in her words made me feel slightly ashamed. "Maybe," I managed, looking at the floor. "I do hope to be worthy of your legacy of magick, in time."

I felt a slight pressure under my chin and I lifted my face to hers. "Magnolia," she said. "You *are* a worthy successor for my spell book and your grandfathers magick. Don't you doubt that for one minute."

"You don't know what happened this summer."

Irene planted her hands on her hips. "Of course I know! I've got ears, don't I?"

I shook my head. "Wait, what?"

"Holy cats girl, I listened to Autumn and Duncan talk about it for a good week afterward! My blood ran cold hearing them describe how Leilah Martin Drake had abducted my great-granddaughter. Do you have any idea how frustrating it has been being trapped here in this house when I wanted to be with you?"

"I guess I never thought about it like that."

"Now you listen to me." Irene got up in my face. "You defended your child, forced that woman to remove her spell from Willow, and you stopped a dangerous adversary. That's something to be proud of— not ashamed of!"

Duly chastised, I folded my hands at my waist. "Yes, ma'am."

Irene narrowed her eyes. "Don't you *ma'am*, me. You sounded exactly like Taylor when you said that."

"Well, bless your heart, sugar," I drawled in my best imitation of my Grandma Taylor.

Irene threw back her head and laughed. "That's absolutely perfect!" She grinned at me. "I see she passed my ring on to you."

I lifted my hand so the sapphire and diamond ring caught the kitchen light. "On my graduation day."

"I made her promise to give it to you, and not

Patricia."

I nodded. "What happened to Mama that made her go dark?"

Irene sighed. "Patricia was made aware of her adoption when she turned eighteen. She'd known me most of her life as her mother's best friend—an honorary aunt. The day I sat and spoke to her about her birth father, and the reasons why we had given her up… well let's say that it didn't go well."

"I can guess," I said wryly. "Mama had been horribly spoiled all her life. She probably was furious thinking she'd been denied anything."

"I'm sorrier than I can say that the only magick you knew growing up was self-serving, dark and twisted," Irene said, placing her hand on my shoulder.

I could actually feel her hand. I didn't understand the metaphysics involved but I found it comforting nonetheless. "Why are you still on this plane, Irene?"

"I won't be, not for very much longer," she said, briskly. "My task is almost complete. There's only one thing left for me to do and then I can join your grandfather on the other side."

"What do you have to finish?"

"I needed to comfort and give my beloved granddaughter some counsel."

I smiled. "I am so happy that I finally got to meet you." I said. "Autumn was right, "You're a hell of a woman."

"It runs in the family," Irene said.

"Why thank you, sugar." I said, and hoped she would laugh. She didn't disappoint me.

Irene moved to the back door looking out for a moment. Then she motioned me over to her side. "You see that handsome man out there?"

"Which one?" I asked.

"The tall lanky one with a mop of hair and a gorgeous beard."

I stood beside her so I could look out the back door with her. "That's Wyatt Hastings," I said.

"He's wonderful with children," Irene said, watching Wyatt toss a ball back and forth to Willow and Morgan in the yard.

I smiled. "Yes, he is. Willow adores him already."

"Maggie." Irene chuckled. "Hear me. Wyatt Hastings is going to be a wonderful father for Willow, *and* he'll give you more children."

"I think your putting the cart before the horse, Irene. Wyatt and I are only dating. We're still getting to know each other."

Irene smiled. "Consider this a bit more counsel from your witchy old grandmother: You'll know him *very* well by the end of the year. Mark my words."

I raised my eyebrows. "We'll see about that."

Irene nudged me with her elbow. "He's a very attractive man...Even if he is in desperate need of a haircut. I love the beard though. Your grandfather had a beard."

"Ah, okay," was the best thing I could think of to

reply.

"I hope you're ready for a couple of rough and tumble little boys. After such a girly girl like Willow, it's certainly going to be different for you."

I felt the impact of her words to the soles of my feet. "Is that a prophecy, or are you teasing me?"

"I'd never tease you. Your boys are waiting impatiently to be born."

Good Lord, I thought. "How soon?"

"Within the next three years."

"One at a time I hope."

"You're not the one who's destined to have twins...not in this generation." Irene tilted her head meaningfully toward Autumn.

I couldn't help the smile. "Does she have any idea?"

"She won't even realize it for another month. Autumn's going to have a rough start...but everything will be alright in the end."

"I'll tell her that you said that. When the time is right."

"By the way," Irene said. "Phillip would be a good name for your first son."

"You're incorrigible." I laughed, despite myself.

"I'm just saying..." She tossed me a wink. "Your grandfather will be delighted."

"I'll be sure and keep that in mind," I said dryly. I suddenly noticed that her image was fading. "Are you leaving?" I reached out, but there was no way for me to touch her.

"Yes." Irene nodded. "It's finally time."

I fought to keep my voice steady. "Thank you for coming to me today. Please tell my grandfather that I said, hello."

"I'm sorry to leave you, Magnolia," Irene said. "But we've waited for so long to be reunited."

"You shouldn't wait any longer." I smiled, and felt tears prick my eyes. "You've helped me. Willow and I are both safe and happy. Go on, enjoy your afterlife."

Irene blew a kiss to me. "Thank you, my love."

"Good journey, Grandma," I said.

She smiled beautifully when I called her *grandma*, and her image began to fade out. As suddenly as she'd appeared, she was gone.

I took a moment to compose myself and wiped the tears from my eyes at Irene's departure. I heard my name being called and I peeped out the door. There was Wyatt, standing in the dusky backyard and smiling at me. God almighty, but the man was striking.

"Come back outside," he said, gesturing for me to come out and rejoin the party.

"Two little boys," I said under my breath. I could almost picture those two dark-haired boys, running around noisily, much as Morgan was doing now. *They'd look like Wyatt,* I knew with a sudden gut hunch.

But their eyes would be like mine.

"One step at a time, honey," I reminded myself.

I took a steadying breath and, with a smile on my face, opened the door to my future.

The End

Turn the page for a sneak peek of Ivy Bishop's new
story.
Of course, this will be a dark and gothic tale. Ivy
wouldn't have it any other way.

Mistletoe & Ivy
Coming November 2019

***

Mistletoe & Ivy

I sat behind the counter of *Enchantments*, staring out the front window. Holiday music played over the speakers in the store, white lights twinkled in the pine garlands that swooped around the walls and on the tree displayed in the front window. The shop smelled cozily of cinnamon and vanilla. It was all picture perfect, inviting, and charming...and I, Ivy Bishop, was bored out of my mind.

You'd think working in an occult store would be a little more exciting. You'd be wrong. It was retail, and more often than not, we had looky-loos and tourists shopping in our store. The serious practitioners came in with a list, quickly made their choices, and got out.

There were three customers in the store at the moment. Two were thumbing through the books, and the third, a high-school age girl, was selecting mini taper candles and placing them carefully in her shopping basket, as if the fate of the world depended on it.

Had to be a new practitioner, I decided.

My intuition was right on the money, as usual. Not only did she purchase the candles, she also bought a 101 type of candle magick book.

Can I call 'em or what? I smiled to myself, rang her

up, and she left the shop all smiles.

I perked up a bit when I noticed the young couple standing by the book case. They appeared to be in the throes of an argument.

What they were arguing about? I wondered, and my imagination bounced as I considered the possibilities. Perhaps one of them had massive gambling debts...or the other was a closeted Witch, and now their partner had just figured it out.

As they moved past the front counter, I caught their words, and was disappointed to discover that they were actually quarreling over which movie to go see. The door closed behind them, leaving me alone in the shop.

I blew out a long breath. Obviously I needed to get out and do something exciting, go have an adventure, *or* get laid.

Sadly none of those things were in my foreseeable future.

I'd been single for the last six months. Nathan Pogue and I had hit a sort of friendly impasse with our relationship. In May, when I'd received my Bachelor's in Photography, Nathan had gotten his Master's degree in Archeology.

I wasn't surprised when he'd been offered a job back in Massachusetts, close to where his family lived. I'd figured it was coming—call me an intuitive. Nathan had been excited about the opportunity, and I'd been happy for him.

As for me, I'd only started working as a part-time

assistant to a local wedding photographer, and I needed at least another year under my belt before I could go solo with my photography career. As my college romance came to a close I'd been a little sad, but it wasn't like a gothic tragedy. It was more of an inevitable thing.

When the time had come for Nathan to go, I'd helped him pack up his belongings and sent him off with a hug and a kiss. He promised he'd call me once he was home and settled. We said all the right things, the *kind* things: Sure, we'd keep in touch, maybe I'd fly out and spend a few weeks with him over the summer.

That sort of thing...But I knew, down in my gut, that it wouldn't happen.

Nathan Pogue had *not* been the love of my life. He'd make some lucky woman really happy, someday. But that woman wasn't me. Was I heartbroken? No. He'd been a great friend and lover for the past couple of years, but we were simply too different. Nathan's family were all extremely private about their Craft. Their tradition was secret, as in they never discussed it with non-believers. Nathan had been very serious and *very discreet* when it came to magick, while I was...

My thoughts trailed off as I caught my reflection in the store mirror. Well, one thing was for certain. I'd never been accused of being subtle.

I looked like what I was. A twenty-something Witch, who had a love affair with gothic-style fashion. I studied my image in the mirror, skimmed a hand through my long brown bob, and noticed a wayward smudge at the outer corner of my eye. Carefully, I wiped it away.

My affection for cosmetics was real and I still dramatically played up my green eyes for all they were worth. The long red and black buffalo plaid shirt I wore was cut like a duster. It skimmed my hips in the front, but swung to my knees in the back. I'd layered it over a midnight scoop-neck tee which framed my pentagram necklace and black crescent pendant nicely. My leggings looked like leather—they weren't—and those were tucked into my over-the-knee black suede boots.

When I was working on a wedding shoot, I toned my makeup down and stuck to classic black slacks, simple blouses and blazers. It made me look more professional, even though I was more likely to be schlepping around equipment and getting folks into position for group shots as the 'assistant'.

If I was lucky, sometimes I got the chance to take candid photos of the wedding party on my own. But still, every time I went with Jillian, I learned something new. She was a hell of a photographer, and I was lucky to have the opportunity to work with her.

However, today I'd volunteered to cover for Terry, our store manager, which had given her the night off. The weekends were typically crazy busy on Main Street between Thanksgiving and Christmas, so she appreciated the down time.

Drumming my fingertips on the counter, I

considered what I could do with myself when I returned home. *I could always rent a movie, or work on finishing up my new apartment in the attic of the manor. I could go crazy and shop for the perfect accessories for my black and white bathroom...*

Yes, my life had truly become that freaking exciting. It was a Wednesday night, in early December, and there wasn't a lot happening in William's Ford.

With a sigh I looked out the front window and told myself to enjoy the quiet. "Otherwise," I muttered., "I'll end up like the old biddies in town." Determinedly, I went to the Yule tree in the front window to make a few adjustments to the ornaments.

The shop door opened. "Ivy!" Sharon Waterman greeted me. "How are you, dear?"

Sharon Waterman was in her sixties. She was the head of the Chamber of Commerce, a cheerful busy-body, and a hell of a lot of fun. "Hello, Mrs. Waterman."

She headed straight for the candle display and picked up a few scented pillar candles. "Have you heard the latest news, dear?" and...she was off.

The hot gossip around town since Thanksgiving weekend had been about the wild animal attack on a boy, I was informed. He'd been on a camping trip in the local woods, and speculation on what sort of animal had attacked him was running rampant.

"Oh," I said. "I hope he'll recover."

Mrs. Waterman continued to fill me in as I rang her

up. "I heard he's expected to make a full recovery," she said. "However, the boys involved were all claiming that it had been a *monster* that attacked them."

"Really?" I'd said with a little laugh, handing her the shopping receipt. The woman had a nose for news, but there wasn't a mean bone in her body.

Sharon Waterman straightened her red scarf. "Yes. A *Monster*. Not since '79 has there been a sighting of that creature in the woods. My father was never taken seriously, you know. And he'd even managed to get a photograph of the beast after his own narrow escape!"

"Beast?" I grinned at her enthusiasm. "A local version of Bigfoot, no doubt?"

"There will always be skeptics, dear." Sharon sniffed. "My father always swore it was no Bigfoot. He'd always told me what he'd seen was *not of this world*."

It was everything I had not to giggle. She was just so damn much fun.

"But unfortunately," she continued, "Since those young men had all been drinking beer, most folks 'round here assume they were drunk, and figure it's all a teenage prank."

"Teenage boys drinking beer in the woods?" I raised an eyebrow. "What are the odds?"

"I hope this doesn't all start up again," she said, tucking her wallet back in her purse. "Those poor boys. You take care, now." Mrs. Waterman gave me a wave and left.

I went to go straighten the candles she'd rifled through, thinking back over what I'd heard. It made me wonder what had *really* happened to those kids. According to Mrs. Waterman, the authorities were claiming it was a mountain lion or perhaps a bear, but both were rare in this part of Missouri, and an attack on a human was practically unheard of.

The bells over the shop door jingled, jolting me out of my thoughts. I turned and saw Eddie O'Connell. "Hey, Eddie!"

"Ivy." He lifted a hand in greeting. "I was wondering if I could talk to you."

"Sure," I gestured to one of the chairs in front of the bookshelves. "Step into my office."

Eddie O'Connell was the younger brother of our family friend Violet O'Connell. I'd known him for years, and if memory served, he was now a Junior at the local high school. A year ago, when I'd been working with his sister Violet, he'd had a bit of a crush on me. While I was happy to see him, I sincerely hoped he wasn't here to ask me out.

Eddie sat, and licked his lips nervously. "Listen, I wasn't sure who else I could ask about this."

"What's up?" Intrigued, I sat across from him.

"I know a couple of years ago you dealt with that evil spirit on campus. Violet told me about it."

"Yes, the ghosts haunting Crowly Hall." I nodded.

He was trying to psych himself up to talk to me. There was a very real anxiety rolling off him. While I didn't consider myself an empath like my sister Holly, I could almost taste the fear that Eddie was battling. Finally he spoke. "I guess you heard about my friend, Hunter Roland, who was attacked in the woods last week."

"Yes. Mrs. Waterman was in a bit ago and told me about it. They think it was an animal attack?"

"The cops are trying to tell us that it was a bear that got him. But I was there and..." He blew out a long breath, trying to compose himself. "Ivy, trust me. It *wasn't* a bear. I saw it."

"You were one of the boys in the woods?" I reached out to him and put a comforting hand on his shoulder. "Eddie, what did you see?"

"I know it wasn't a bear," he said. "It had a long tail, was *huge*, had dark shaggy fur, and most importantly..." Eddie reached under his shirt and withdrew a silver-toned pentagram. "I think it was afraid of my amulet."

"Why do you think that?" I asked, studying the pendant.

"Because my pentagram lit up when I got close to it. I hit the thing with a big branch from the fire and that got its attention. But when my pentagram swung free, it glowed. Really brightly. I've never seen my pendant do that before, and I think *that* is what made the monster let go of Hunter."

"I see," I said. My mind was racing as I sat back in my chair. *I'd once seen my own pentagram react in a similar way a few years ago...*

"I didn't know who else to go to," Eddie said. "No one believes me. My family is so mad about what happened. They think I'm making all of this up to try and get out of trouble for swiping my dad's beer from the garage."

"Were you drunk that night?" I asked softly.

"No I wasn't! None of us were." Eddie shot to his feet and started to leave. "I thought *you* at least would believe me."

"Before you stomp off." I held up a hand. "I never said that I didn't believe you."

Eddie paused and looked back over his shoulder.

"Eddie," I sighed. "I know what it's like to have folks roll their eyes and assume you're being dramatic or making things up."

"Okay," he said, sounding suspicious.

He looked so young standing there, with his shoulders hunched in his letterman's jacket, I thought. "Why don't you sit down, and tell me everything that happened that night."

Eddie took a seat again and told me about their camping trip, and the details on what had happened to his friends. The more he talked, the more intrigued I became. After we spoke, he announced he had to get back home. I walked him to the door, promised I would be in touch, and told him that everything would be okay.

Flashing a confident smile, I waved goodbye to him, even as my mind raced. It was hardly a coincidence that

Mrs. Waterman had mentioned the creature in the woods just before Eddie had arrived. "No such thing as coincidence," I murmured, recalling what my mom had always said.

I grabbed a notepad and started to write everything down. Everything I could recall from my conversation with Mrs. Waterman, and then with Eddie. I covered three pages with notes in what seemed like no time at all.

If what Mrs. Waterman said was true, then Eddie and his friends *weren't* the first ones to come across a monster in the woods. I flipped back a page and studied the notes from my conversation.

I circled the words *the creature was not of this world*. I underlined the words, *Not since '79*. "Which means," I said, as I thought it over, "there's probably a newspaper article about her father's experience. Or perhaps a copy of the picture she'd spoken about, somewhere."

Mrs. Waterman had described her father's experience as a 'narrow escape', and after hearing from Eddie about the seriousness of Hunter's injuries, I was inclined to believe her.

Now, all I had to do was start digging. Rubbing my hands together, I headed to the store's computer and booted it up.

This was what I'd been waiting for. A mystery to solve, and a little paranormal adventure to sink my teeth into.

This, I decided, was exactly what I needed.

Mistletoe & Ivy
Legacy Of Magick, Book 10
By Ellen Dugan

Coming November 2019

CPSIA information can be obtained
at www.ICGtesting.com
Printed in the USA
BVHW082126010119
536803BV00001B/34/P